PECULIAR WOODS

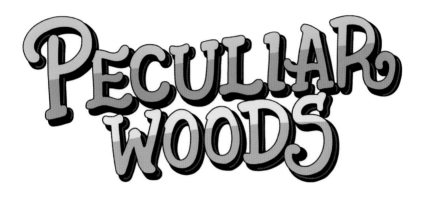

PECULIAR WOODS

∽ The Ancient Underwater City ∽

Andrés J. Colmenares

Andrews McMeel
PUBLISHING®

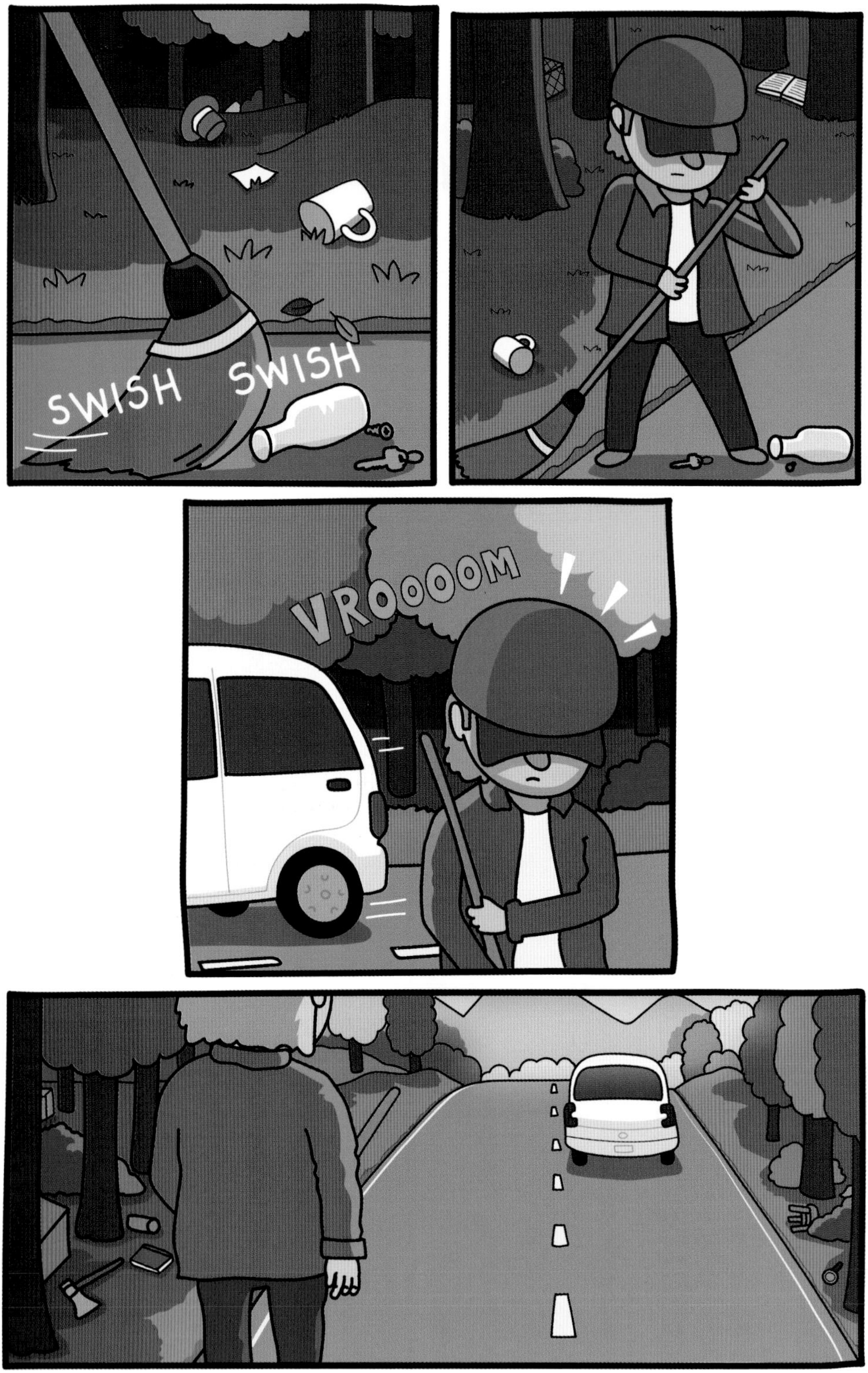
SWISH SWISH
VROOOOM

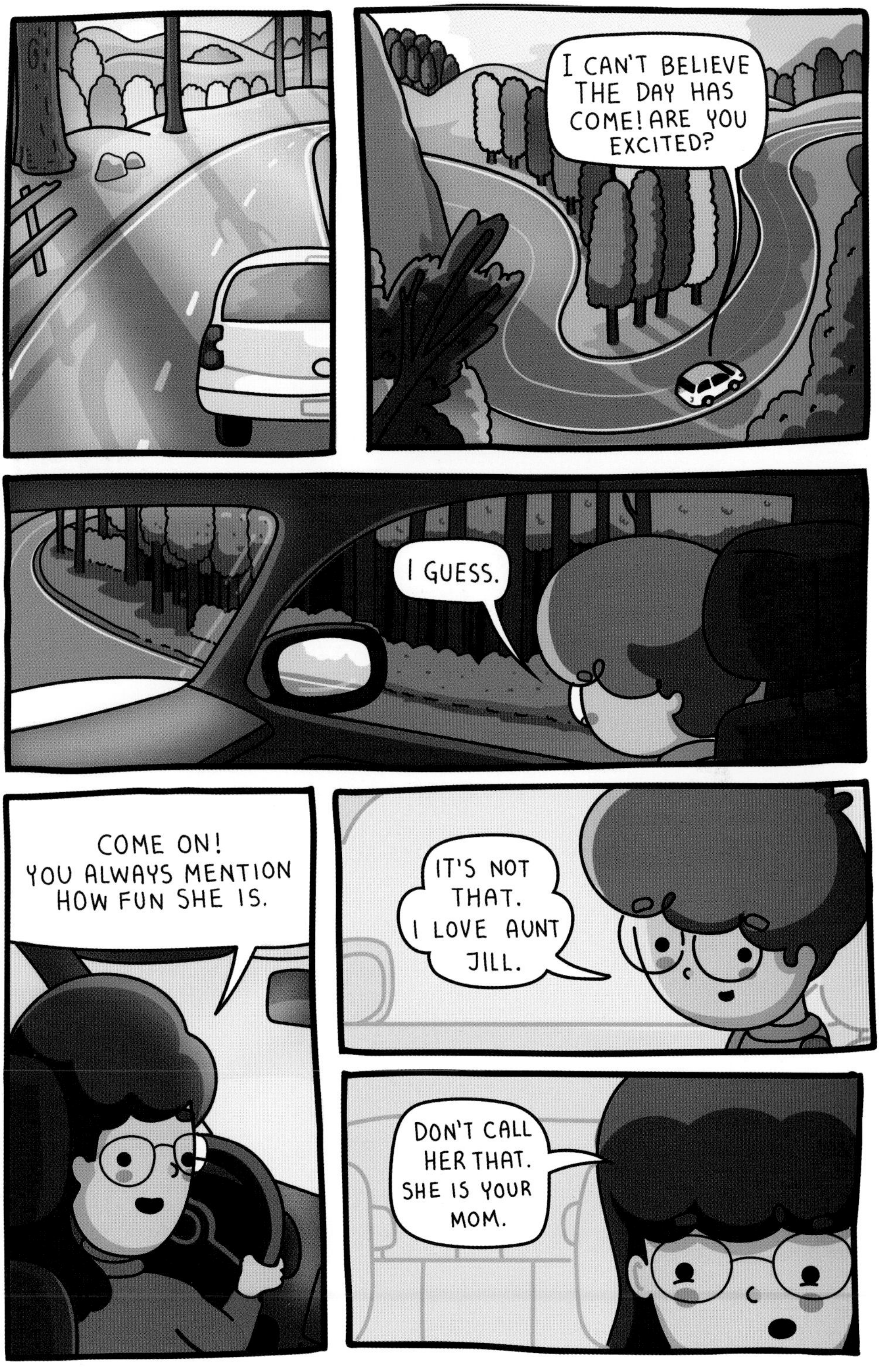
I CAN'T BELIEVE THE DAY HAS COME! ARE YOU EXCITED?
I GUESS.
COME ON! YOU ALWAYS MENTION HOW FUN SHE IS.
IT'S NOT THAT. I LOVE AUNT JILL.
DON'T CALL HER THAT. SHE IS YOUR MOM.

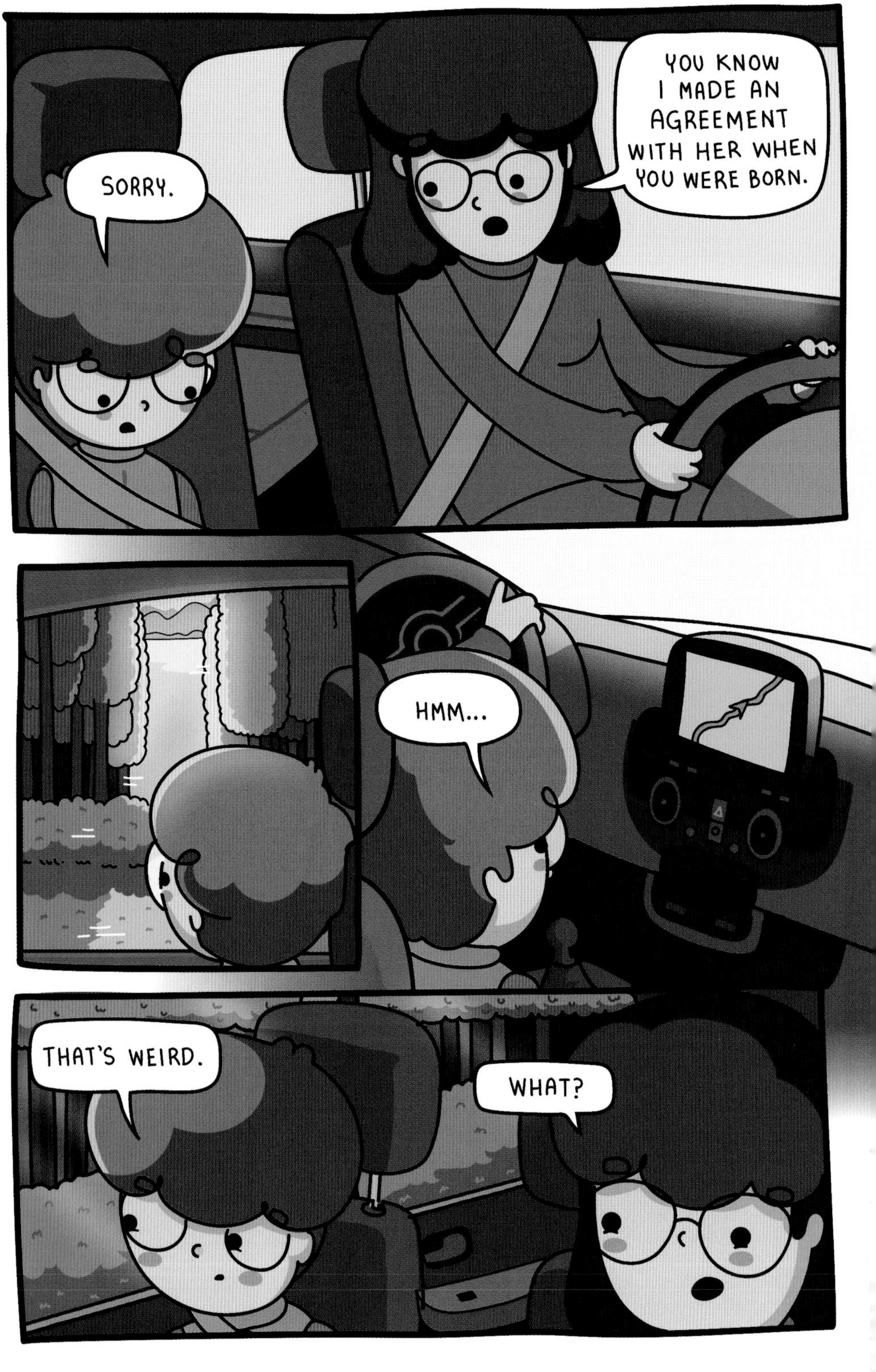
YOU KNOW I MADE AN AGREEMENT WITH HER WHEN YOU WERE BORN.
SORRY.
HMM...
THAT'S WEIRD.
WHAT?

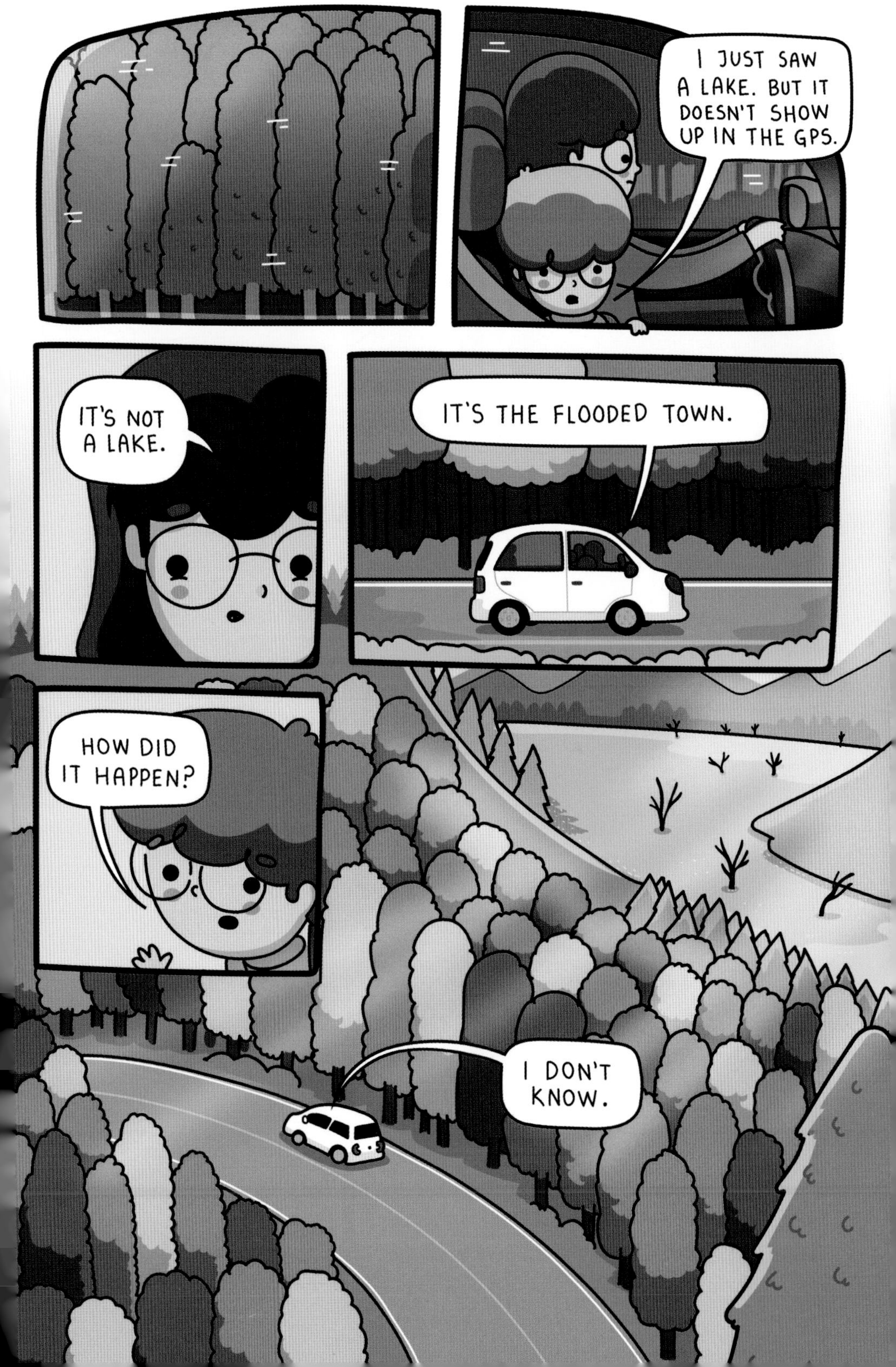
I JUST SAW A LAKE. BUT IT DOESN'T SHOW UP IN THE GPS.
IT'S NOT A LAKE.
IT'S THE FLOODED TOWN.
HOW DID IT HAPPEN?
I DON'T KNOW.

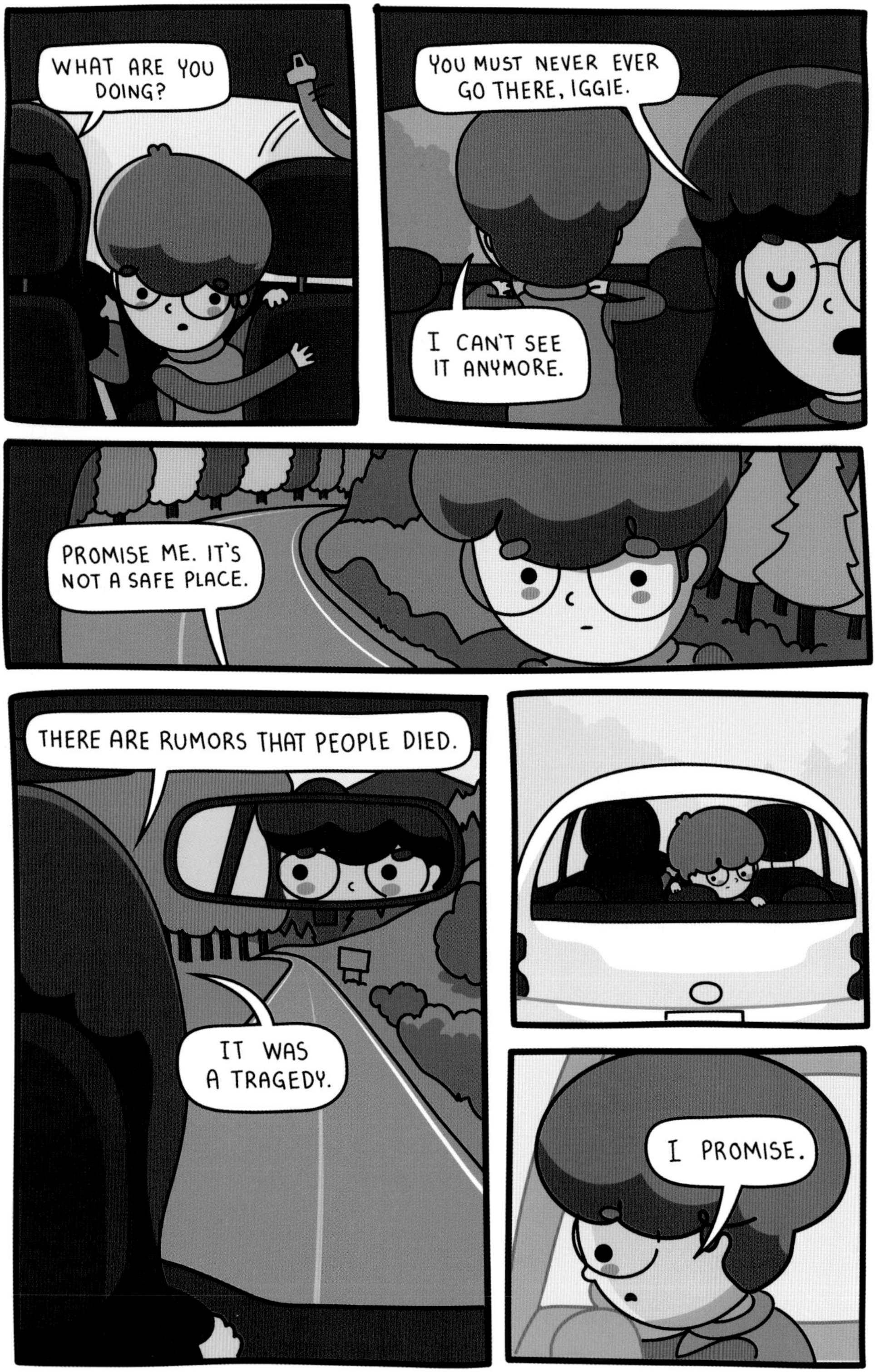
WHAT ARE YOU DOING?
YOU MUST NEVER EVER GO THERE, IGGIE.
I CAN'T SEE IT ANYMORE.
PROMISE ME. IT'S NOT A SAFE PLACE.
THERE ARE RUMORS THAT PEOPLE DIED.
IT WAS A TRAGEDY.
I PROMISE.

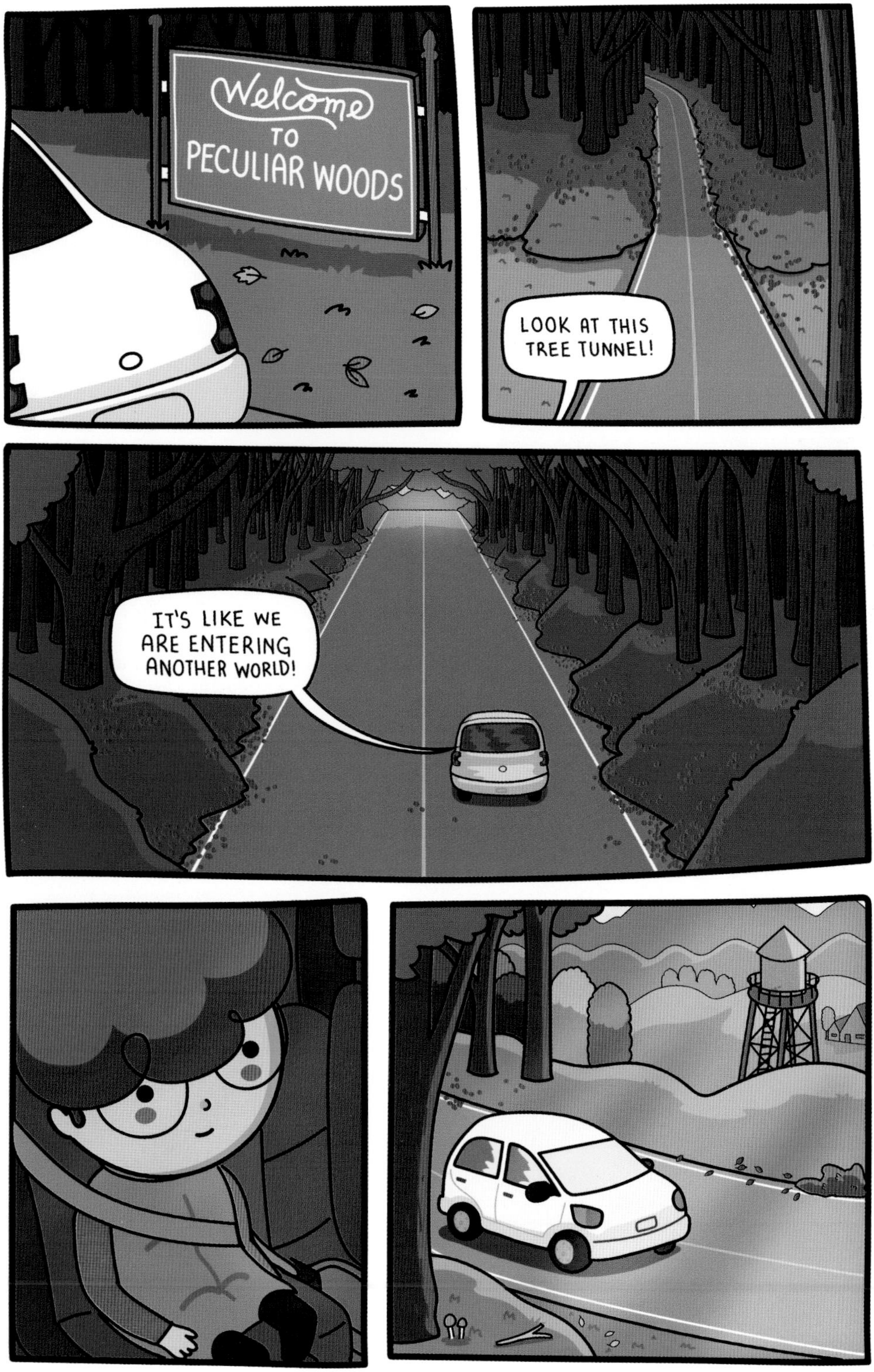
Welcome
TO
PECULIAR WOODS
LOOK AT THIS TREE TUNNEL!
IT'S LIKE WE ARE ENTERING ANOTHER WORLD!

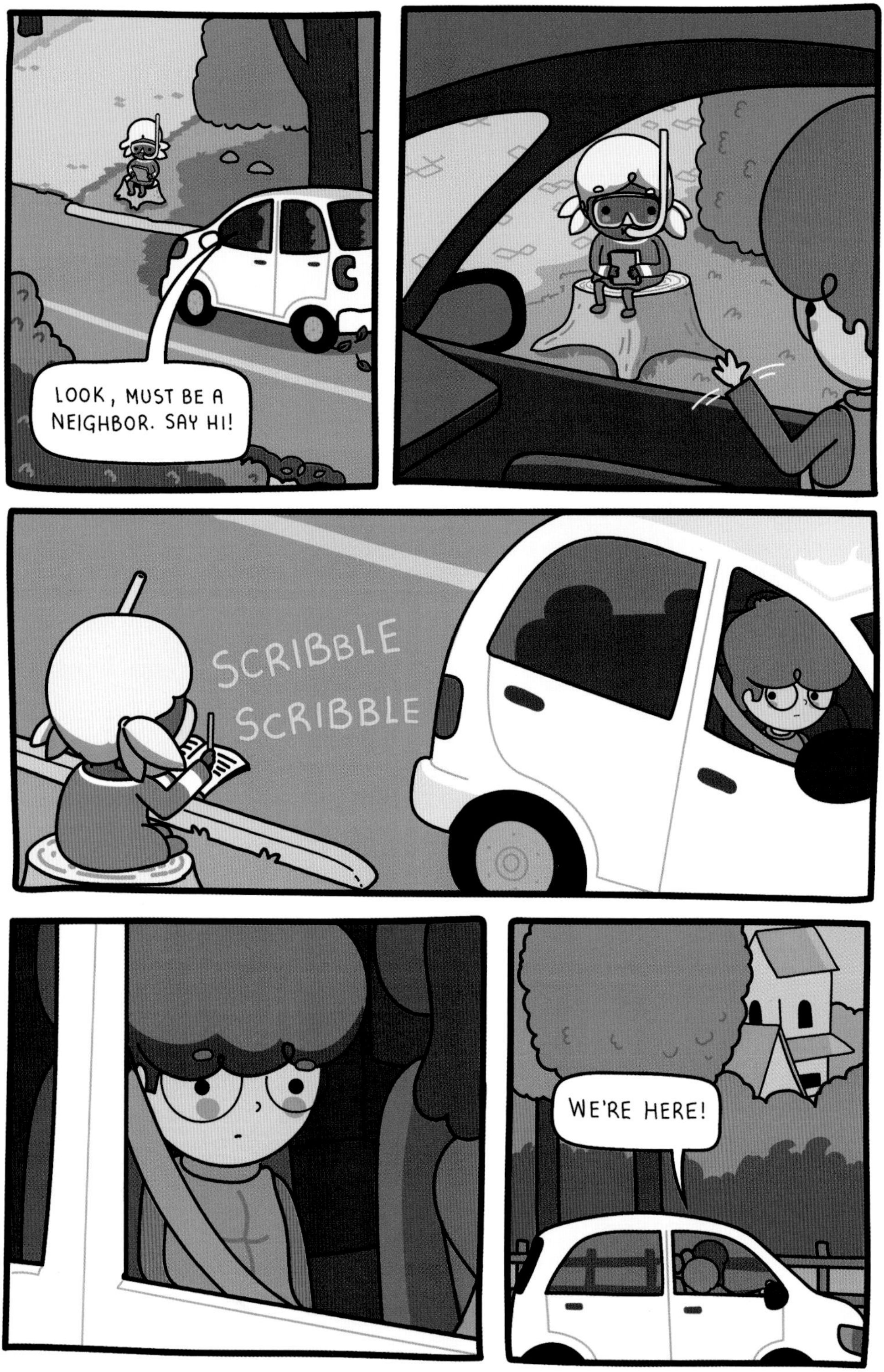
LOOK, MUST BE A NEIGHBOR. SAY HI!
SCRIBBLE SCRIBBLE
WE'RE HERE!

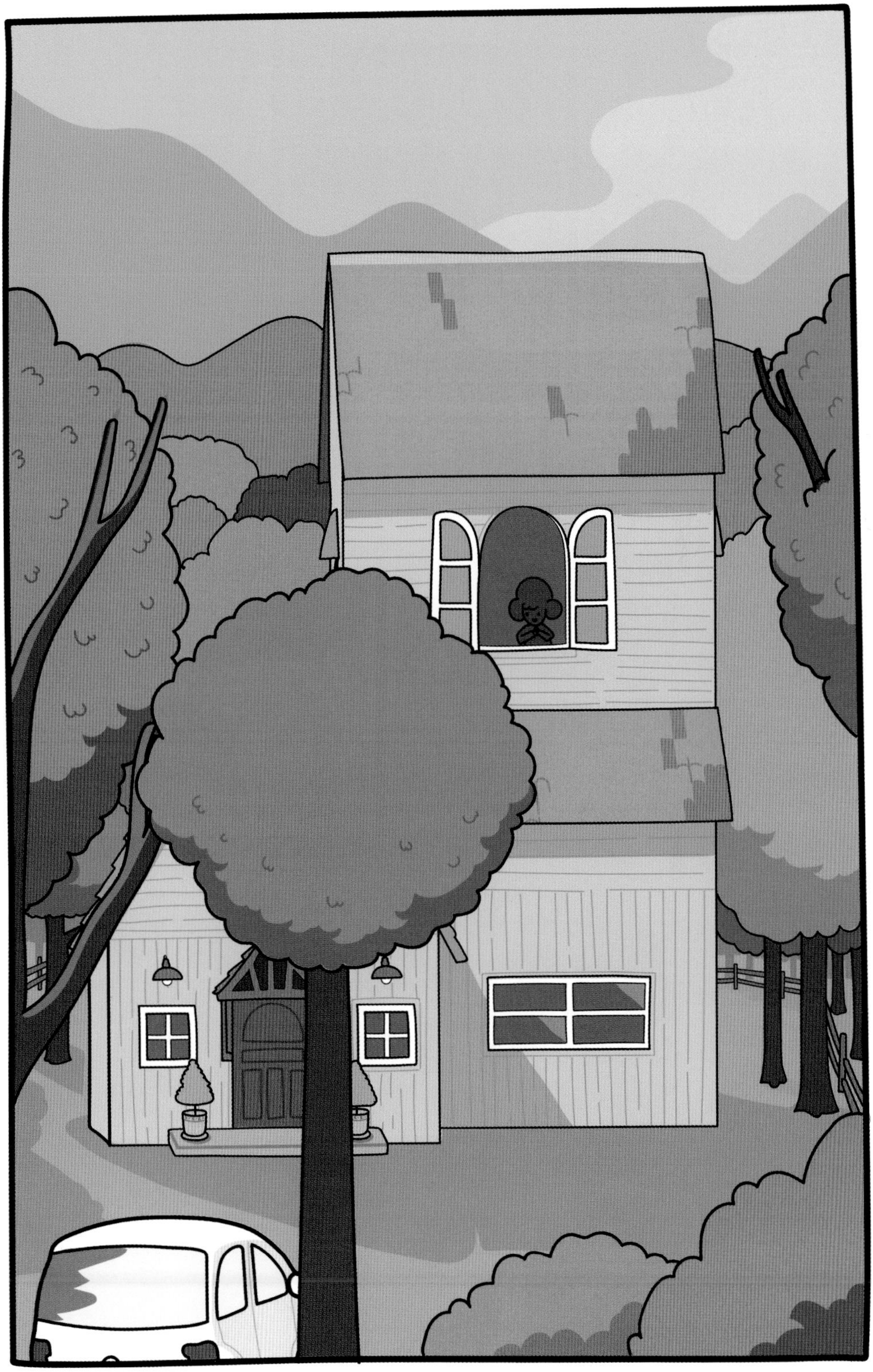

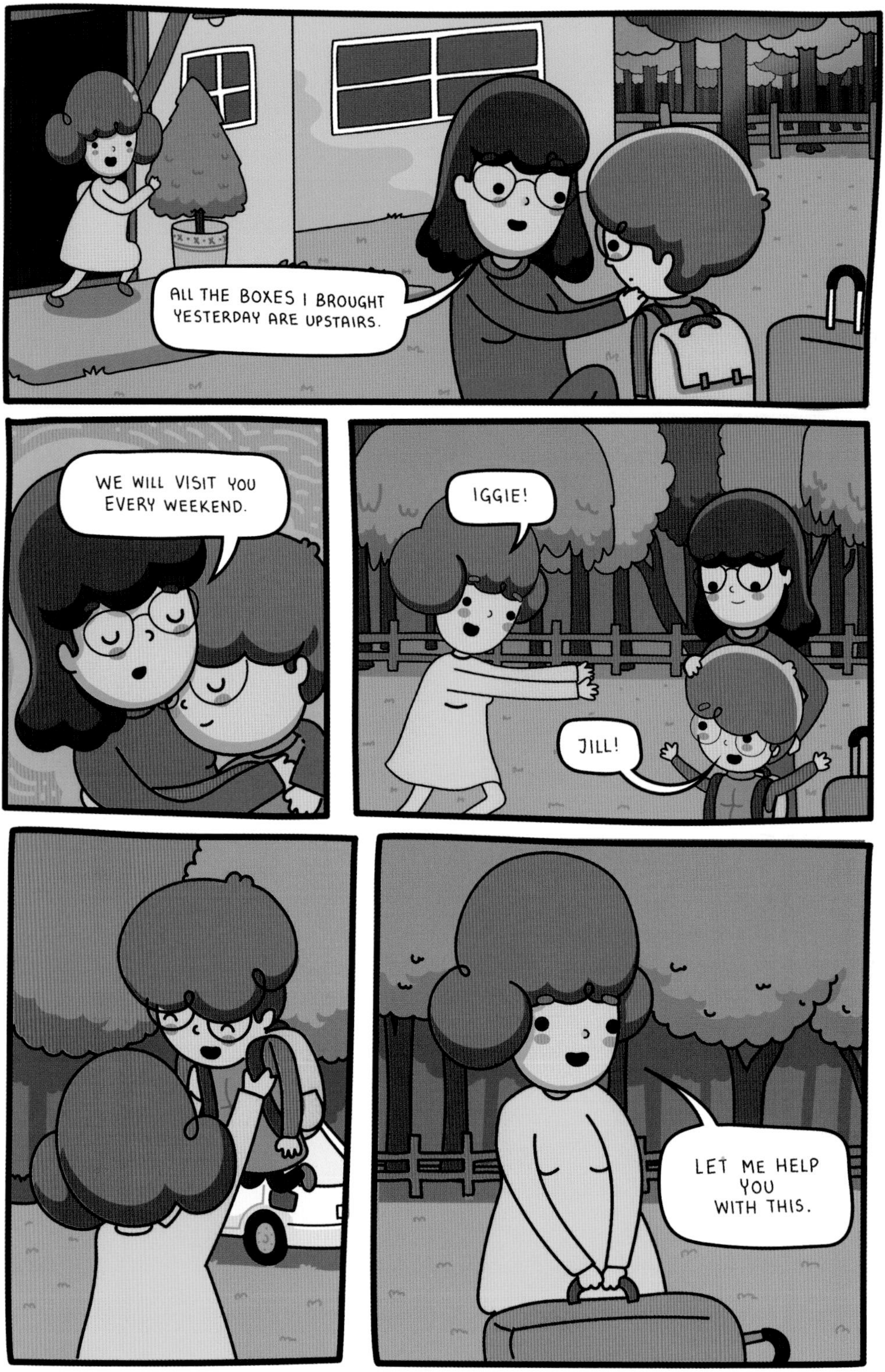
ALL THE BOXES I BROUGHT YESTERDAY ARE UPSTAIRS.
WE WILL VISIT YOU EVERY WEEKEND.
IGGIE!
JILL!
LET ME HELP YOU WITH THIS.

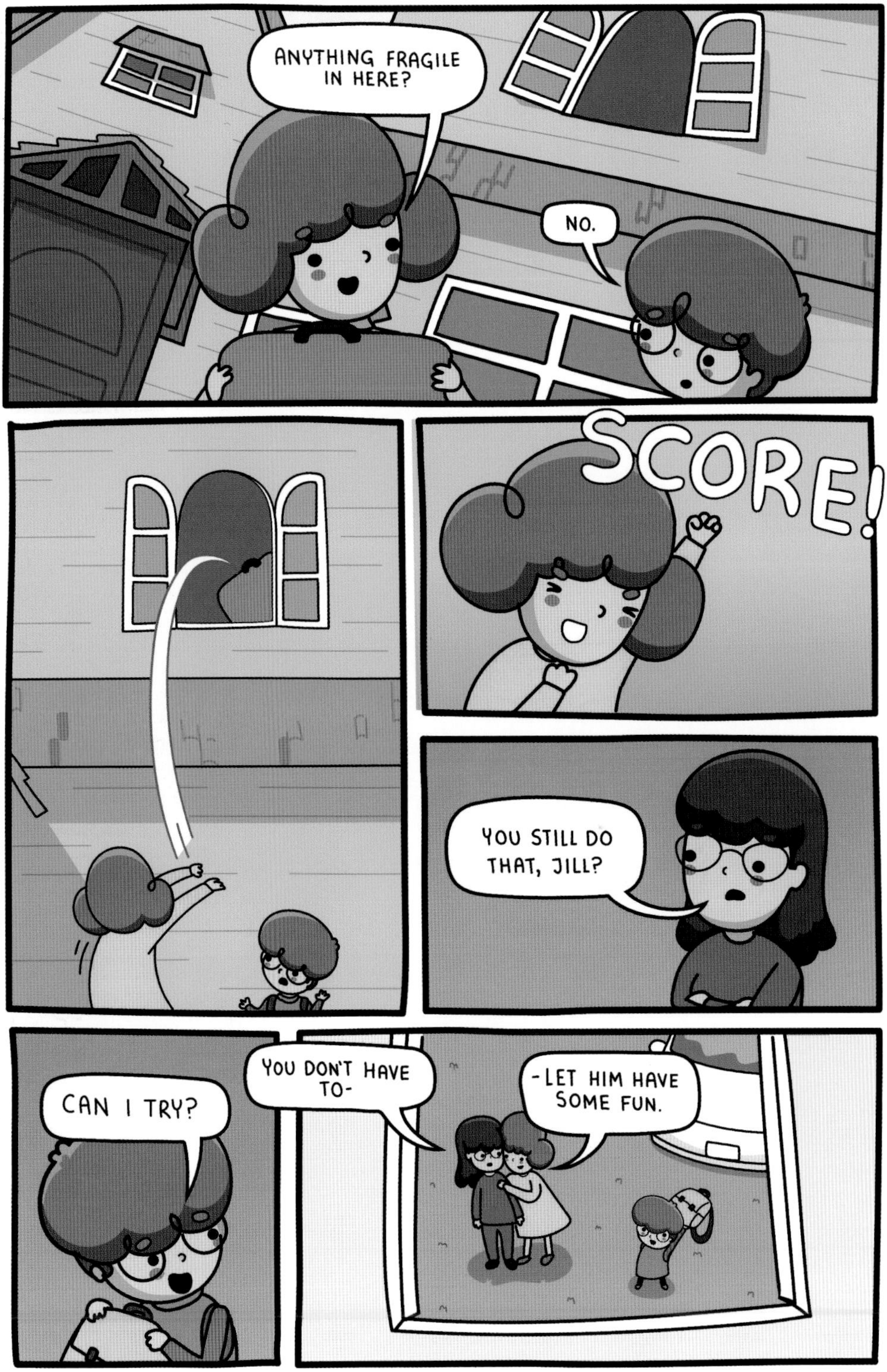
ANYTHING FRAGILE IN HERE?
NO.
SCORE!
YOU STILL DO THAT, JILL?
CAN I TRY?
YOU DON'T HAVE TO-
-LET HIM HAVE SOME FUN.

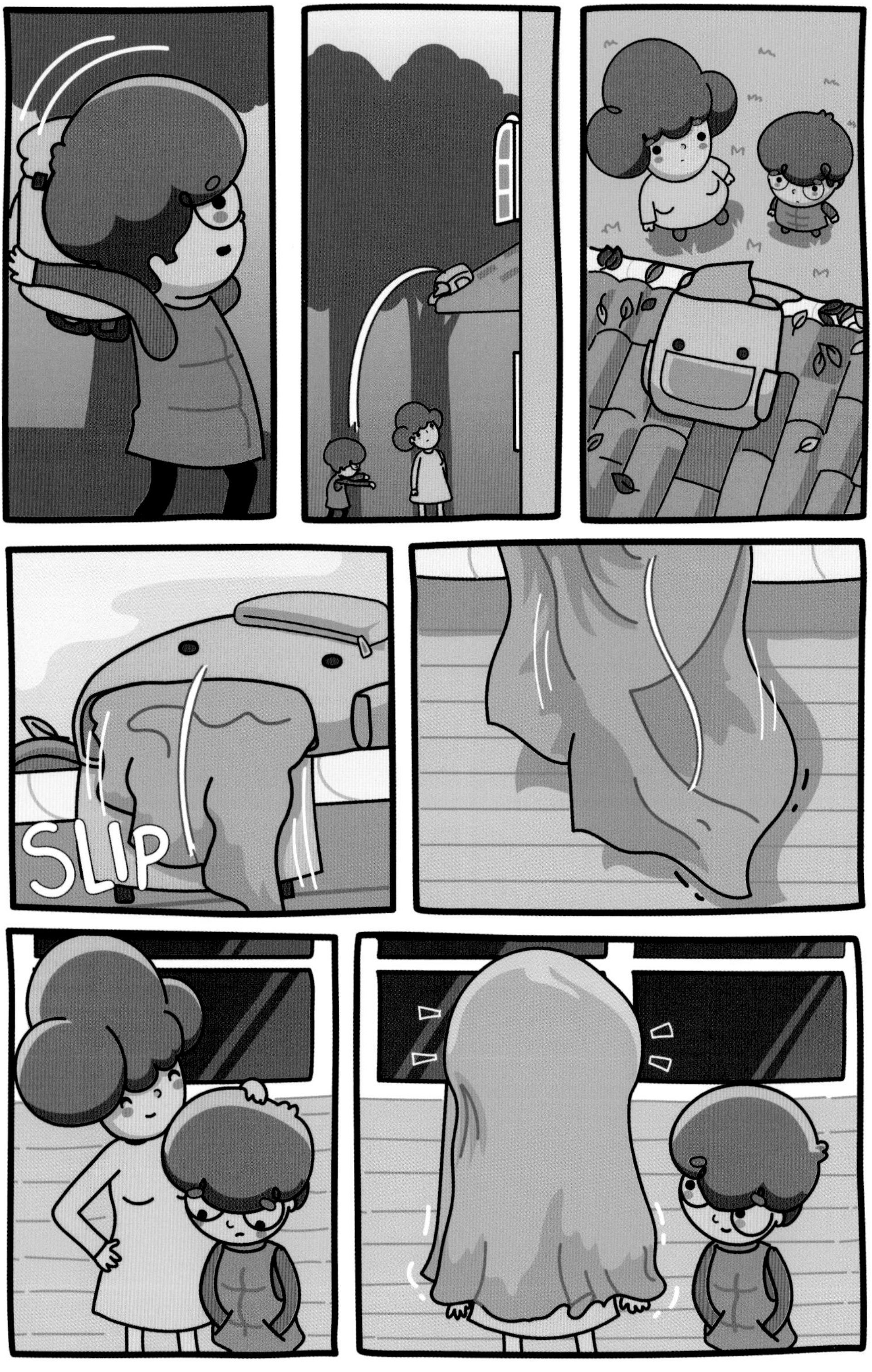
SLIP

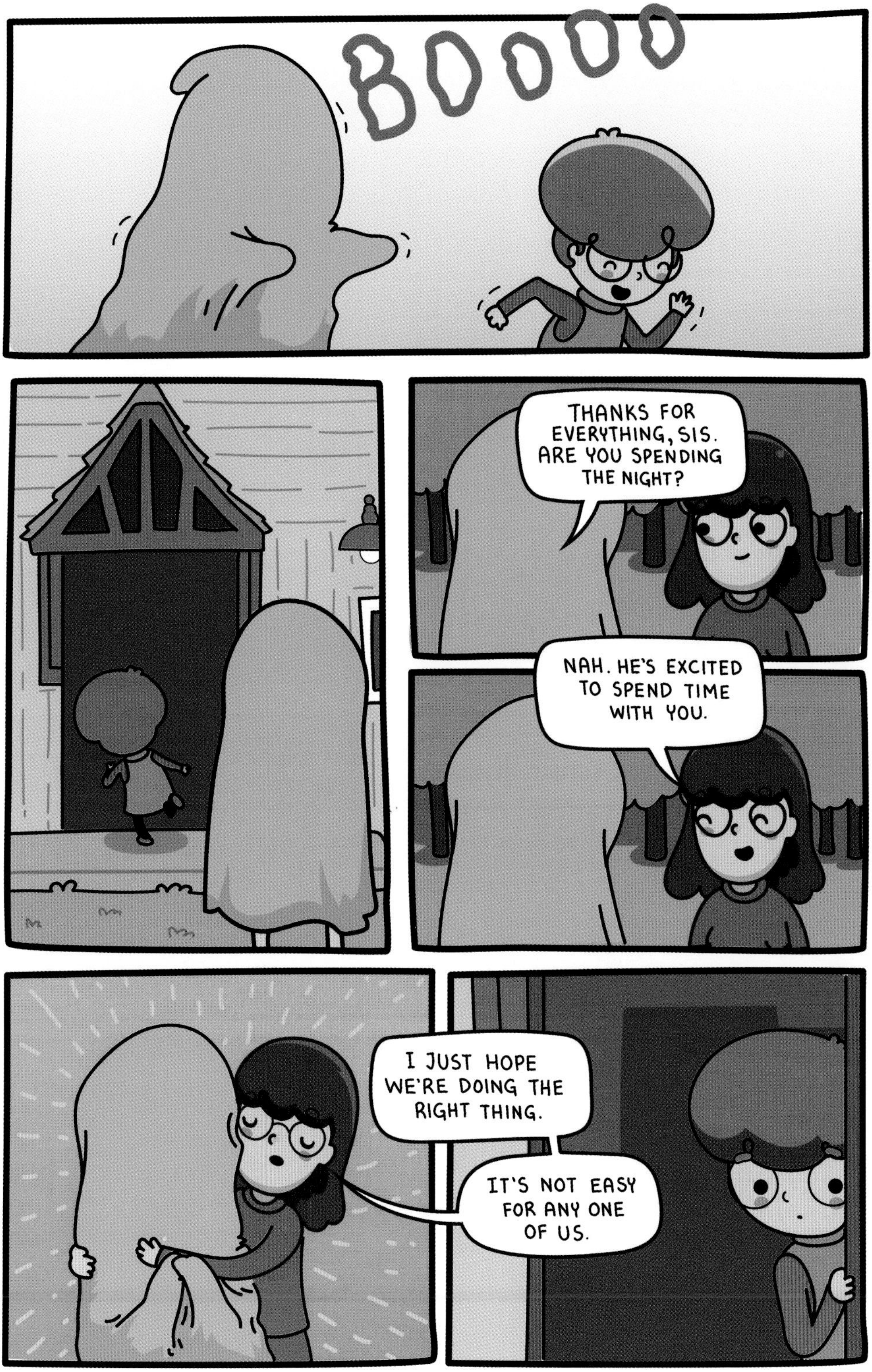
BOOOO
THANKS FOR EVERYTHING, SIS. ARE YOU SPENDING THE NIGHT?
NAH. HE'S EXCITED TO SPEND TIME WITH YOU.
I JUST HOPE WE'RE DOING THE RIGHT THING.
IT'S NOT EASY FOR ANY ONE OF US.

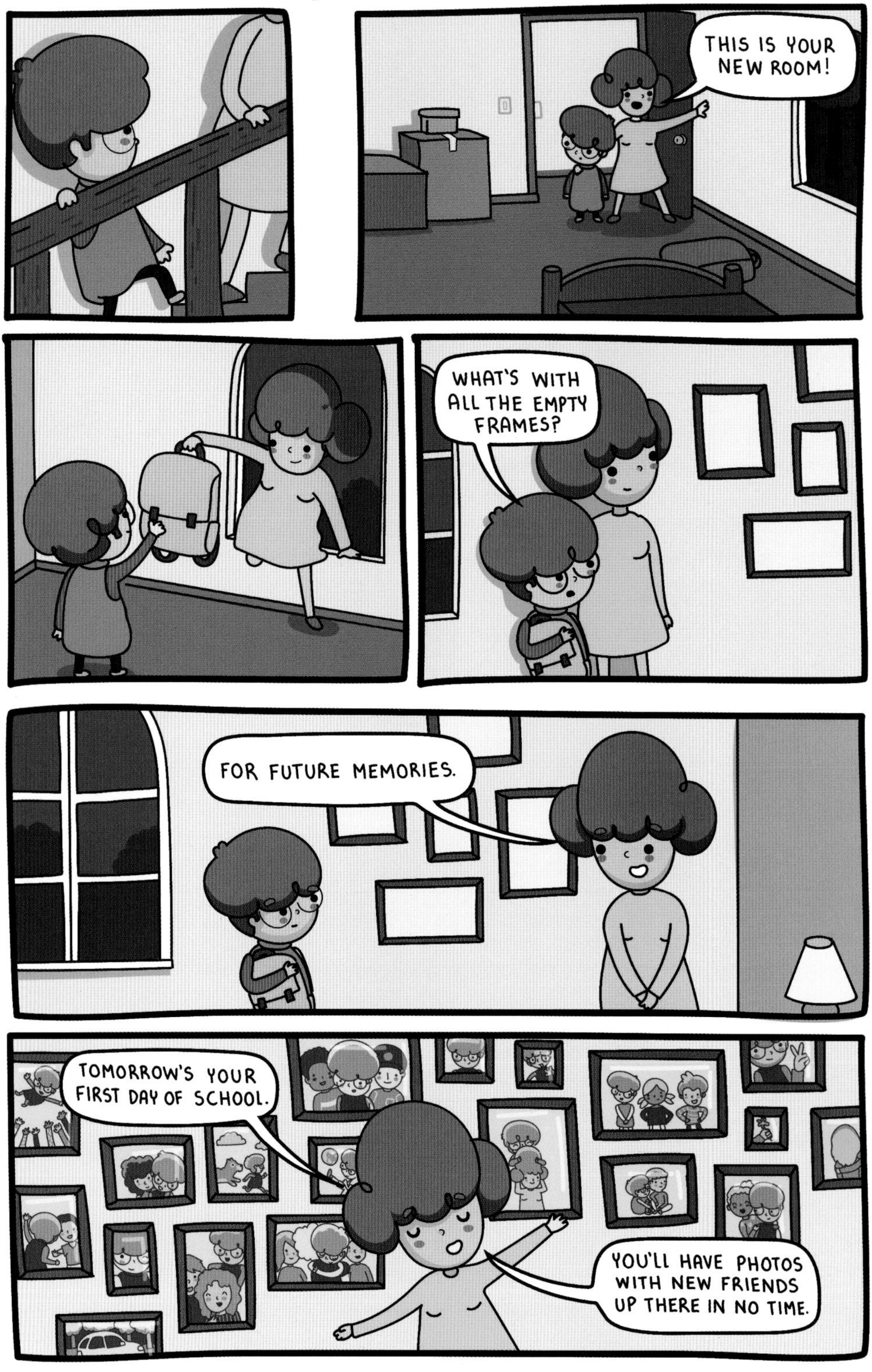
THIS IS YOUR NEW ROOM!
WHAT'S WITH ALL THE EMPTY FRAMES?
FOR FUTURE MEMORIES.
TOMORROW'S YOUR FIRST DAY OF SCHOOL.
YOU'LL HAVE PHOTOS WITH NEW FRIENDS UP THERE IN NO TIME.

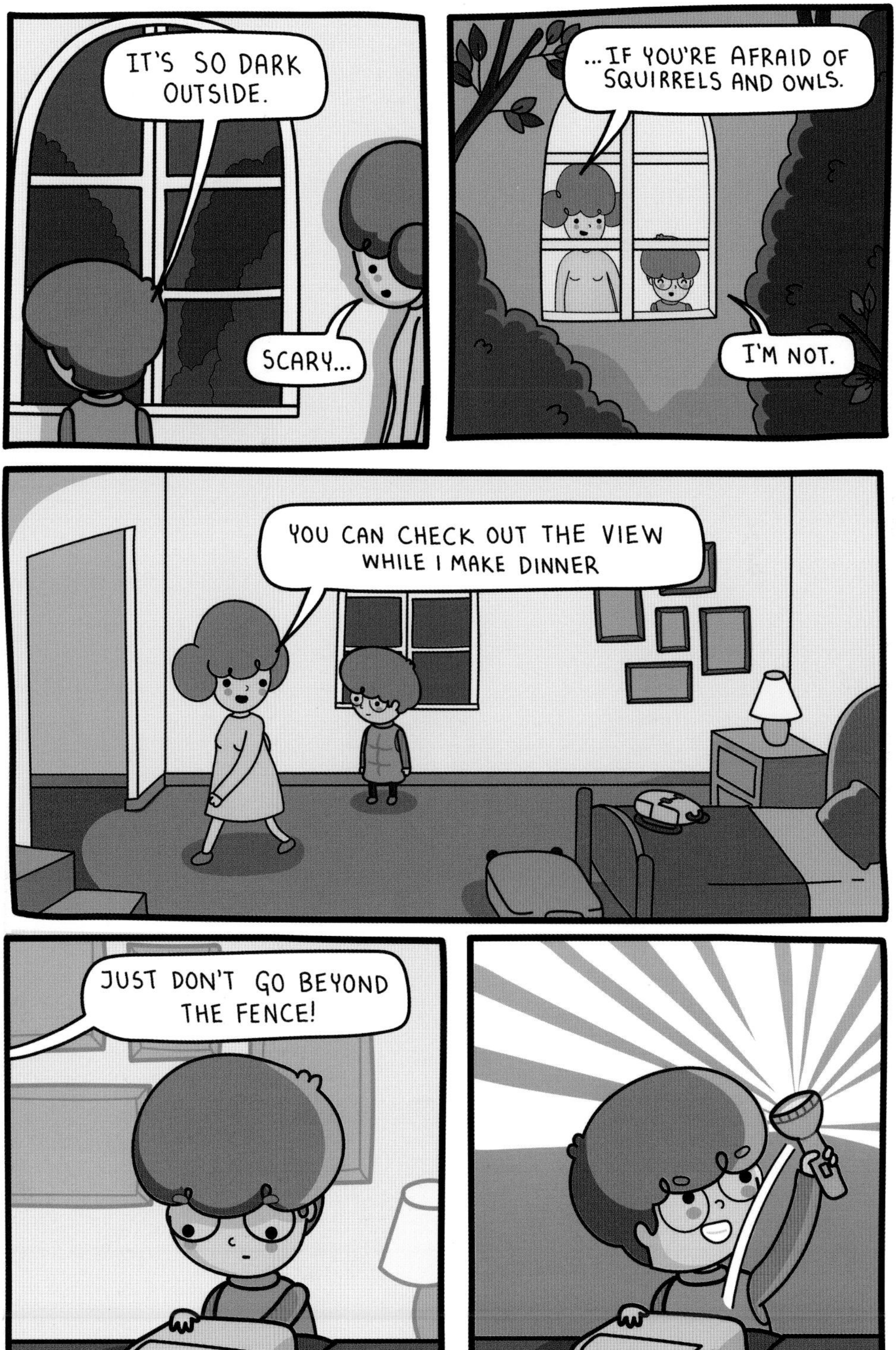
IT'S SO DARK OUTSIDE.
SCARY...
...IF YOU'RE AFRAID OF SQUIRRELS AND OWLS.
I'M NOT.
YOU CAN CHECK OUT THE VIEW WHILE I MAKE DINNER
JUST DON'T GO BEYOND THE FENCE!

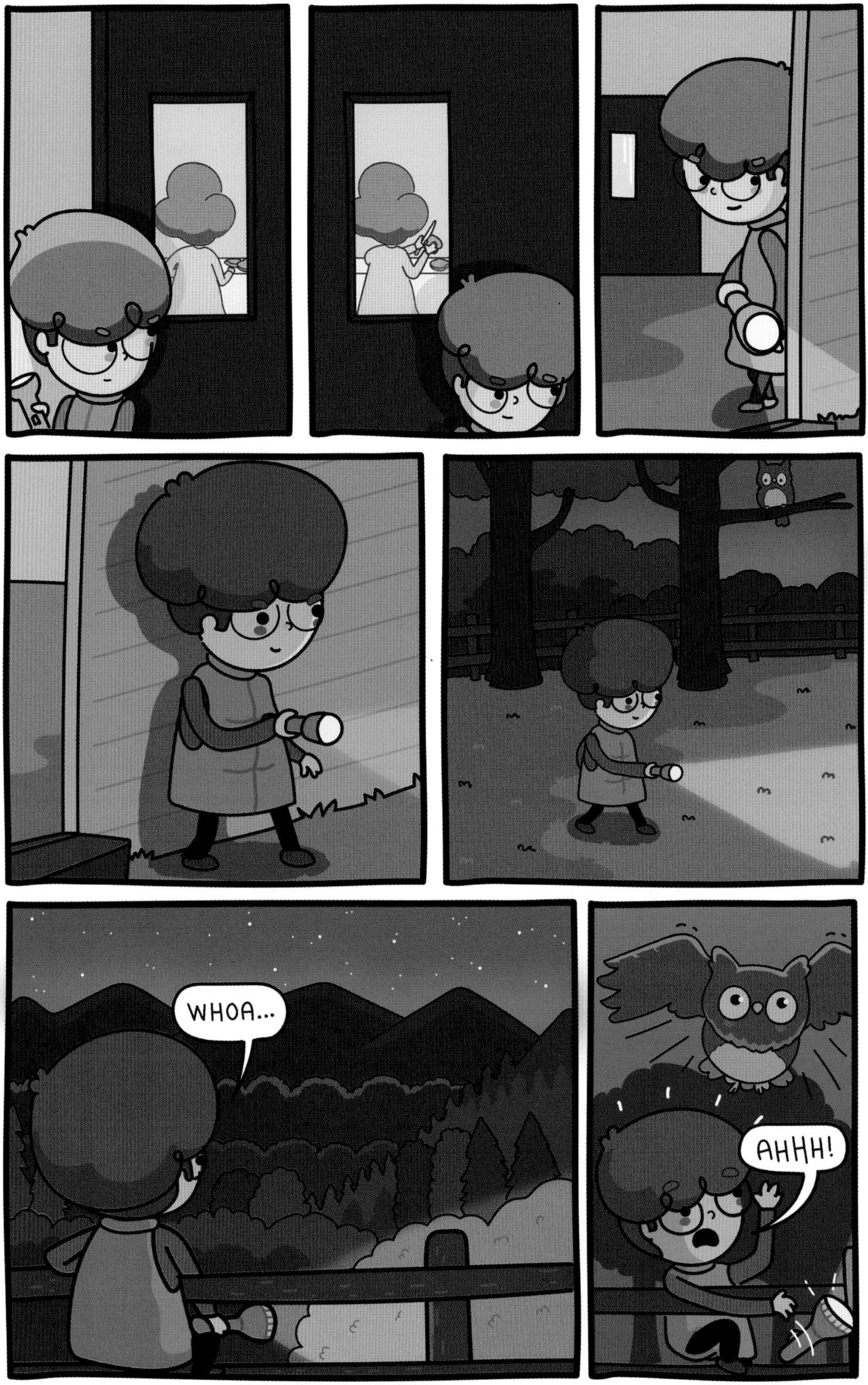
WHOA...
AHHH!

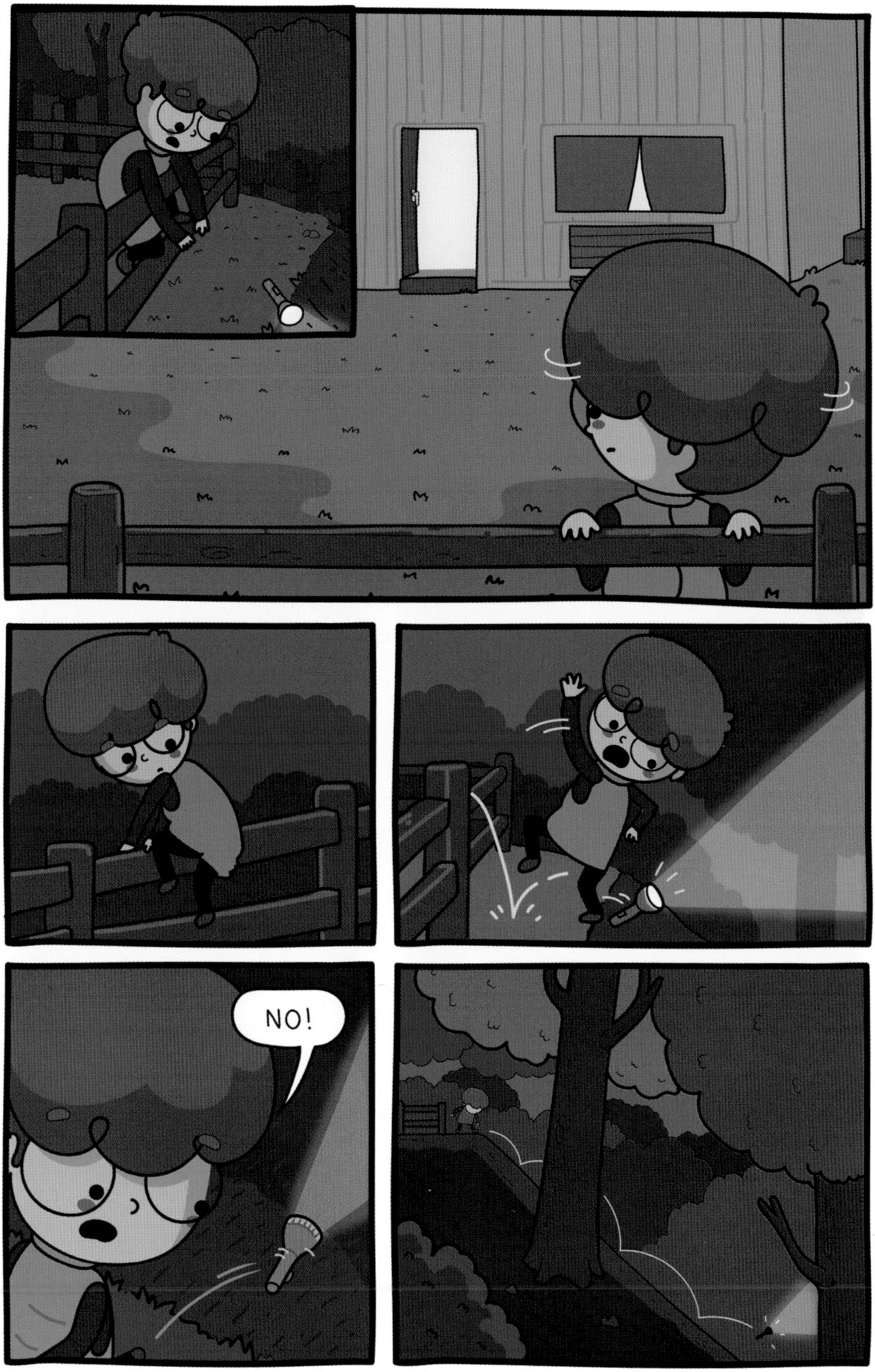
NO!

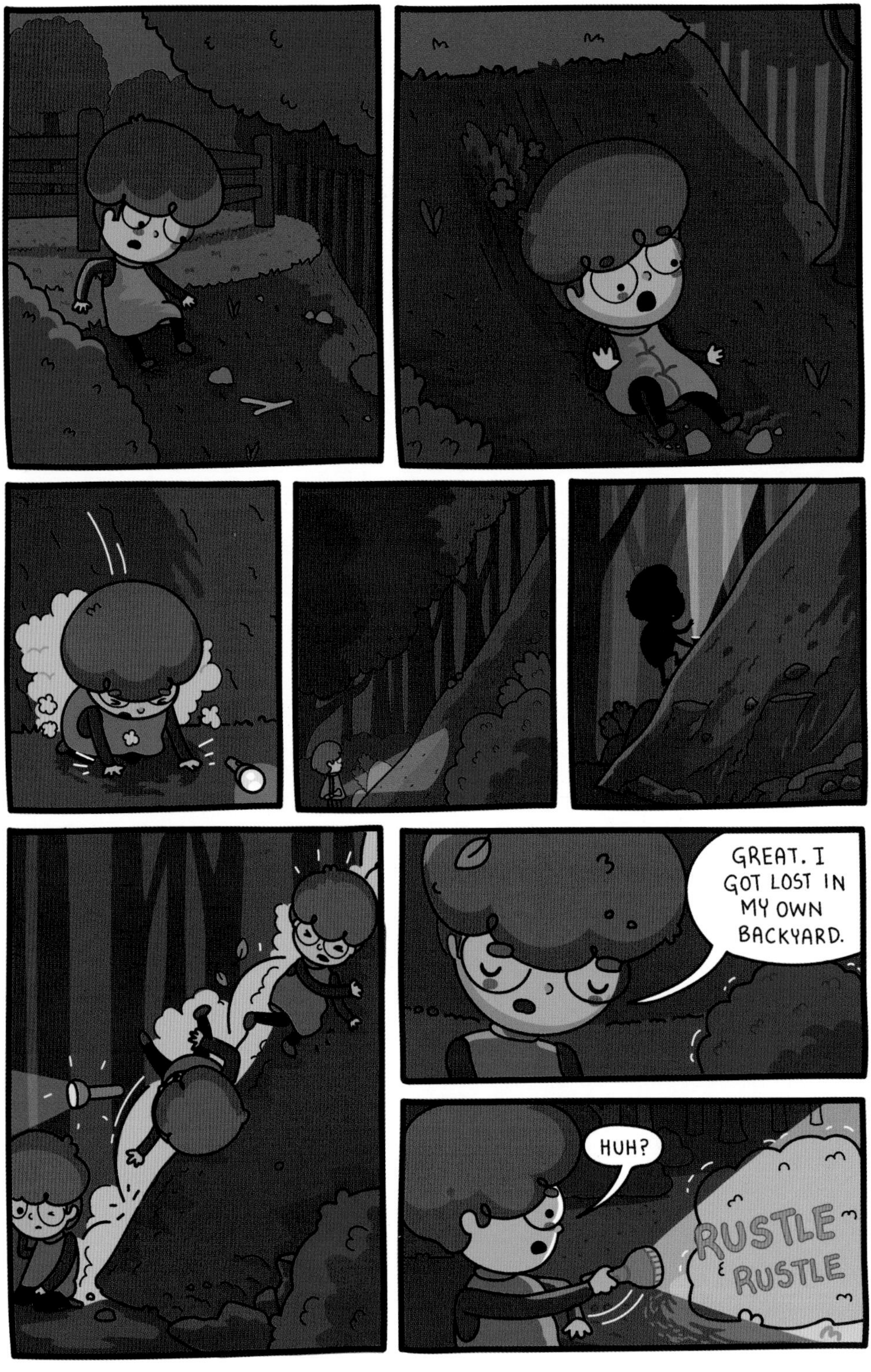
GREAT. I GOT LOST IN MY OWN BACKYARD.
HUH?
RUSTLE
RUSTLE

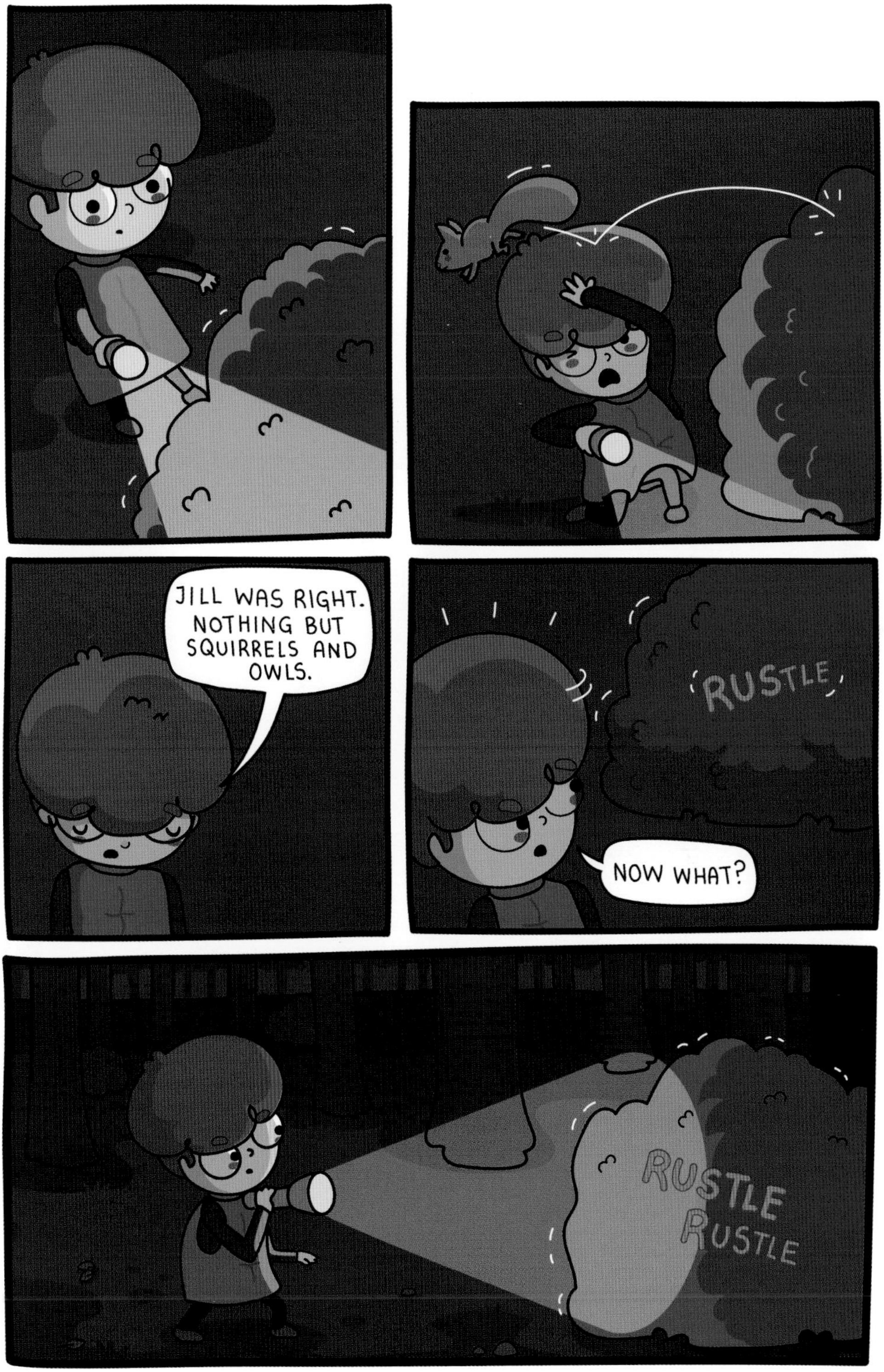
JILL WAS RIGHT. NOTHING BUT SQUIRRELS AND OWLS.
RUSTLE
NOW WHAT?
RUSTLE
RUSTLE

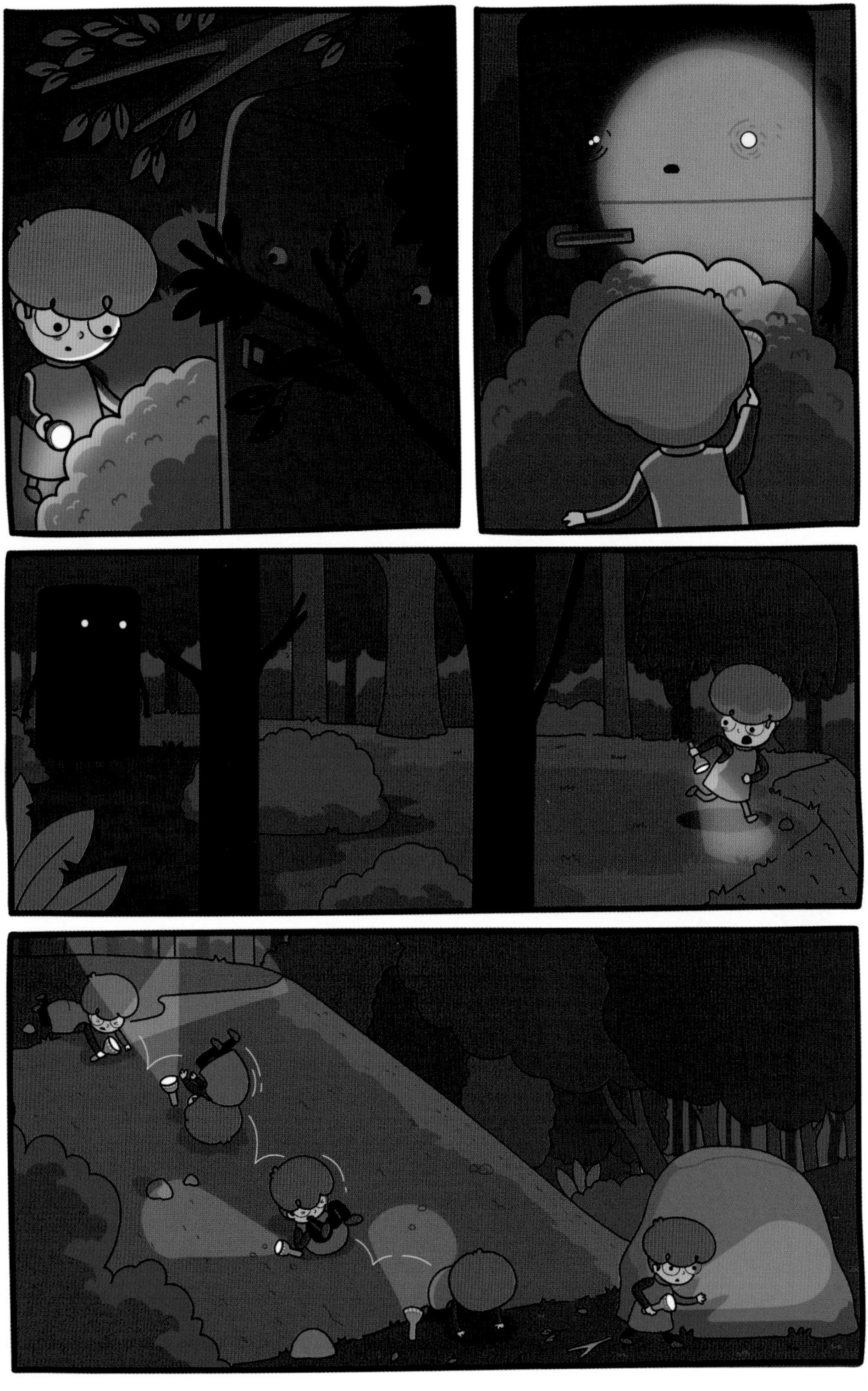

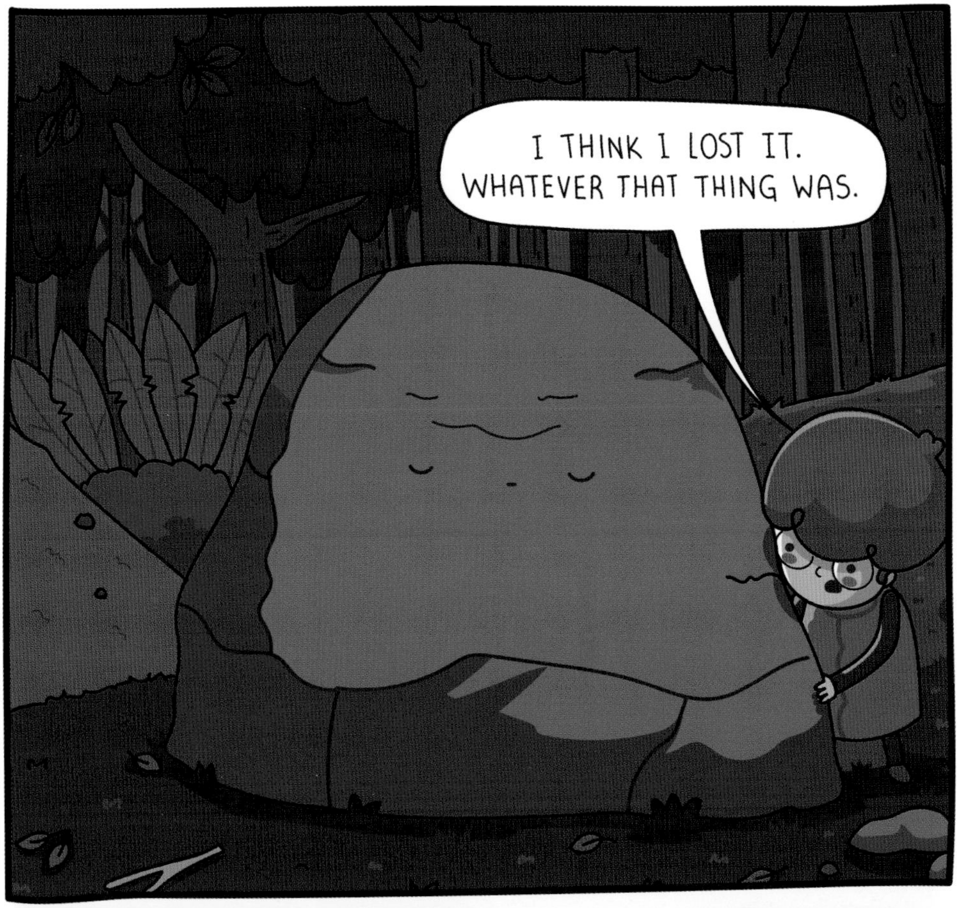
I THINK I LOST IT. WHATEVER THAT THING WAS.

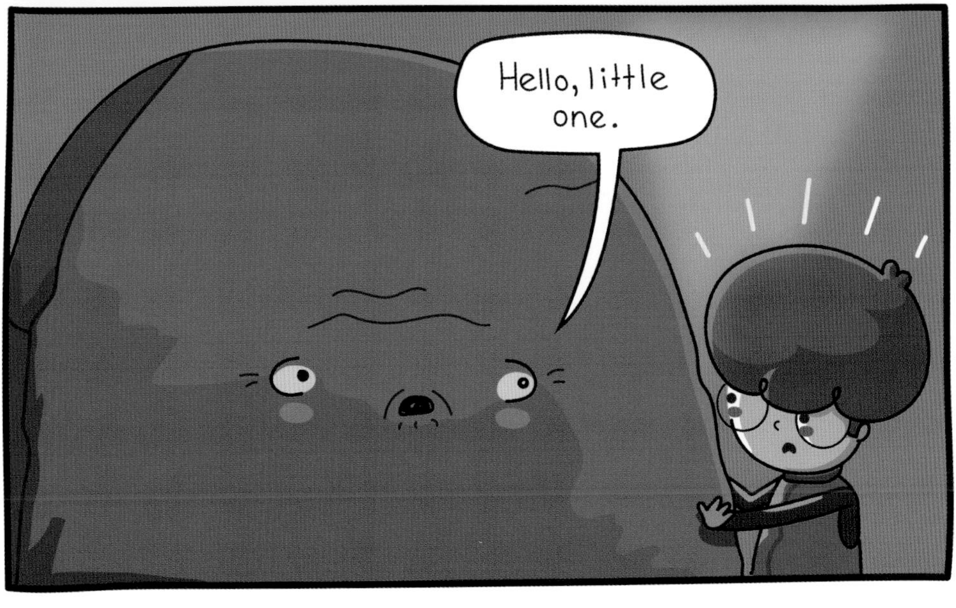
Hello, little one.

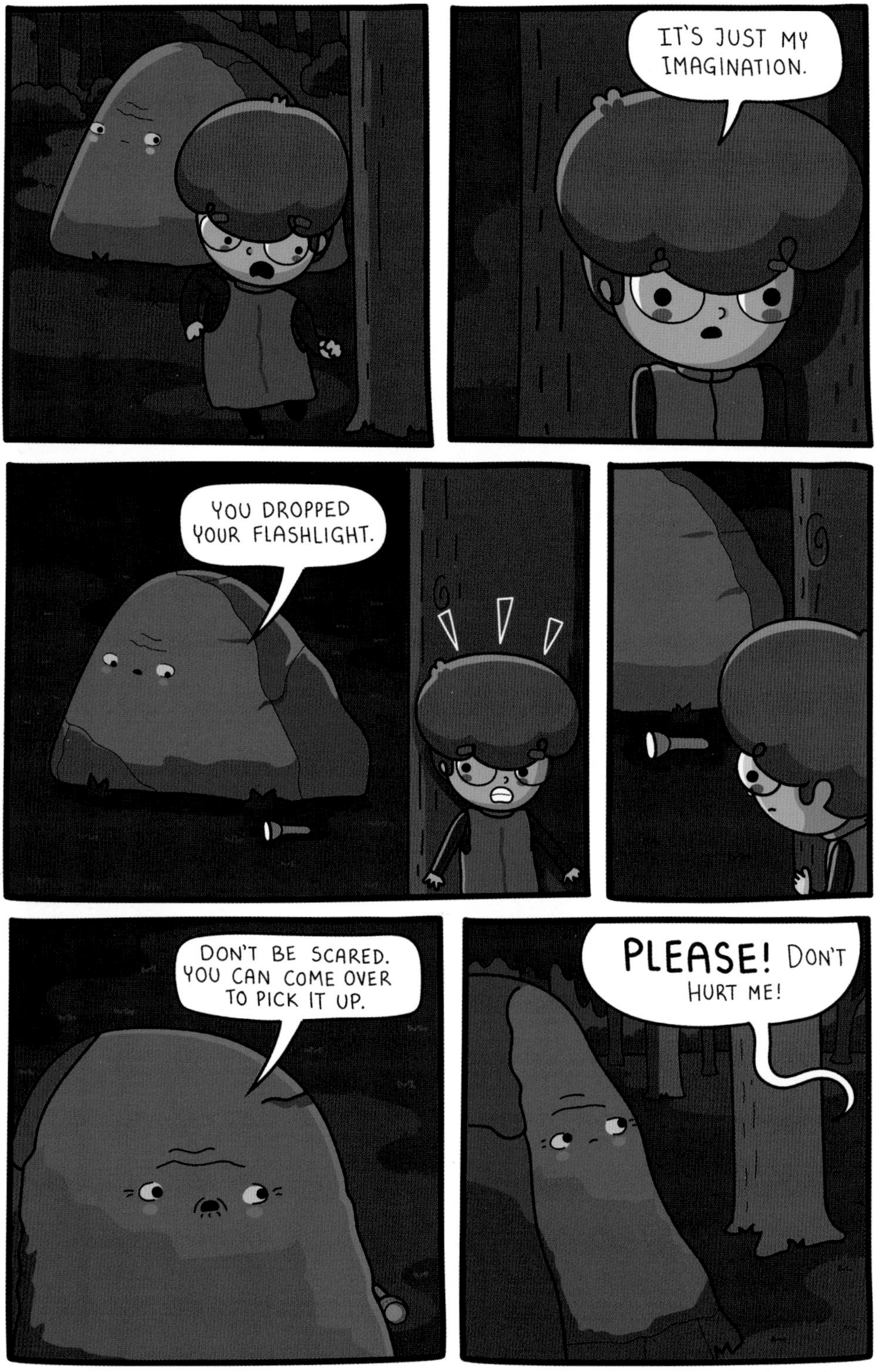
IT'S JUST MY IMAGINATION.
YOU DROPPED YOUR FLASHLIGHT.
DON'T BE SCARED. YOU CAN COME OVER TO PICK IT UP.
PLEASE! DON'T HURT ME!

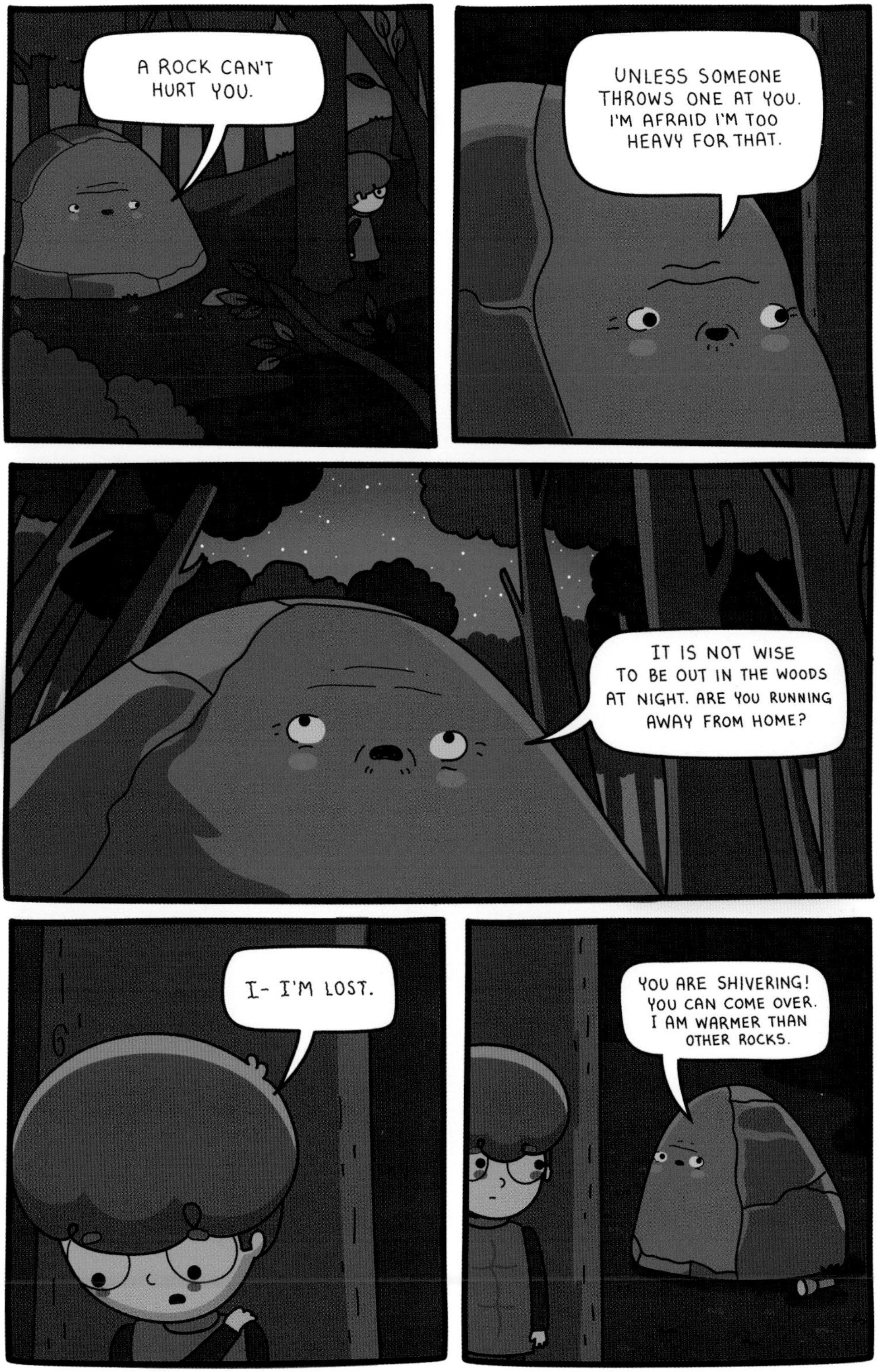
A ROCK CAN'T HURT YOU.
UNLESS SOMEONE THROWS ONE AT YOU. I'M AFRAID I'M TOO HEAVY FOR THAT.
IT IS NOT WISE TO BE OUT IN THE WOODS AT NIGHT. ARE YOU RUNNING AWAY FROM HOME?
I- I'M LOST.
YOU ARE SHIVERING! YOU CAN COME OVER. I AM WARMER THAN OTHER ROCKS.

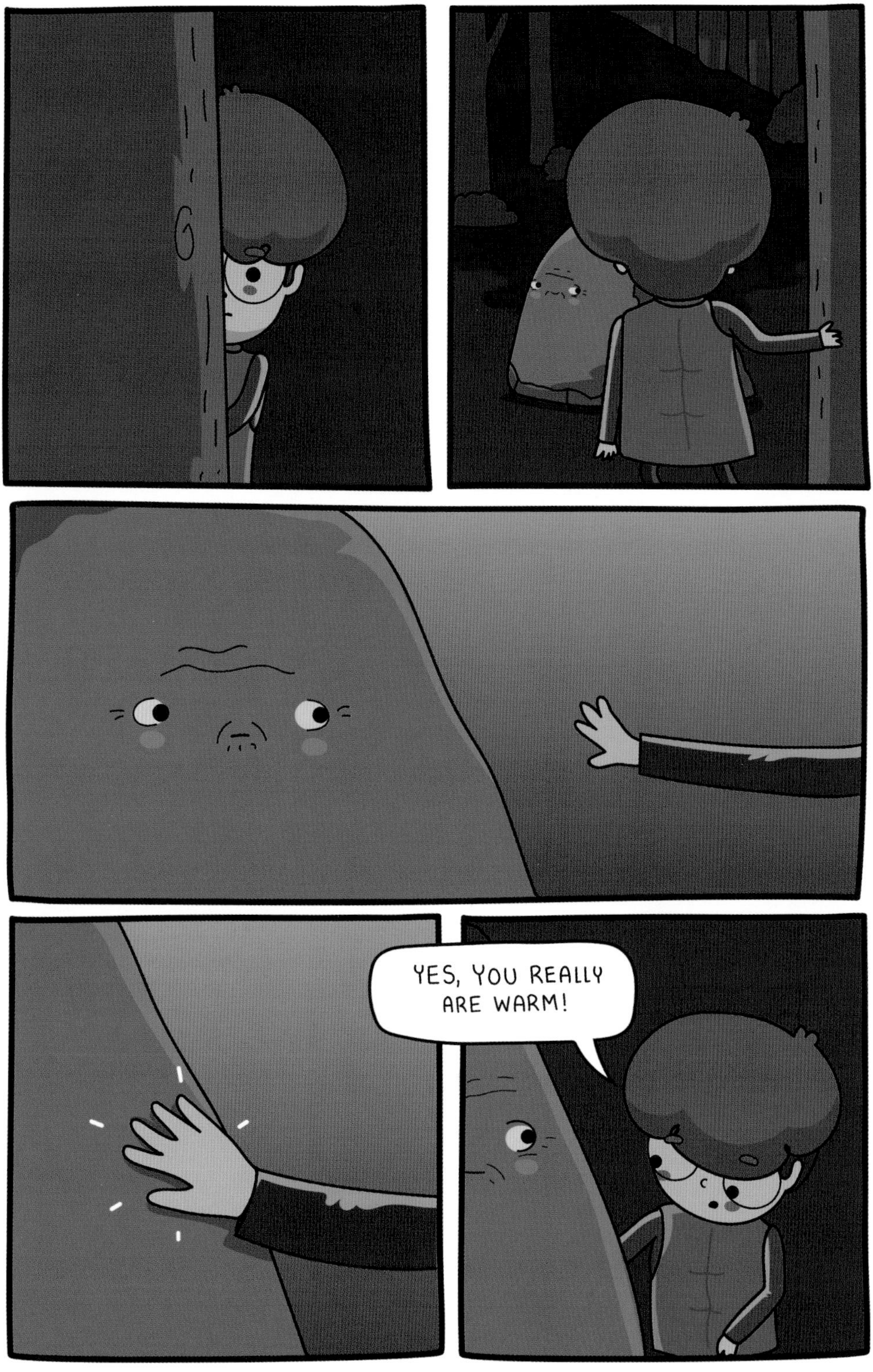
YES, YOU REALLY ARE WARM!

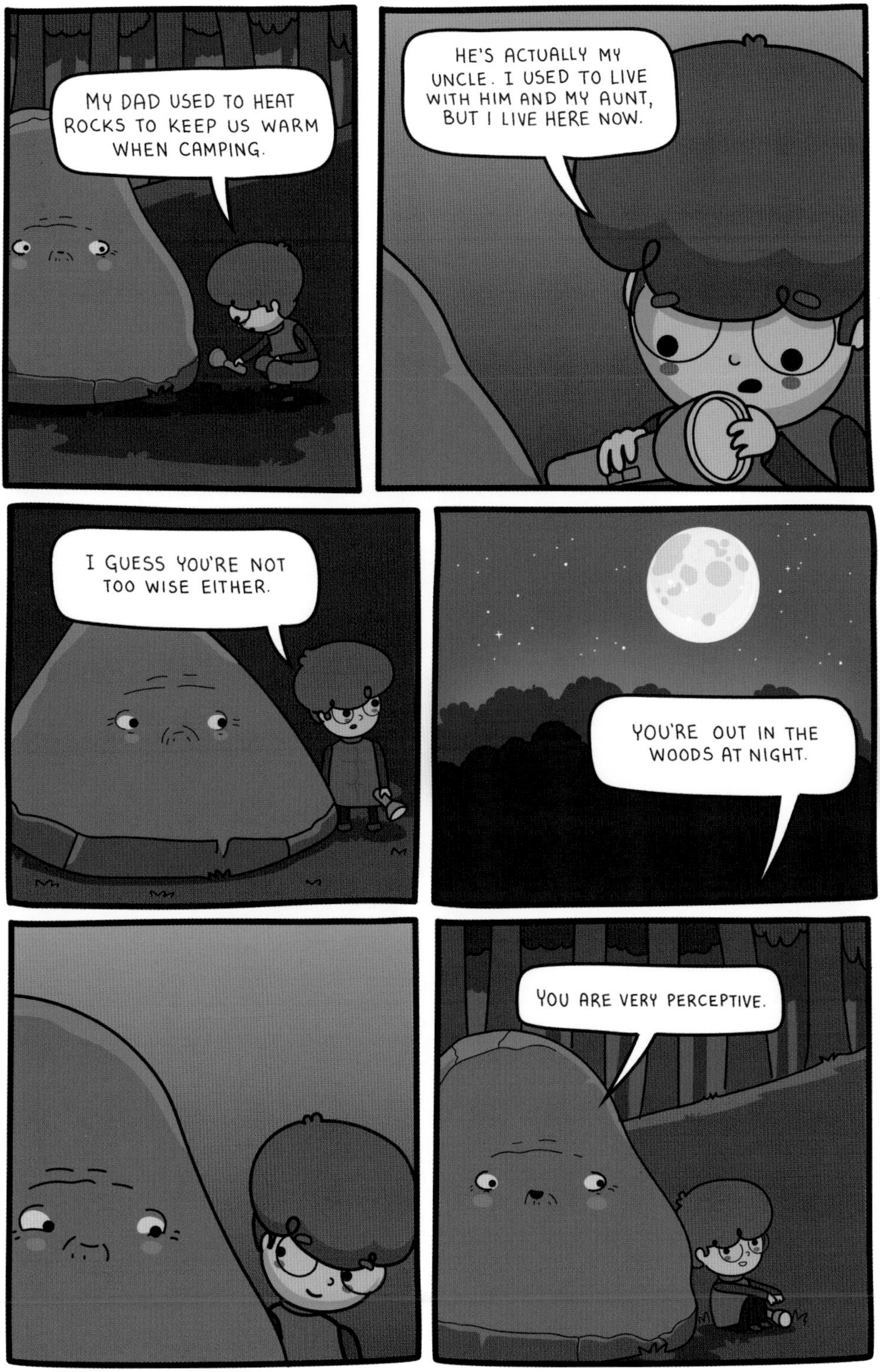
MY DAD USED TO HEAT ROCKS TO KEEP US WARM WHEN CAMPING.
HE'S ACTUALLY MY UNCLE. I USED TO LIVE WITH HIM AND MY AUNT, BUT I LIVE HERE NOW.
I GUESS YOU'RE NOT TOO WISE EITHER.
YOU'RE OUT IN THE WOODS AT NIGHT.
YOU ARE VERY PERCEPTIVE.

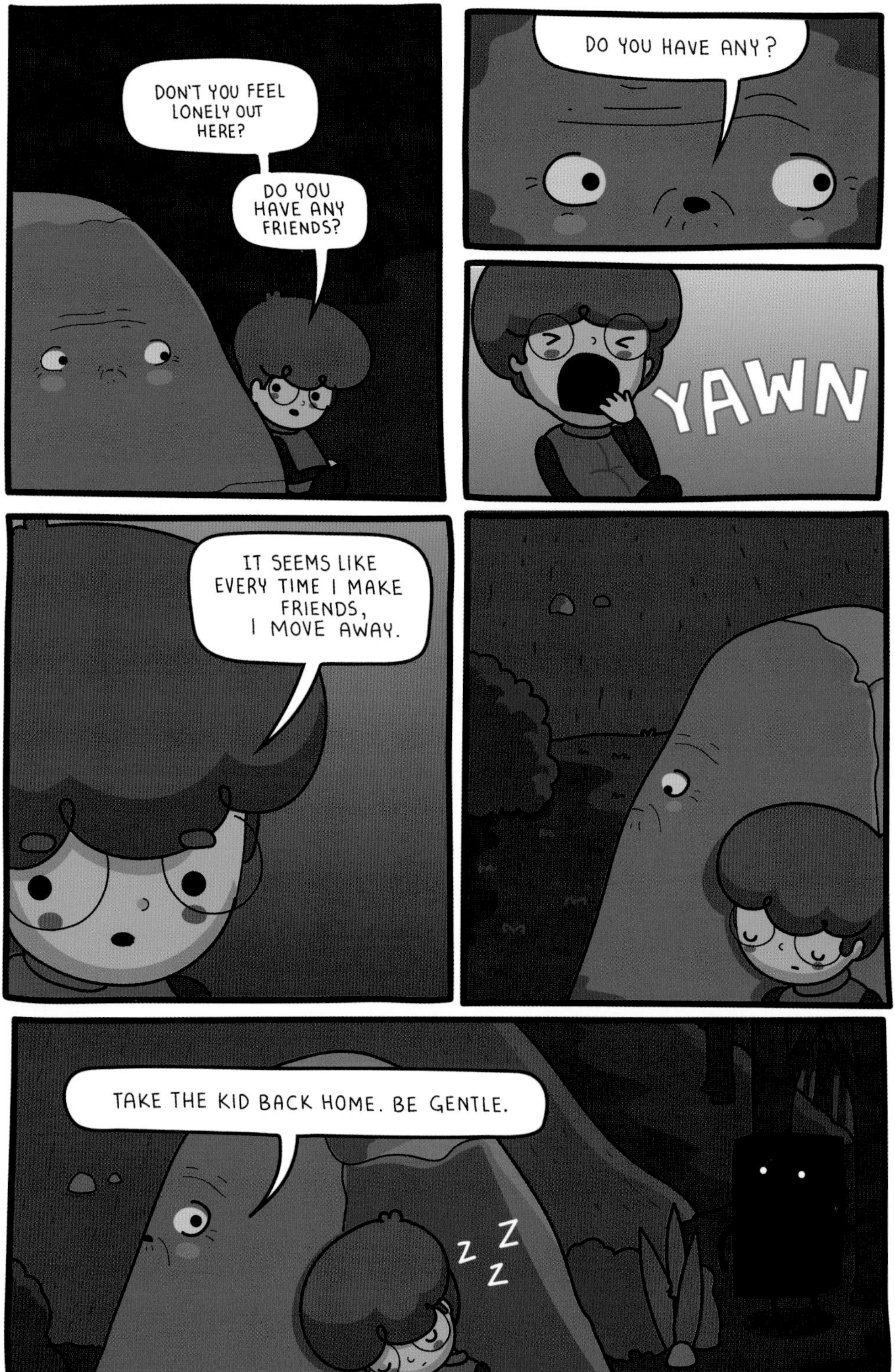
DON'T YOU FEEL LONELY OUT HERE?
DO YOU HAVE ANY FRIENDS?
DO YOU HAVE ANY?
YAWN
IT SEEMS LIKE EVERY TIME I MAKE FRIENDS, I MOVE AWAY.
TAKE THE KID BACK HOME. BE GENTLE.
Z Z Z

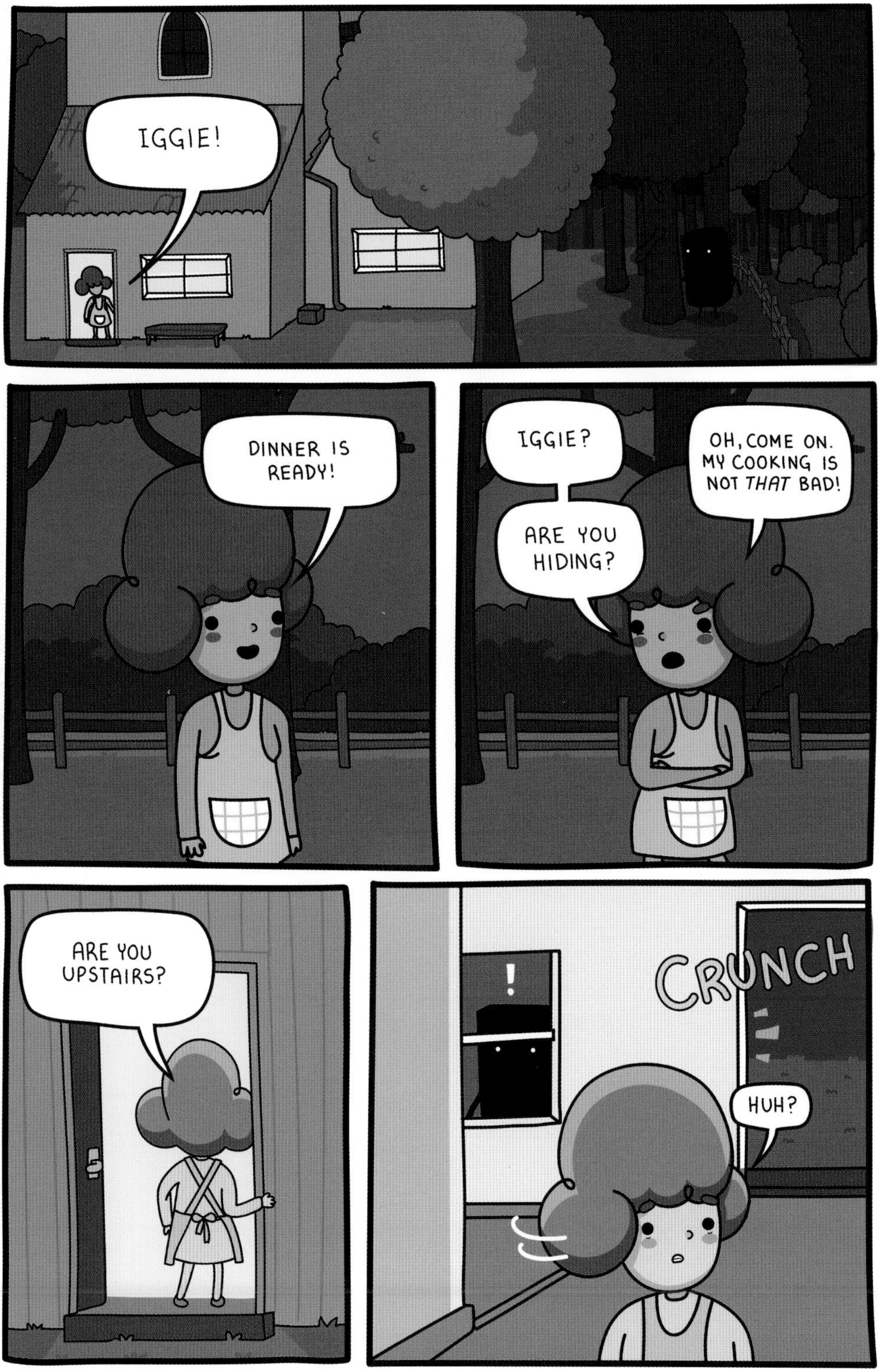
IGGIE!
DINNER IS READY!
IGGIE?
ARE YOU HIDING?
OH, COME ON. MY COOKING IS NOT *THAT* BAD!
ARE YOU UPSTAIRS?
!
CRUNCH
HUH?

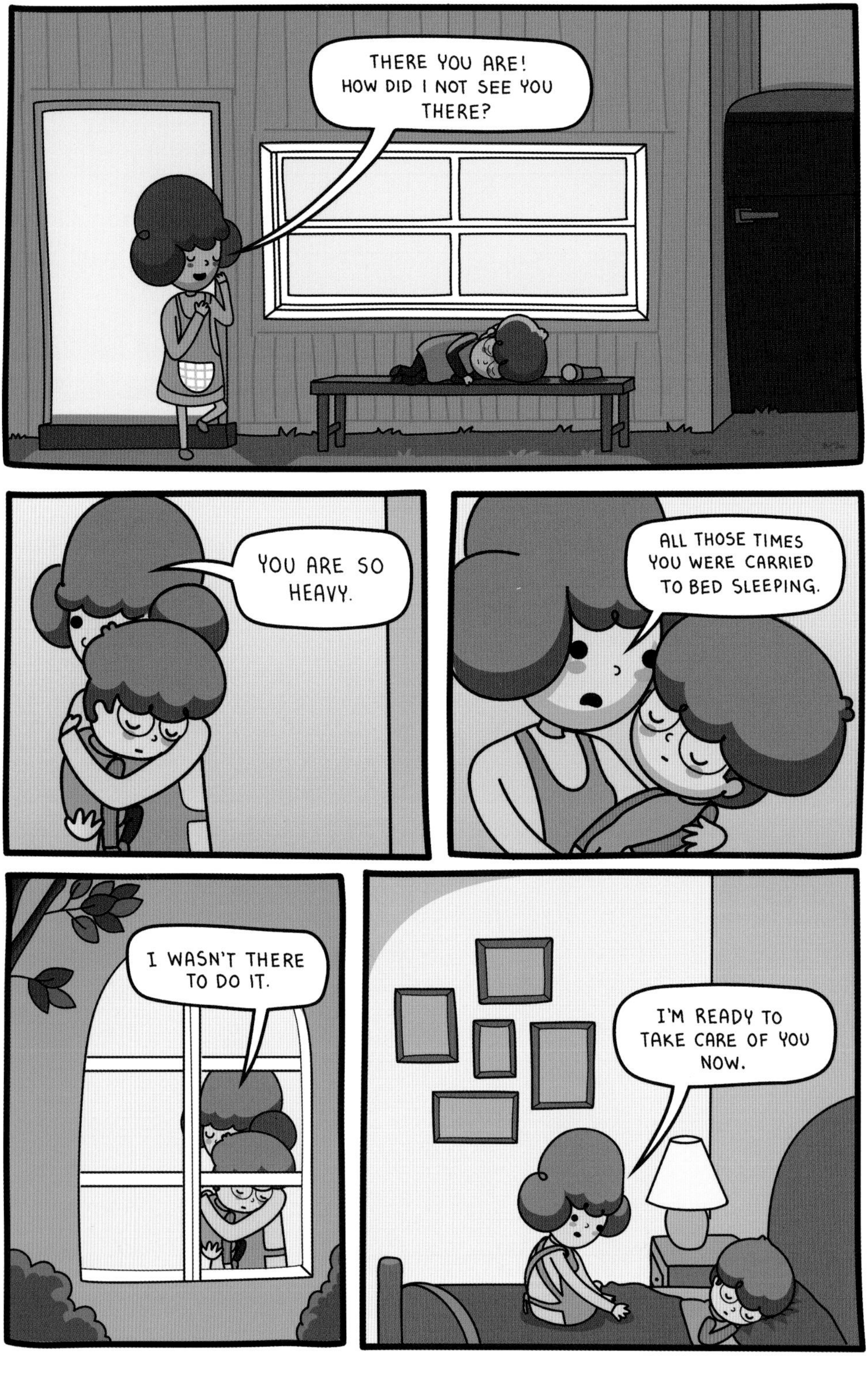
THERE YOU ARE! HOW DID I NOT SEE YOU THERE?
YOU ARE SO HEAVY.
ALL THOSE TIMES YOU WERE CARRIED TO BED SLEEPING.
I WASN'T THERE TO DO IT.
I'M READY TO TAKE CARE OF YOU NOW.

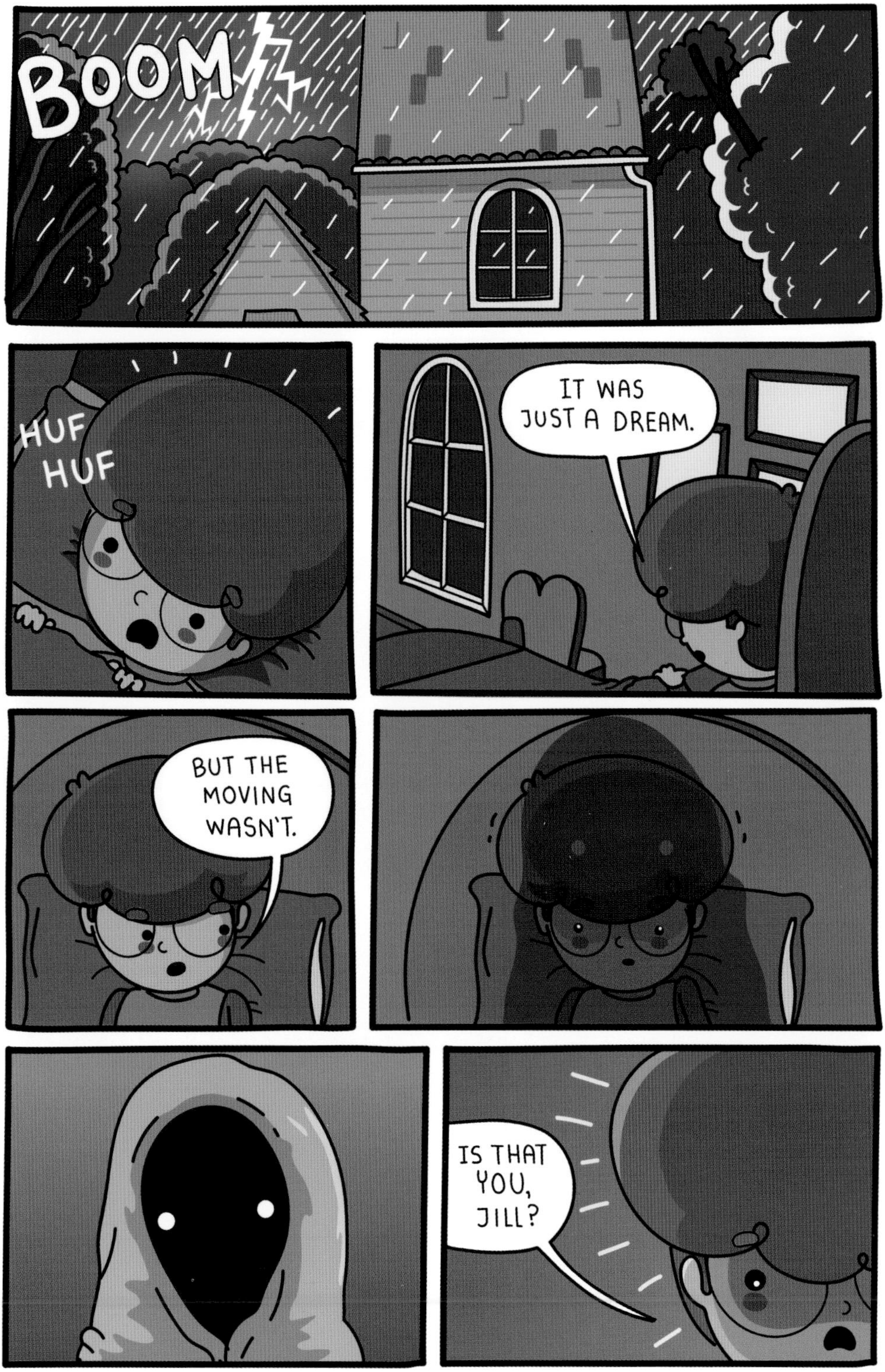
BOOM
HUF HUF
IT WAS JUST A DREAM.
BUT THE MOVING WASN'T.
IS THAT YOU, JILL?

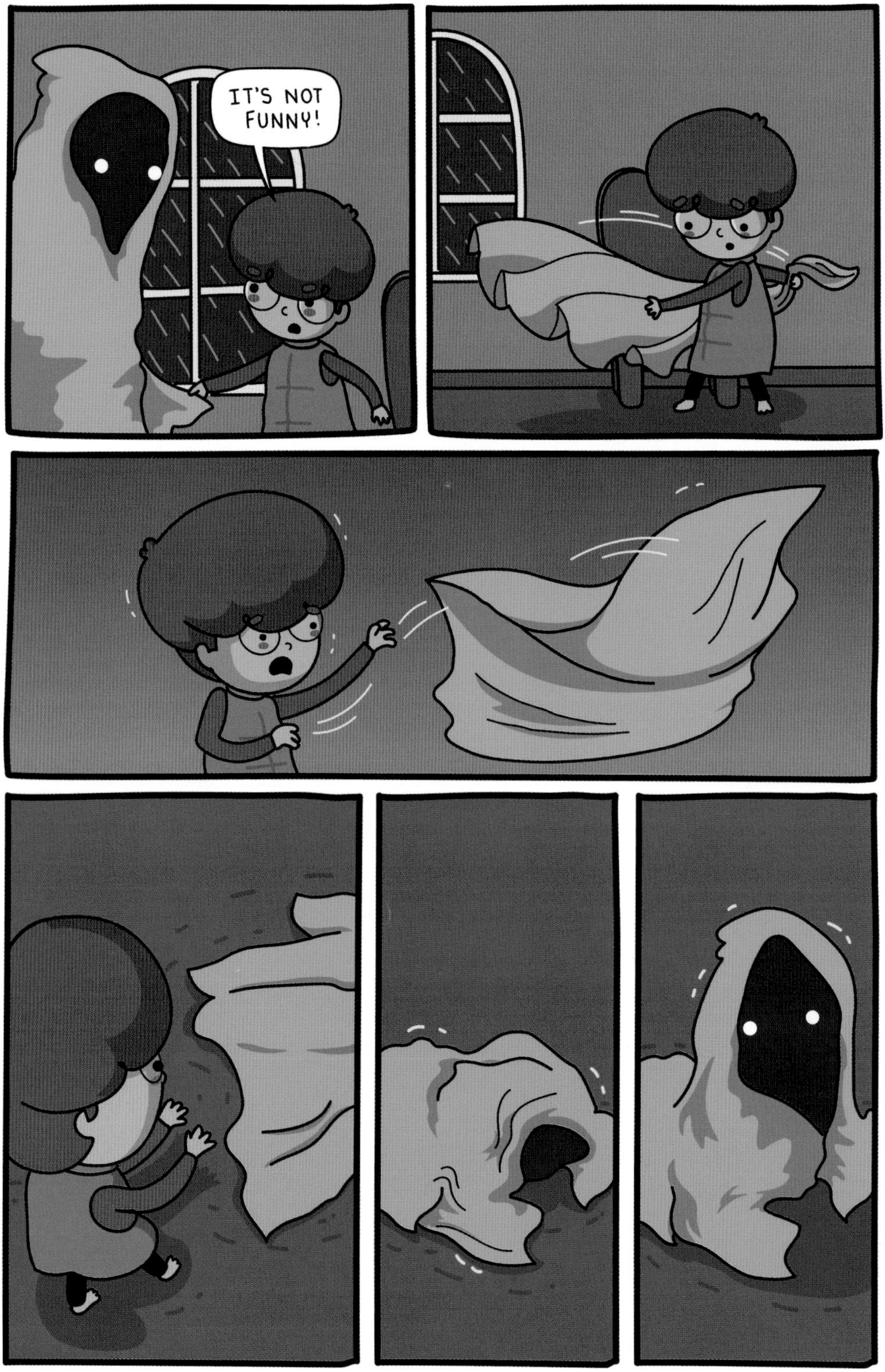
IT'S NOT FUNNY!

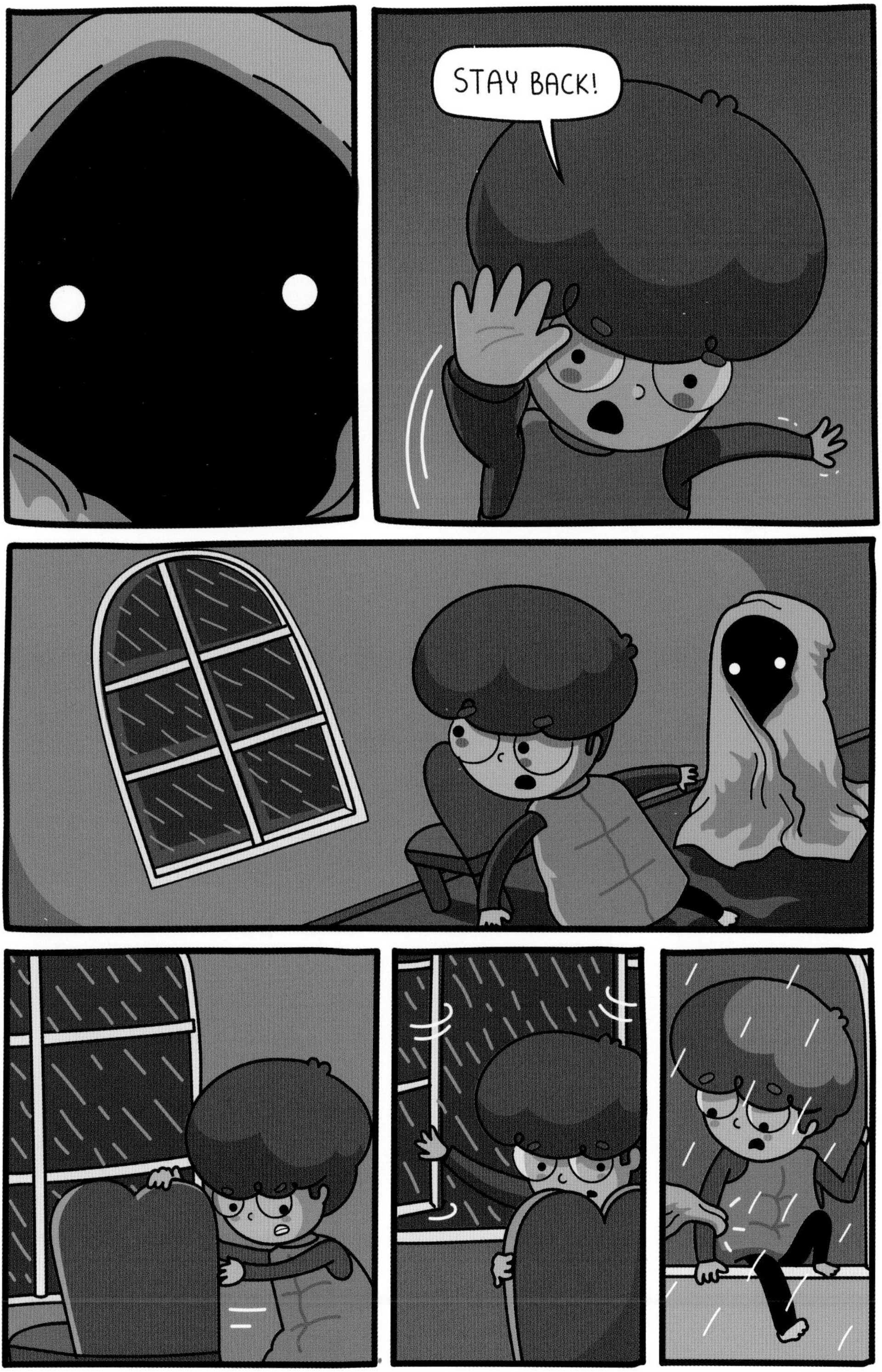
STAY BACK!

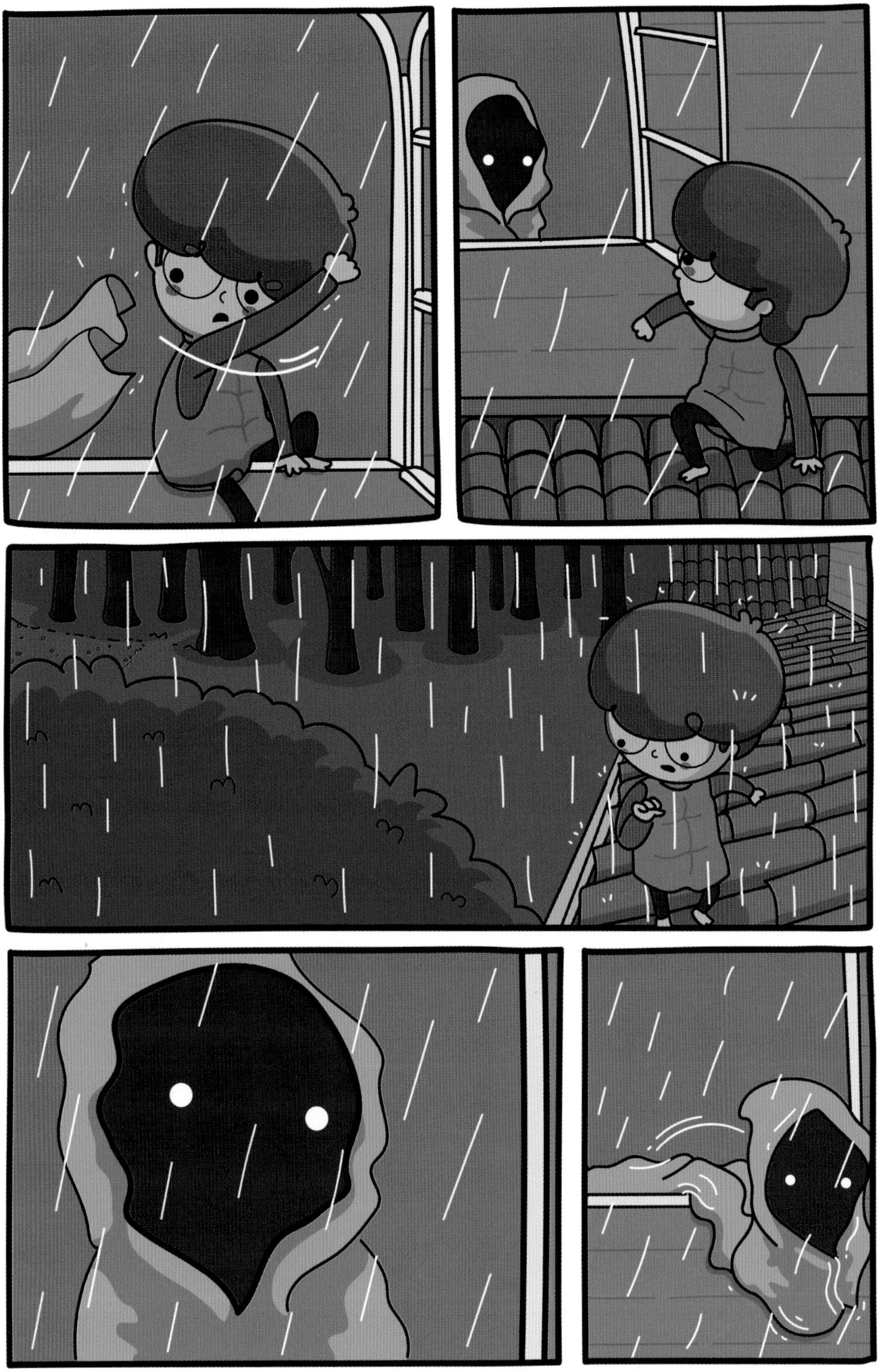

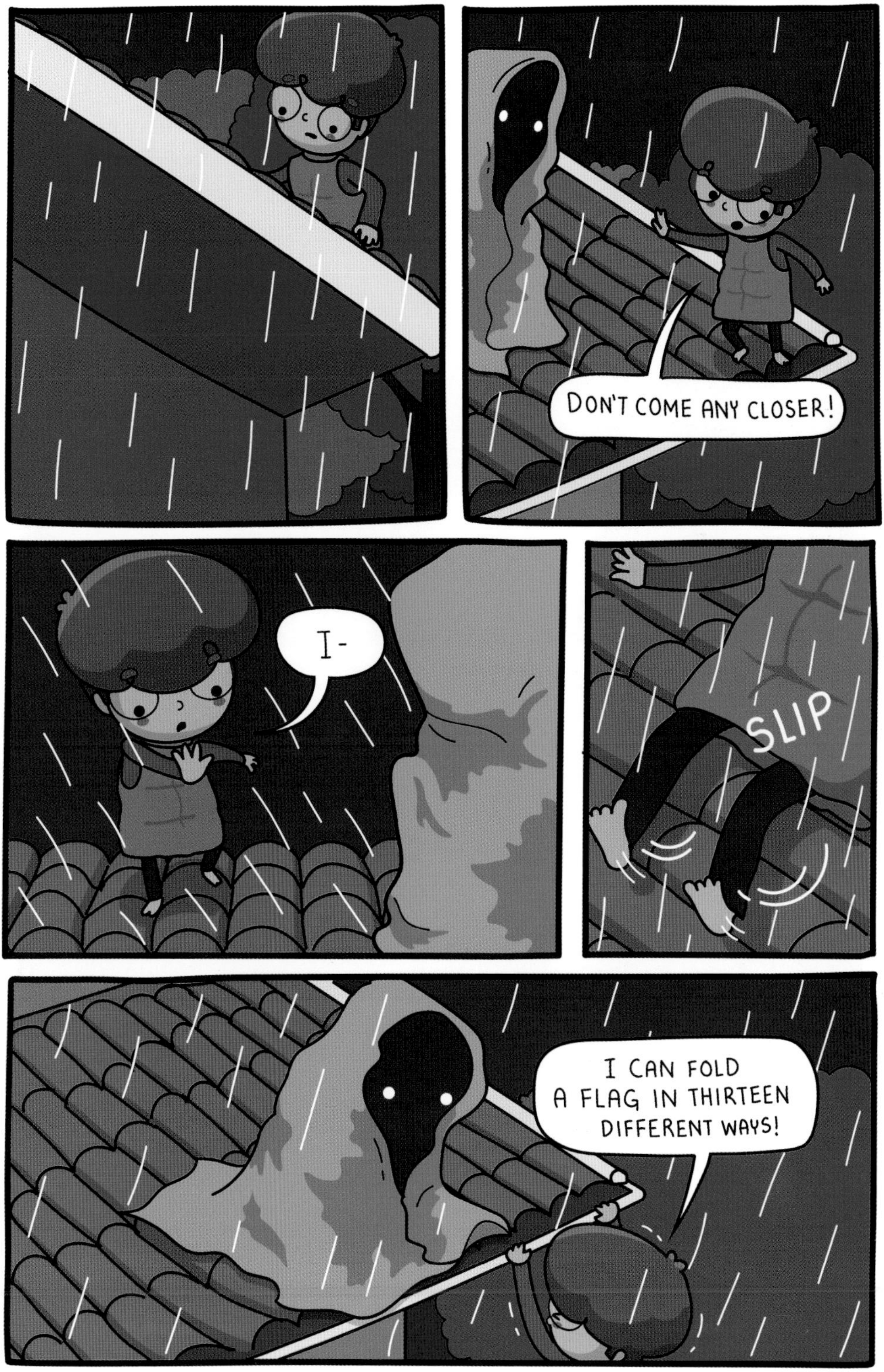
DON'T COME ANY CLOSER!
I-
SLIP
I CAN FOLD A FLAG IN THIRTEEN DIFFERENT WAYS!

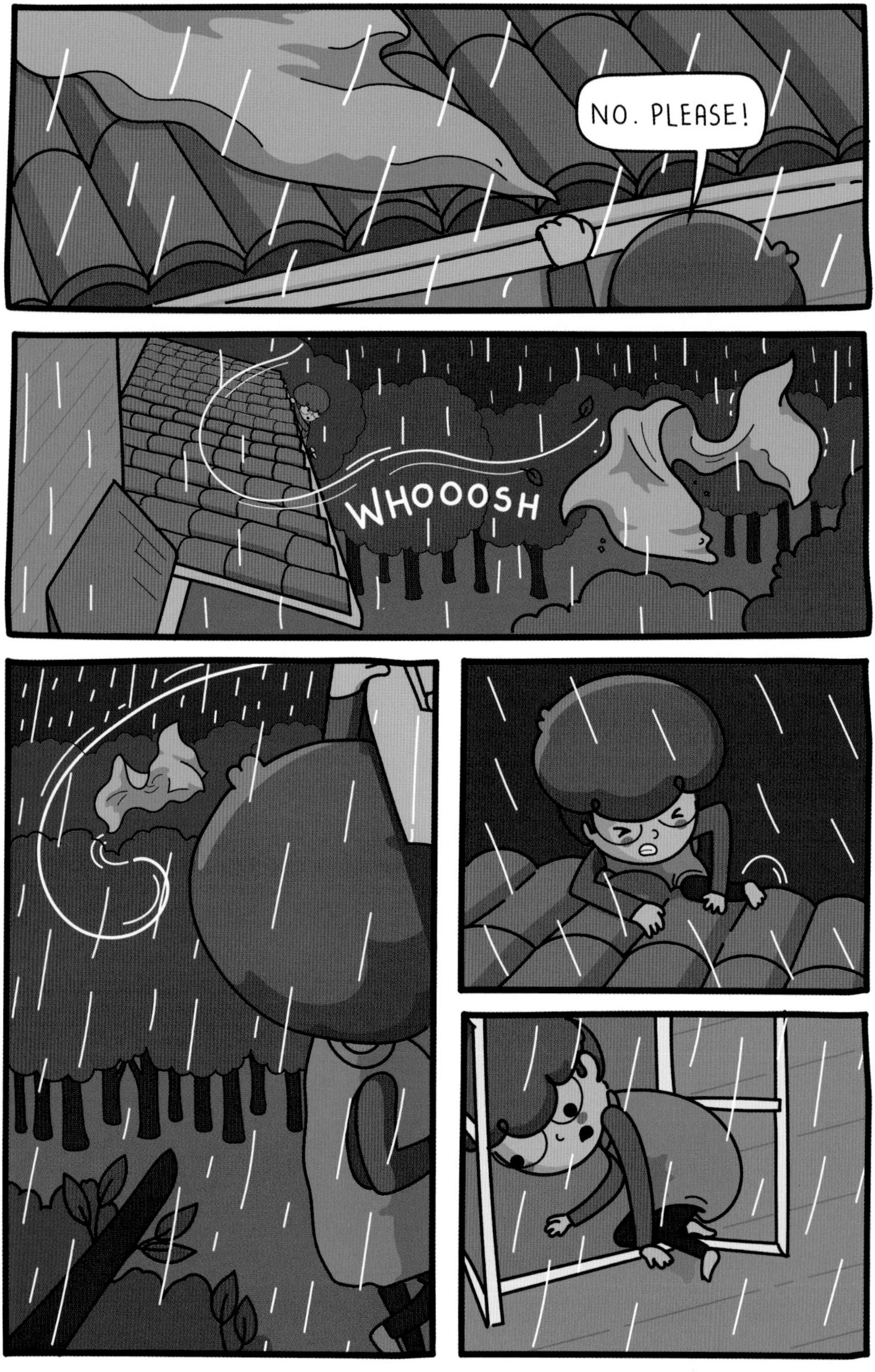
NO. PLEASE!
WHOOOSH

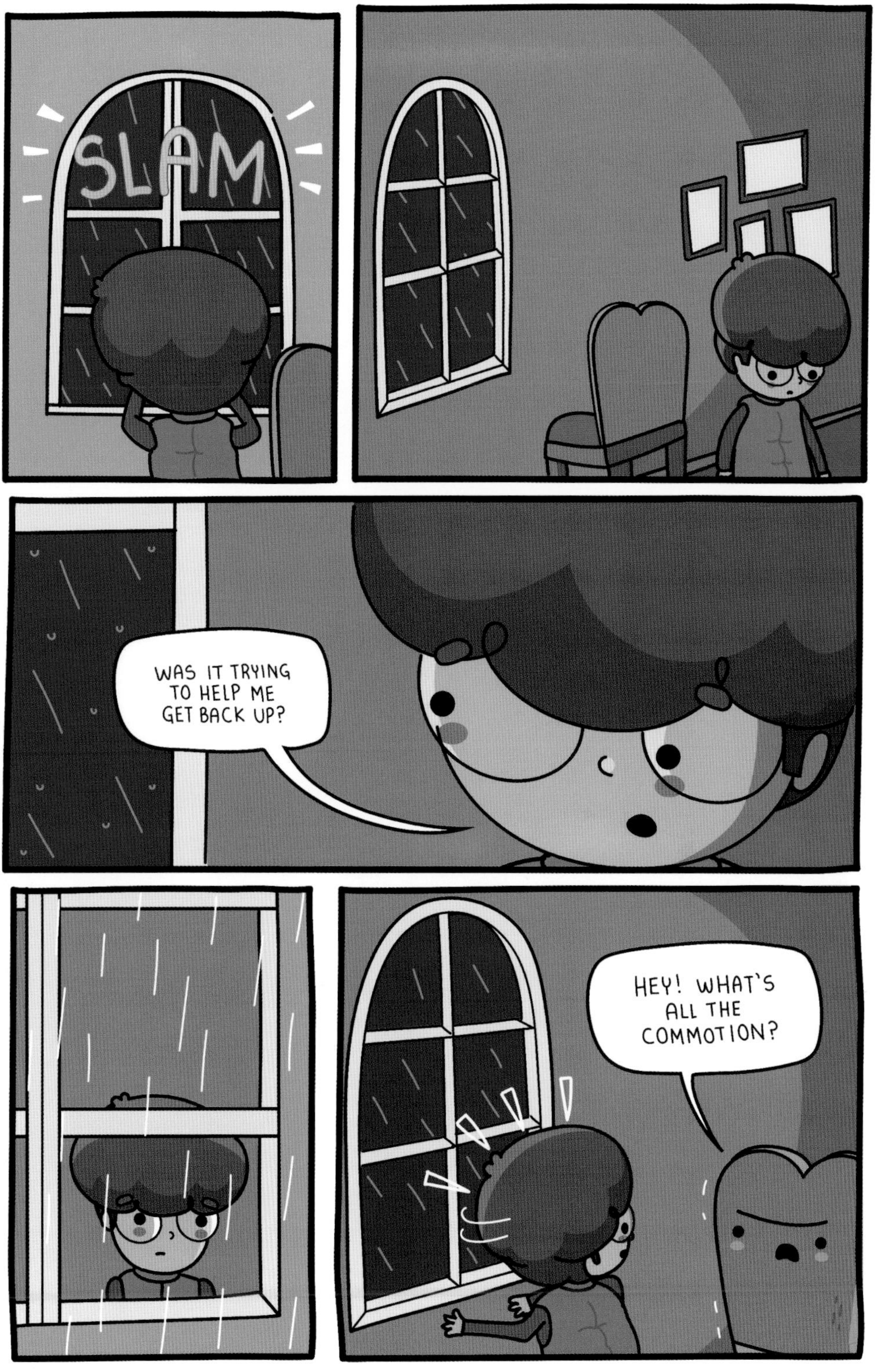
SLAM
WAS IT TRYING TO HELP ME GET BACK UP?
HEY! WHAT'S ALL THE COMMOTION?

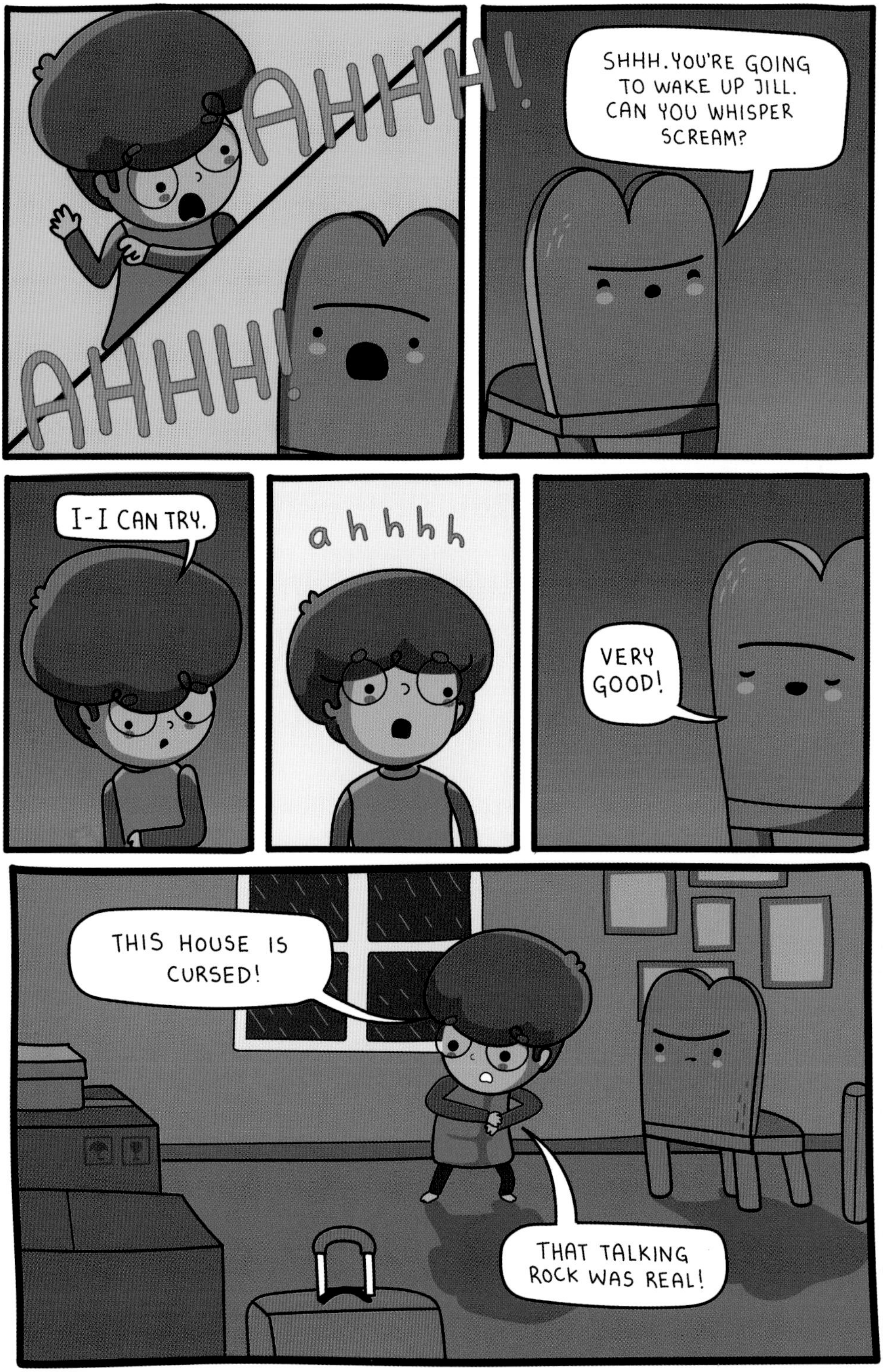
AHHHH!
AHHHH!
SHHH. YOU'RE GOING TO WAKE UP JILL. CAN YOU WHISPER SCREAM?
I-I CAN TRY.
a h h h h
VERY GOOD!
THIS HOUSE IS CURSED!
THAT TALKING ROCK WAS REAL!

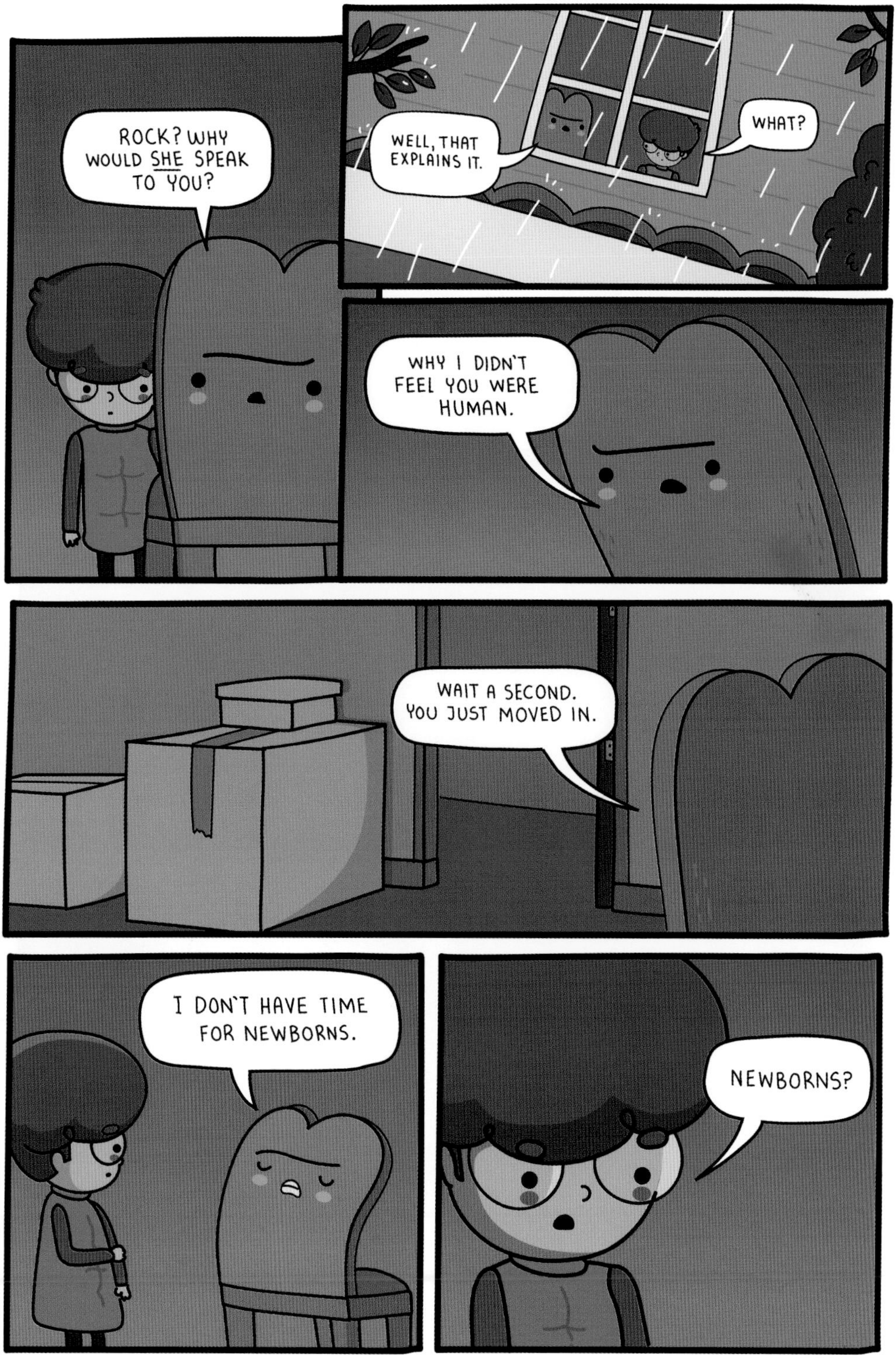
ROCK? WHY WOULD SHE SPEAK TO YOU?
WELL, THAT EXPLAINS IT.
WHAT?
WHY I DIDN'T FEEL YOU WERE HUMAN.
WAIT A SECOND. YOU JUST MOVED IN.
I DON'T HAVE TIME FOR NEWBORNS.
NEWBORNS?

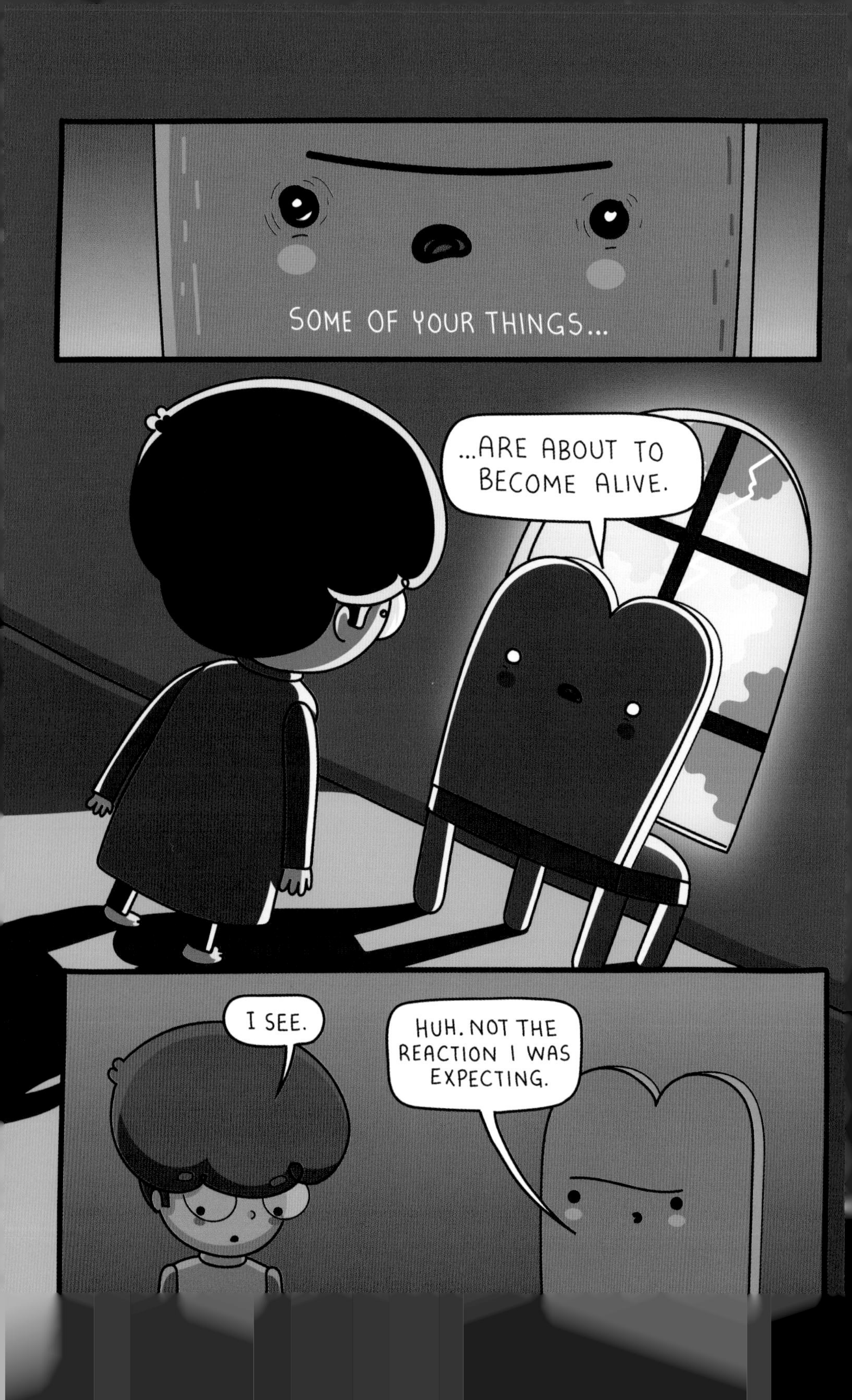
SOME OF YOUR THINGS...
...ARE ABOUT TO BECOME ALIVE.
I SEE.
HUH. NOT THE REACTION I WAS EXPECTING.

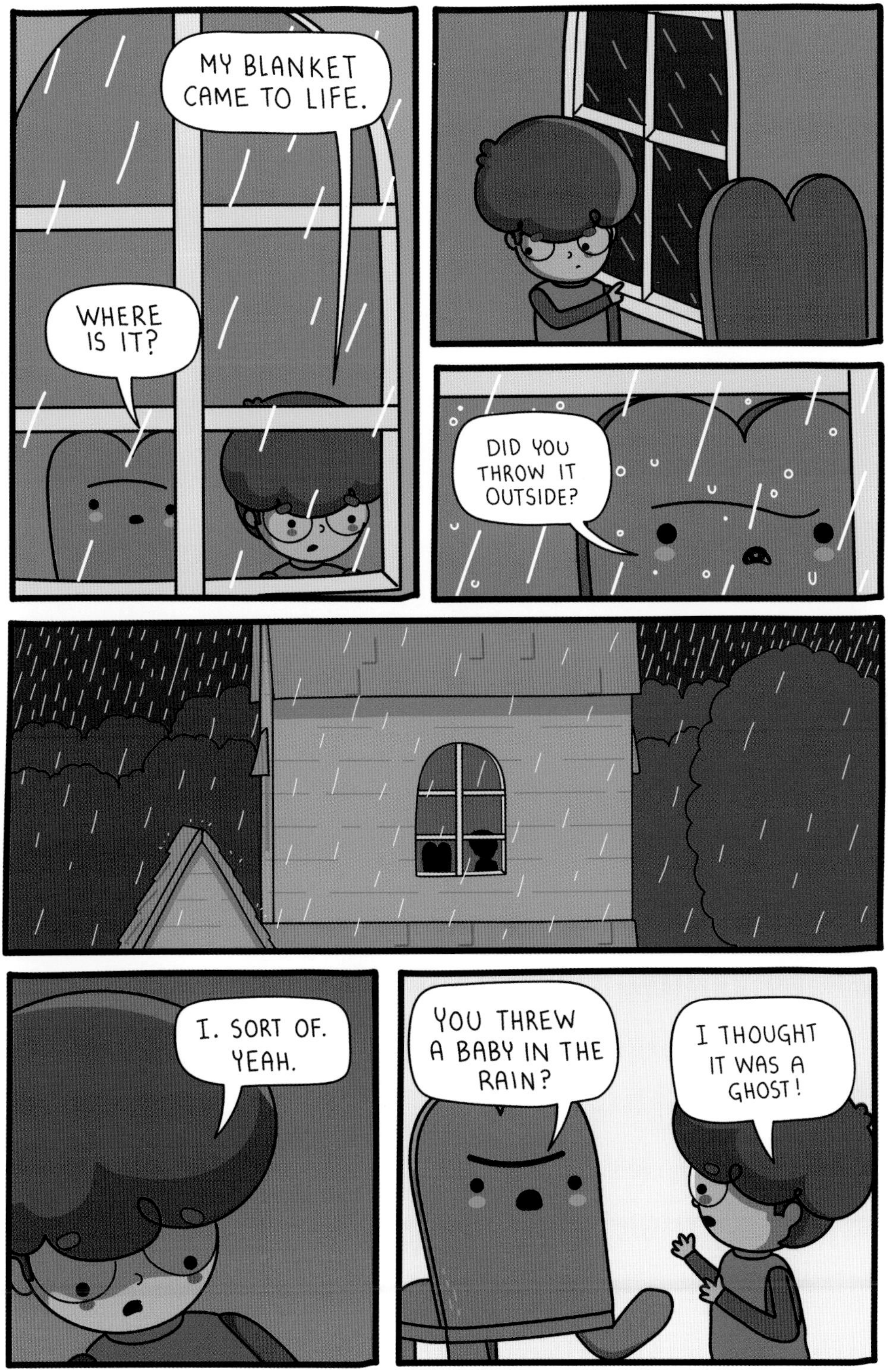
MY BLANKET CAME TO LIFE.
WHERE IS IT?
DID YOU THROW IT OUTSIDE?
I. SORT OF. YEAH.
YOU THREW A BABY IN THE RAIN?
I THOUGHT IT WAS A GHOST!

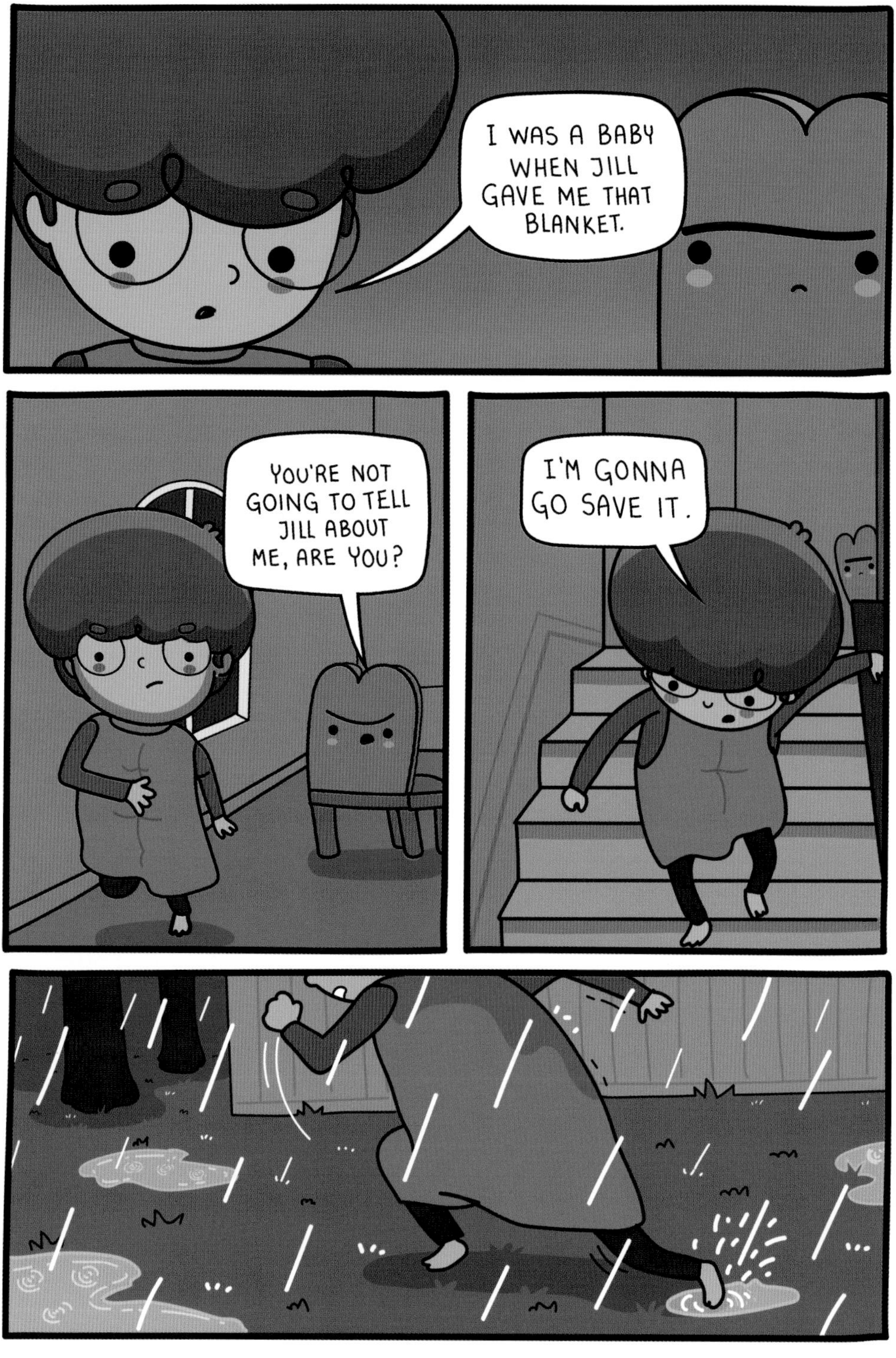
I WAS A BABY WHEN JILL GAVE ME THAT BLANKET.
YOU'RE NOT GOING TO TELL JILL ABOUT ME, ARE YOU?
I'M GONNA GO SAVE IT.

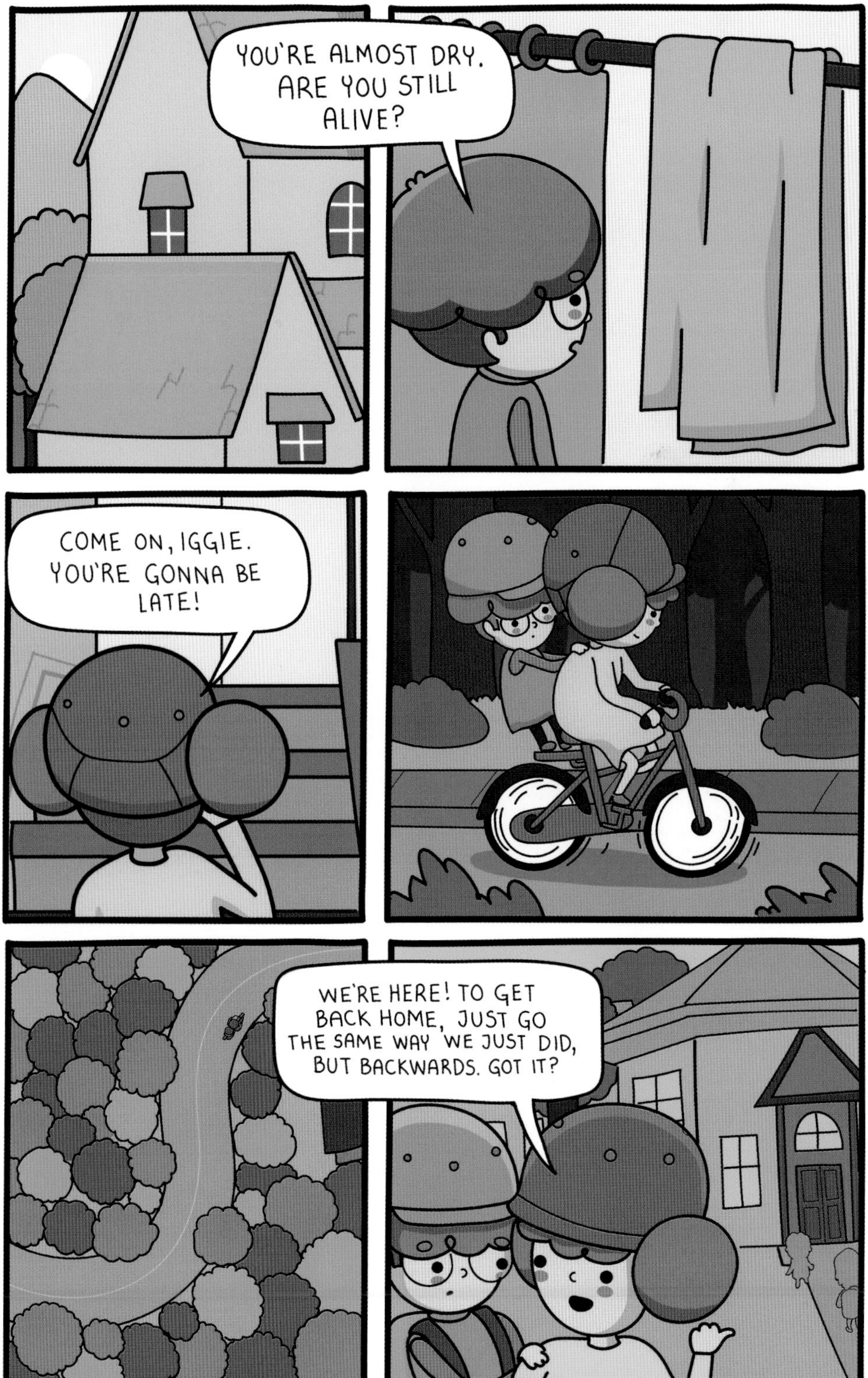
YOU'RE ALMOST DRY. ARE YOU STILL ALIVE?
COME ON, IGGIE. YOU'RE GONNA BE LATE!
WE'RE HERE! TO GET BACK HOME, JUST GO THE SAME WAY WE JUST DID, BUT BACKWARDS. GOT IT?

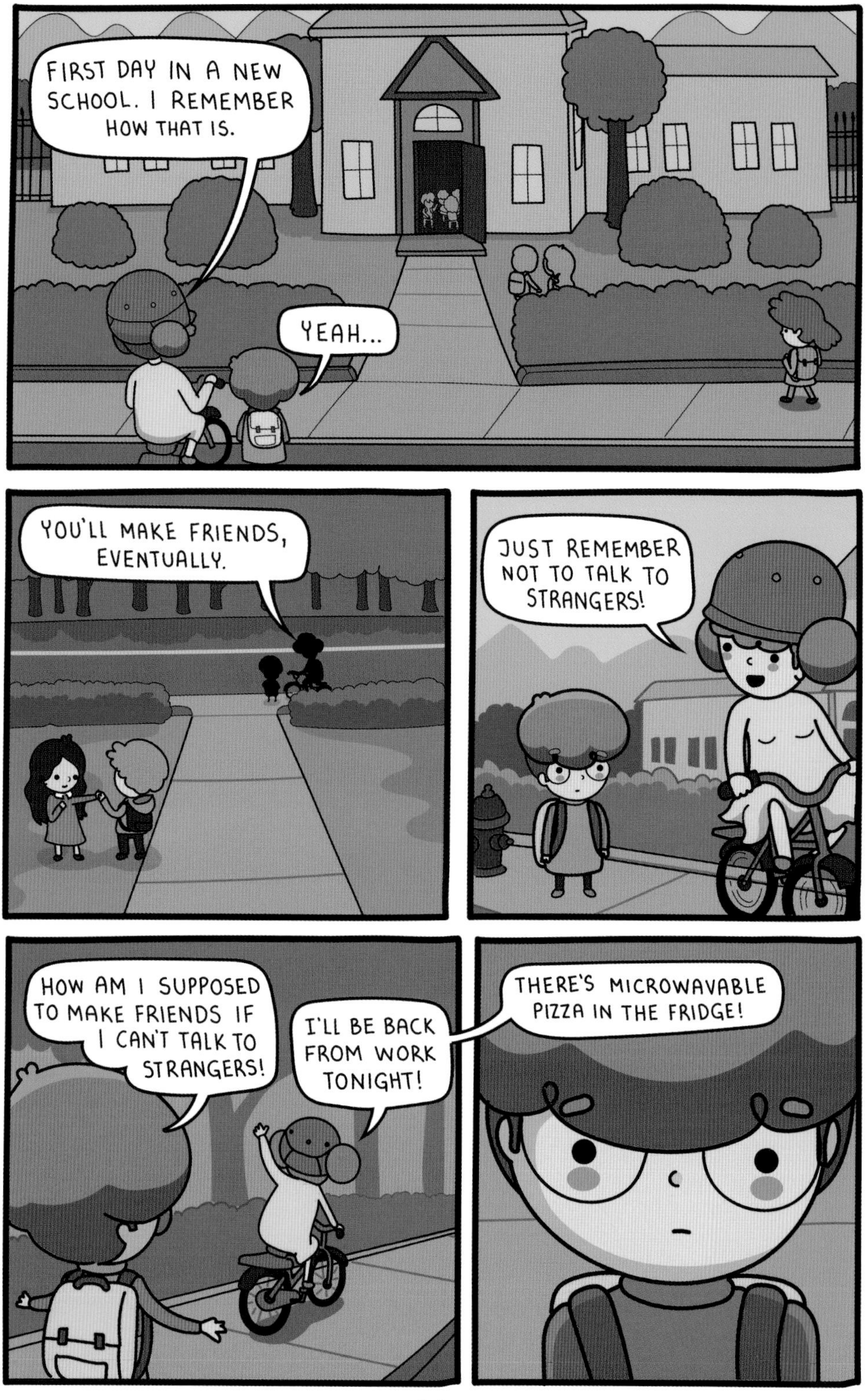
FIRST DAY IN A NEW SCHOOL. I REMEMBER HOW THAT IS.
YEAH...
YOU'LL MAKE FRIENDS, EVENTUALLY.
JUST REMEMBER NOT TO TALK TO STRANGERS!
HOW AM I SUPPOSED TO MAKE FRIENDS IF I CAN'T TALK TO STRANGERS!
I'LL BE BACK FROM WORK TONIGHT!
THERE'S MICROWAVABLE PIZZA IN THE FRIDGE!

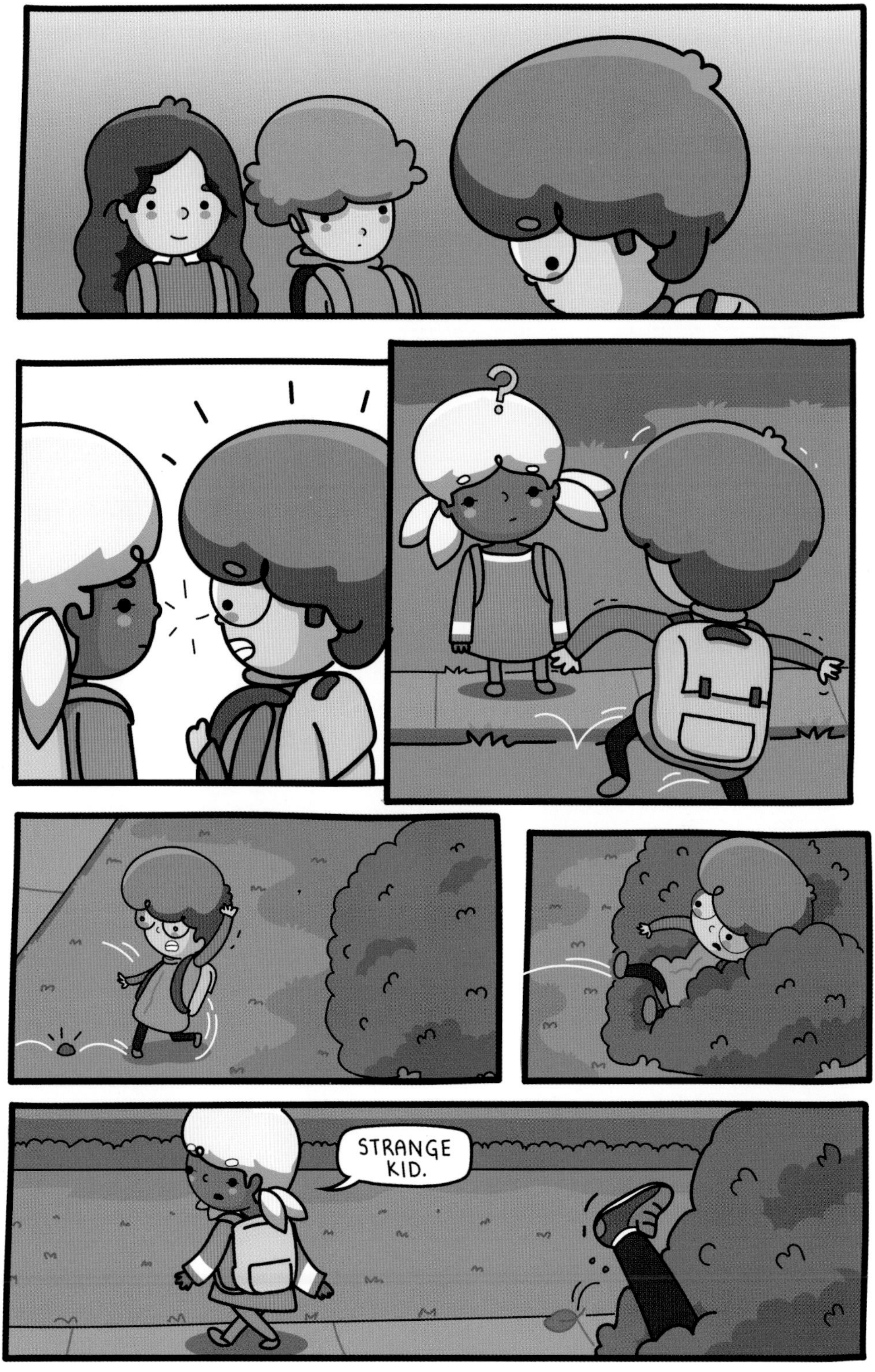
STRANGE KID.

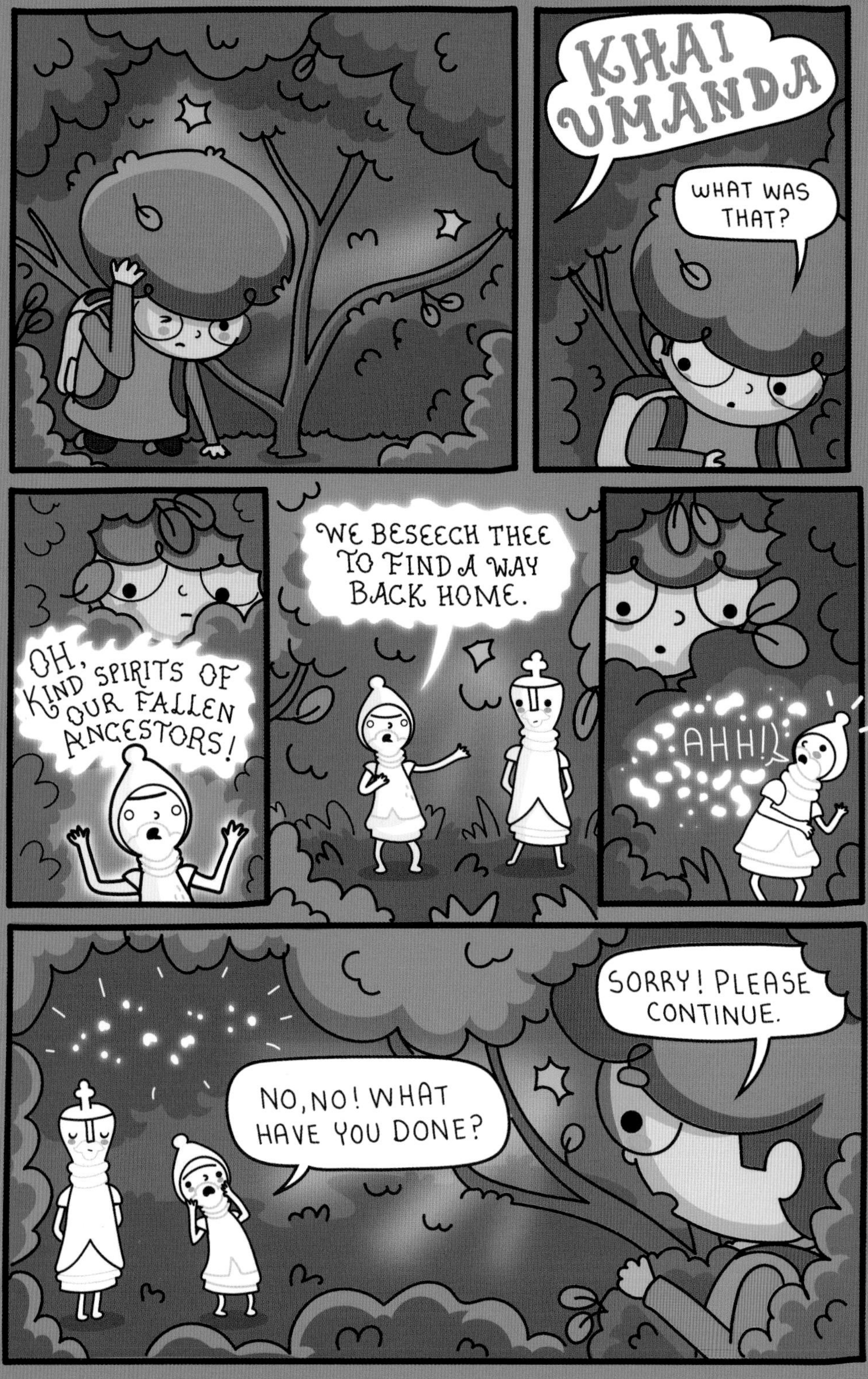
KHAI UMANDA
WHAT WAS THAT?
OH, KIND SPIRITS OF OUR FALLEN ANCESTORS!
WE BESEECH THEE TO FIND A WAY BACK HOME.
AHH!
SORRY! PLEASE CONTINUE.
NO, NO! WHAT HAVE YOU DONE?

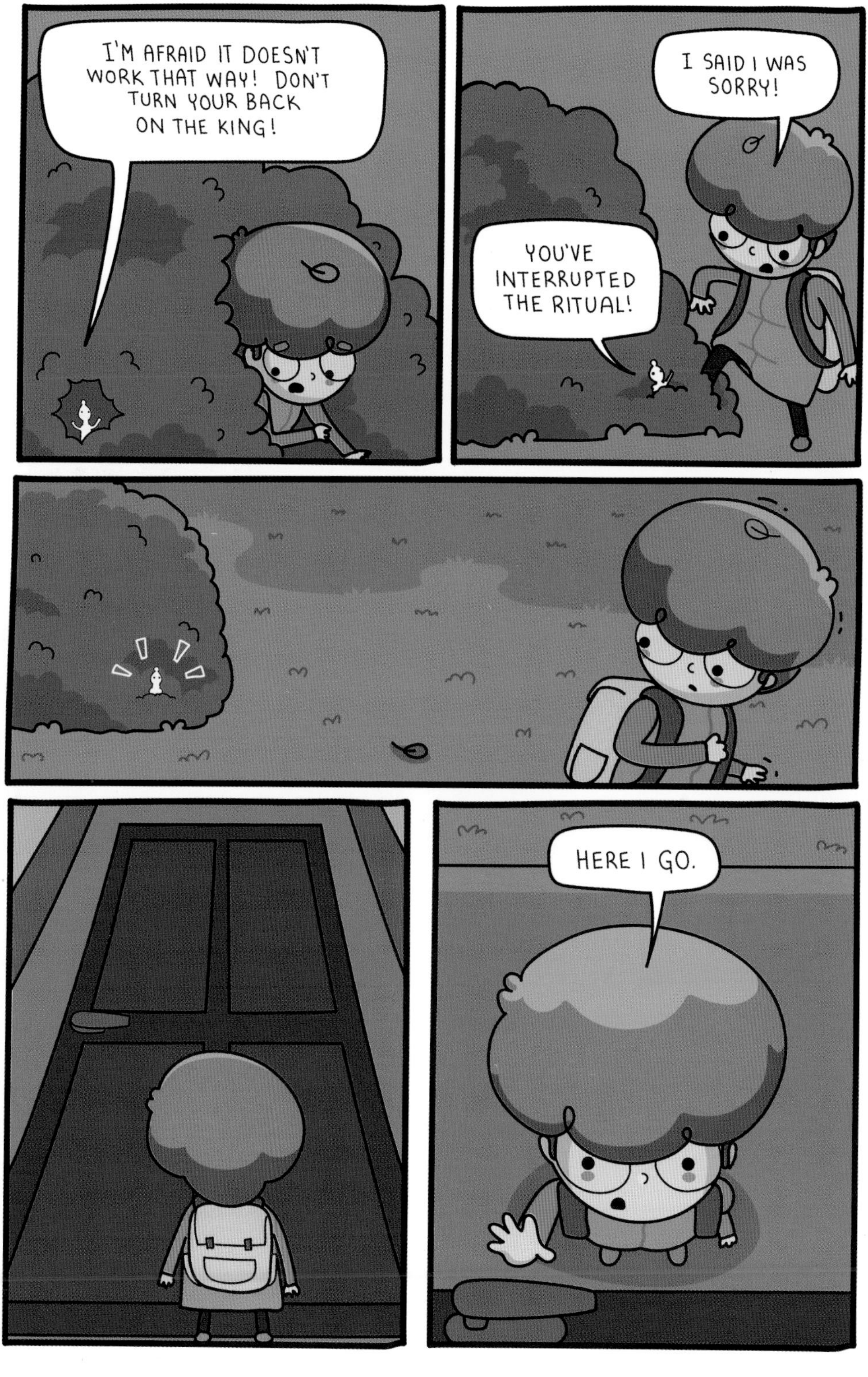
I'M AFRAID IT DOESN'T WORK THAT WAY! DON'T TURN YOUR BACK ON THE KING!
I SAID I WAS SORRY!
YOU'VE INTERRUPTED THE RITUAL!
HERE I GO.

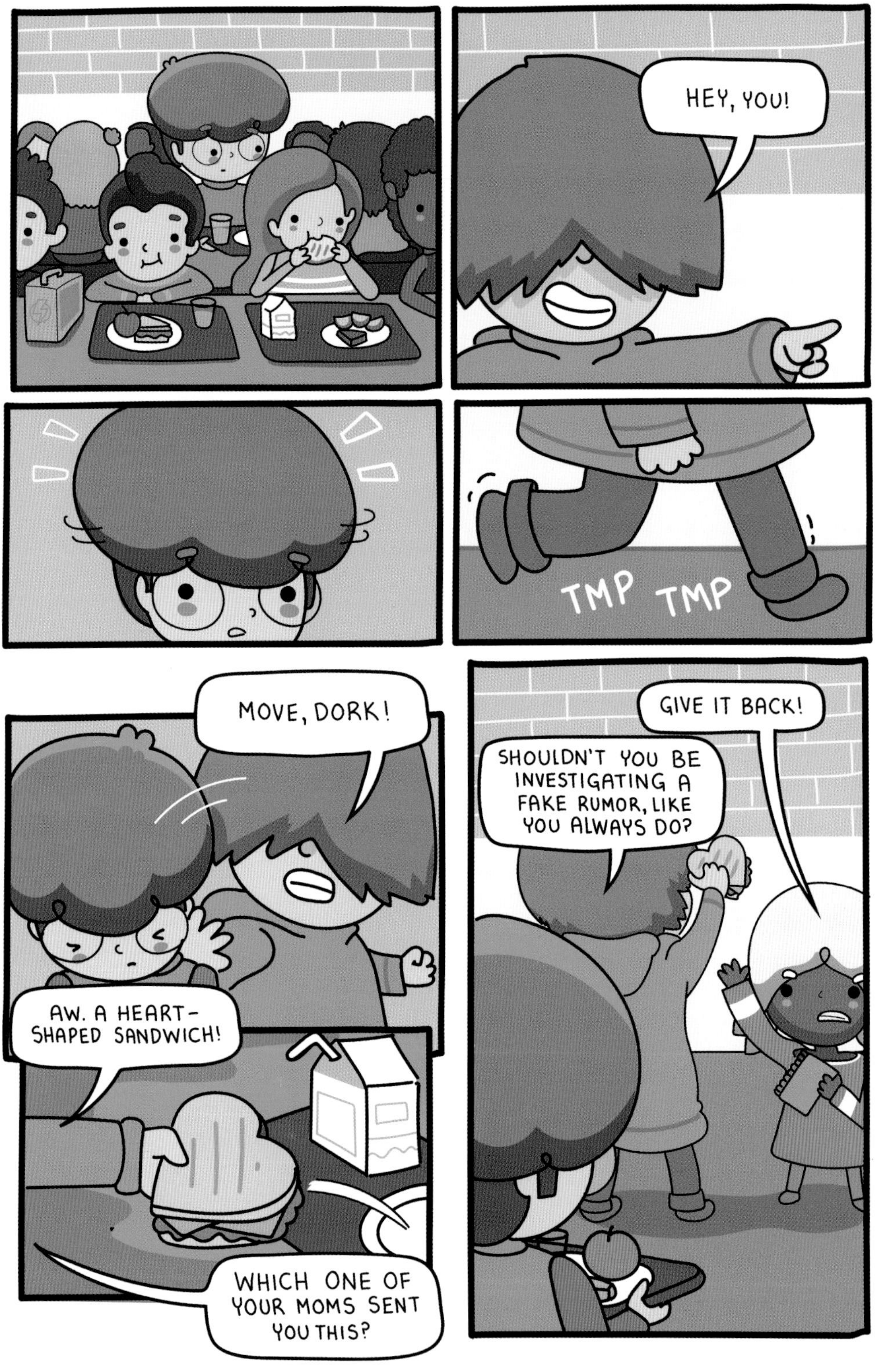
HEY, YOU!
TMP TMP
MOVE, DORK!
AW. A HEART-SHAPED SANDWICH!
WHICH ONE OF YOUR MOMS SENT YOU THIS?
GIVE IT BACK!
SHOULDN'T YOU BE INVESTIGATING A FAKE RUMOR, LIKE YOU ALWAYS DO?

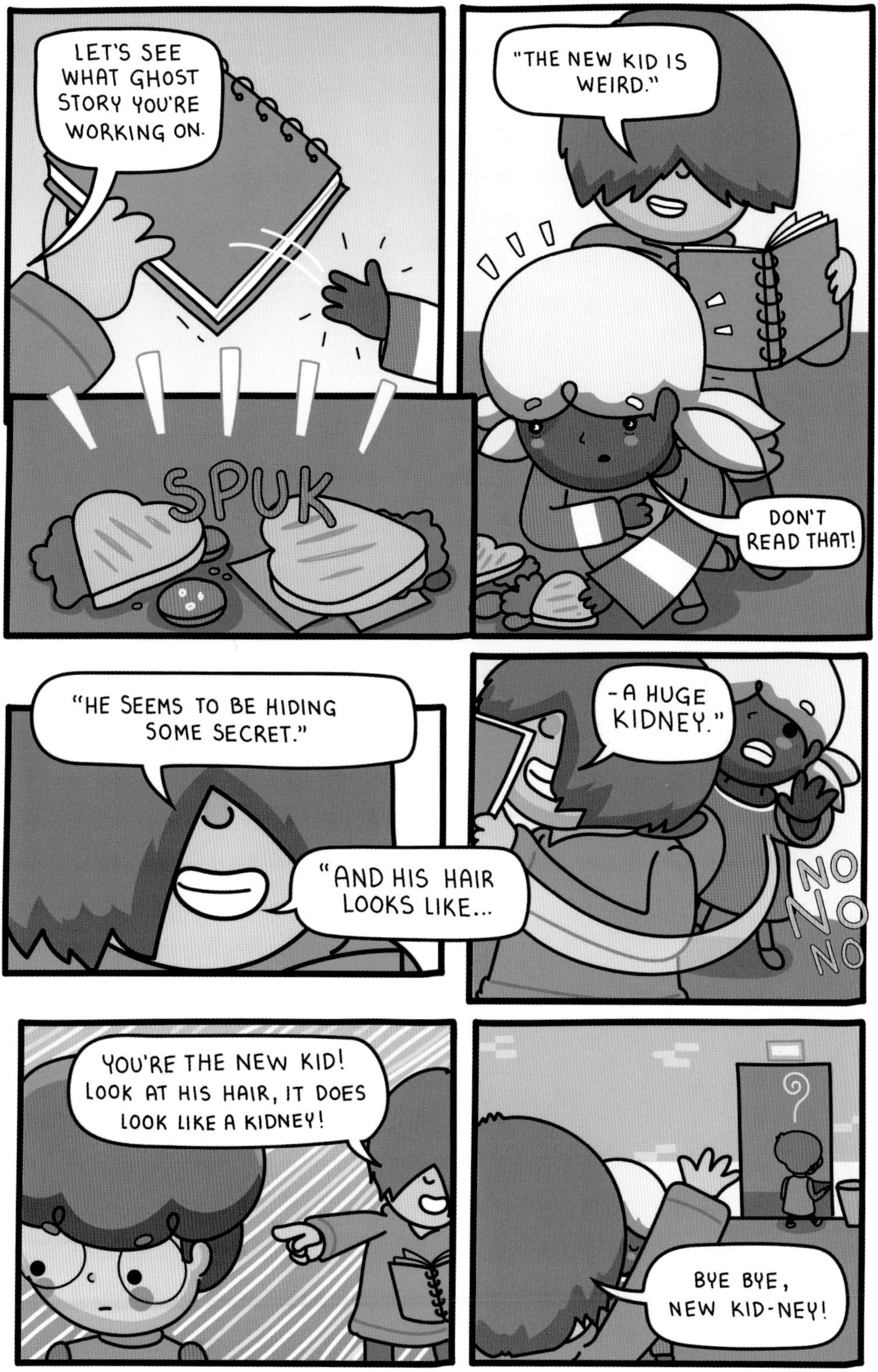
LET'S SEE WHAT GHOST STORY YOU'RE WORKING ON.
SPUK
"THE NEW KID IS WEIRD."
DON'T READ THAT!
"HE SEEMS TO BE HIDING SOME SECRET."
"AND HIS HAIR LOOKS LIKE...
-A HUGE KIDNEY."
NO NO NO
YOU'RE THE NEW KID! LOOK AT HIS HAIR, IT DOES LOOK LIKE A KIDNEY!
BYE BYE, NEW KID-NEY!

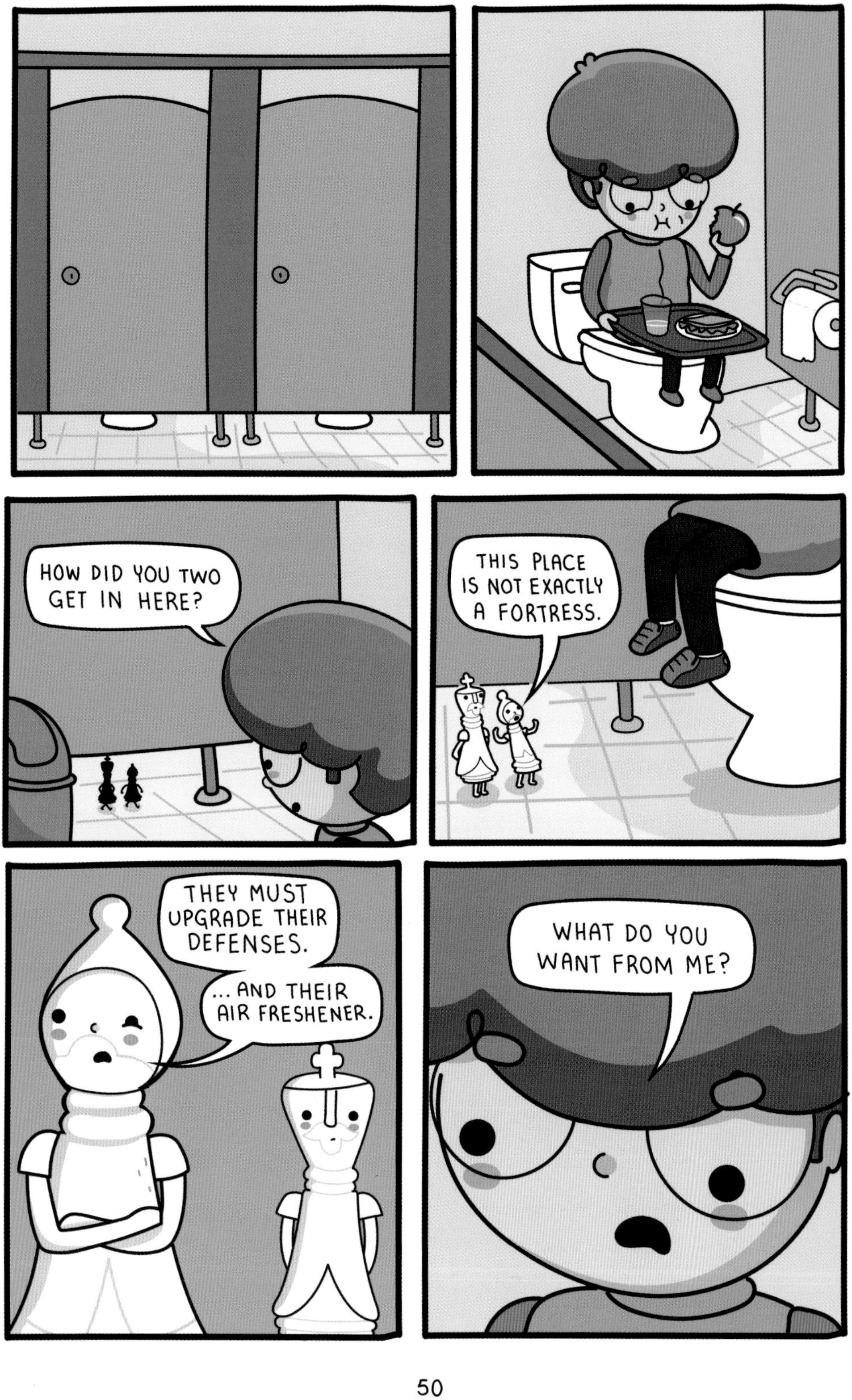
HOW DID YOU TWO GET IN HERE?
THIS PLACE IS NOT EXACTLY A FORTRESS.
THEY MUST UPGRADE THEIR DEFENSES.
... AND THEIR AIR FRESHENER.
WHAT DO YOU WANT FROM ME?

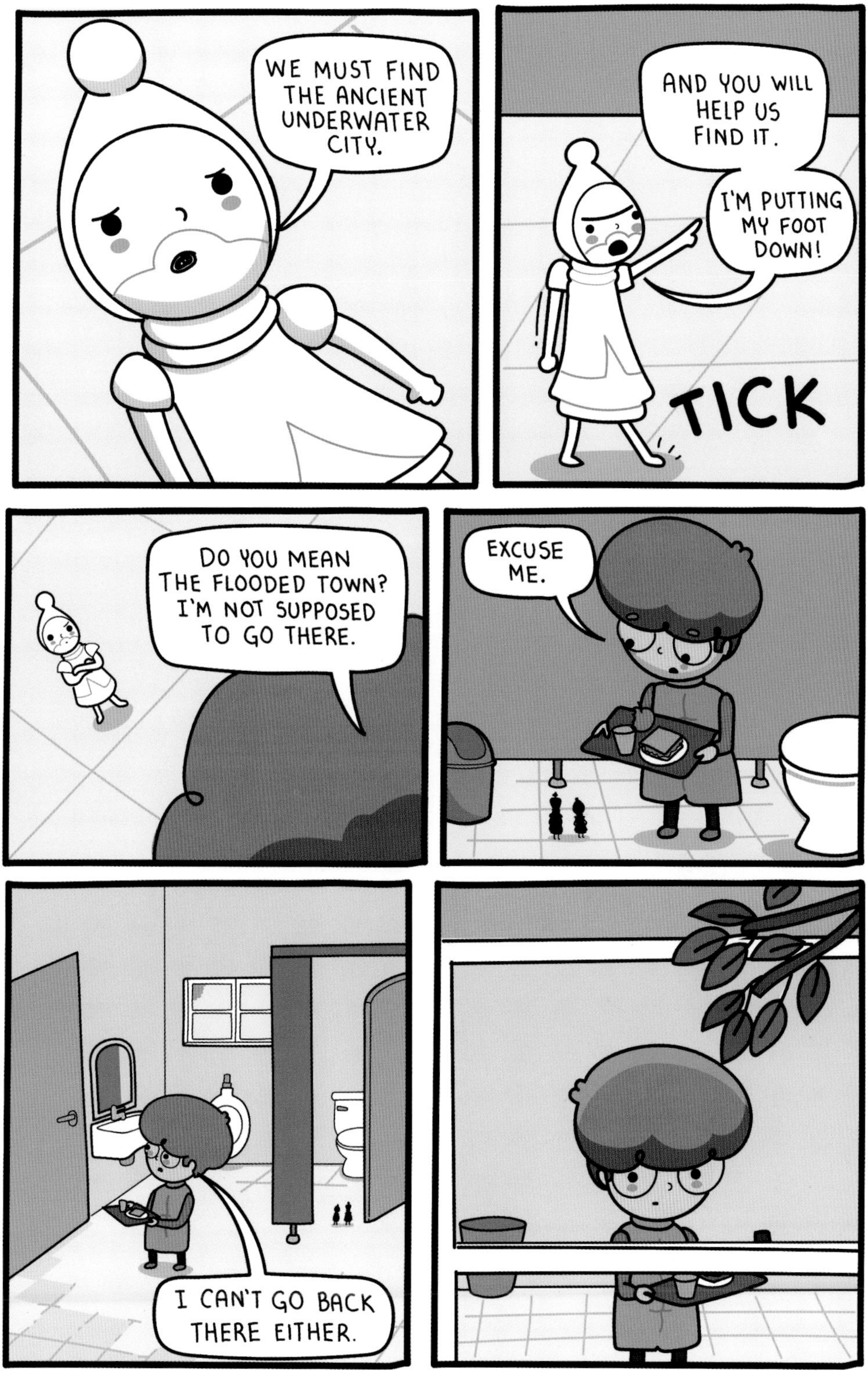
WE MUST FIND THE ANCIENT UNDERWATER CITY.
AND YOU WILL HELP US FIND IT.
I'M PUTTING MY FOOT DOWN!
TICK
DO YOU MEAN THE FLOODED TOWN? I'M NOT SUPPOSED TO GO THERE.
EXCUSE ME.
I CAN'T GO BACK THERE EITHER.

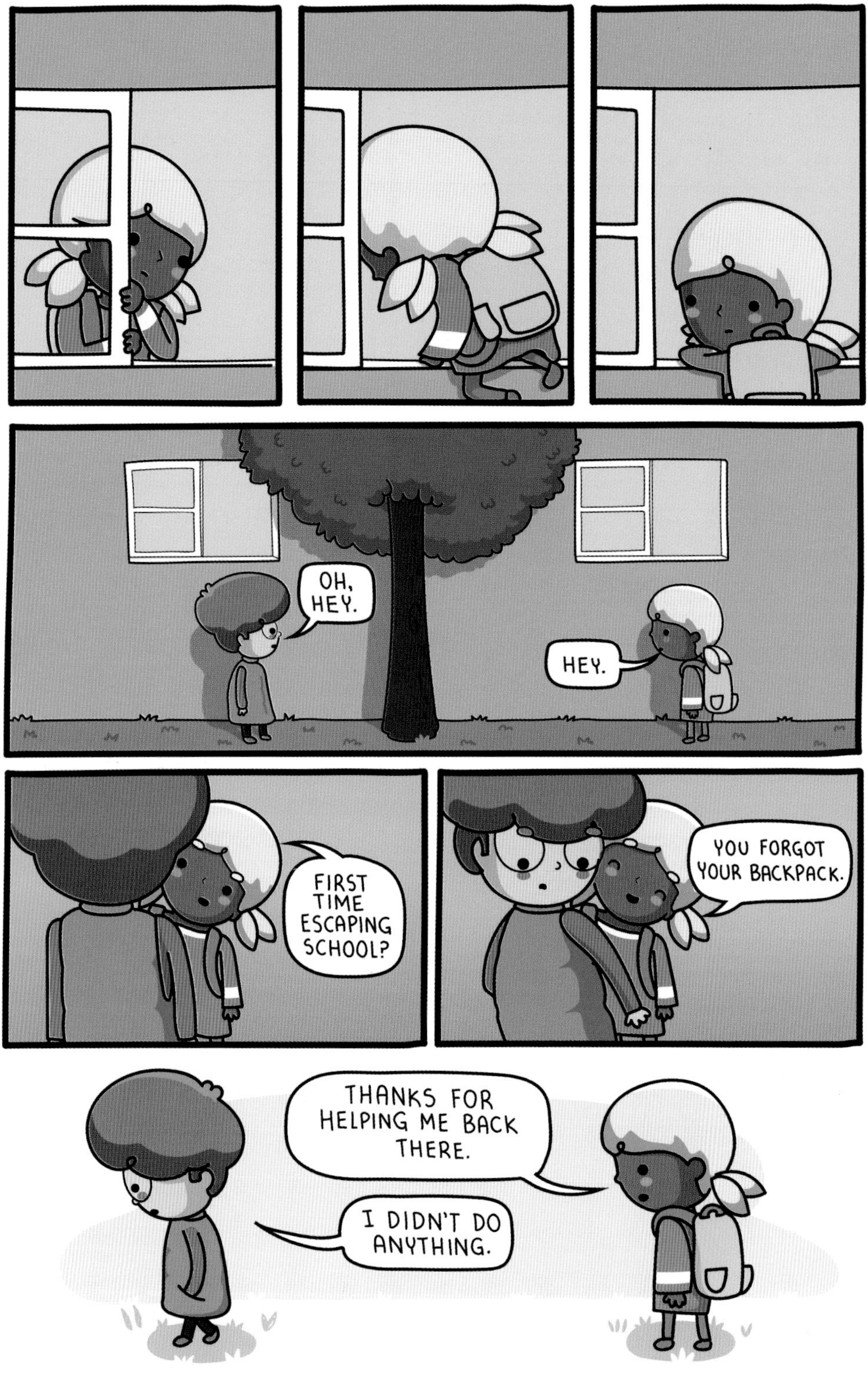
OH, HEY.
HEY.
FIRST TIME ESCAPING SCHOOL?
YOU FORGOT YOUR BACKPACK.
THANKS FOR HELPING ME BACK THERE.
I DIDN'T DO ANYTHING.

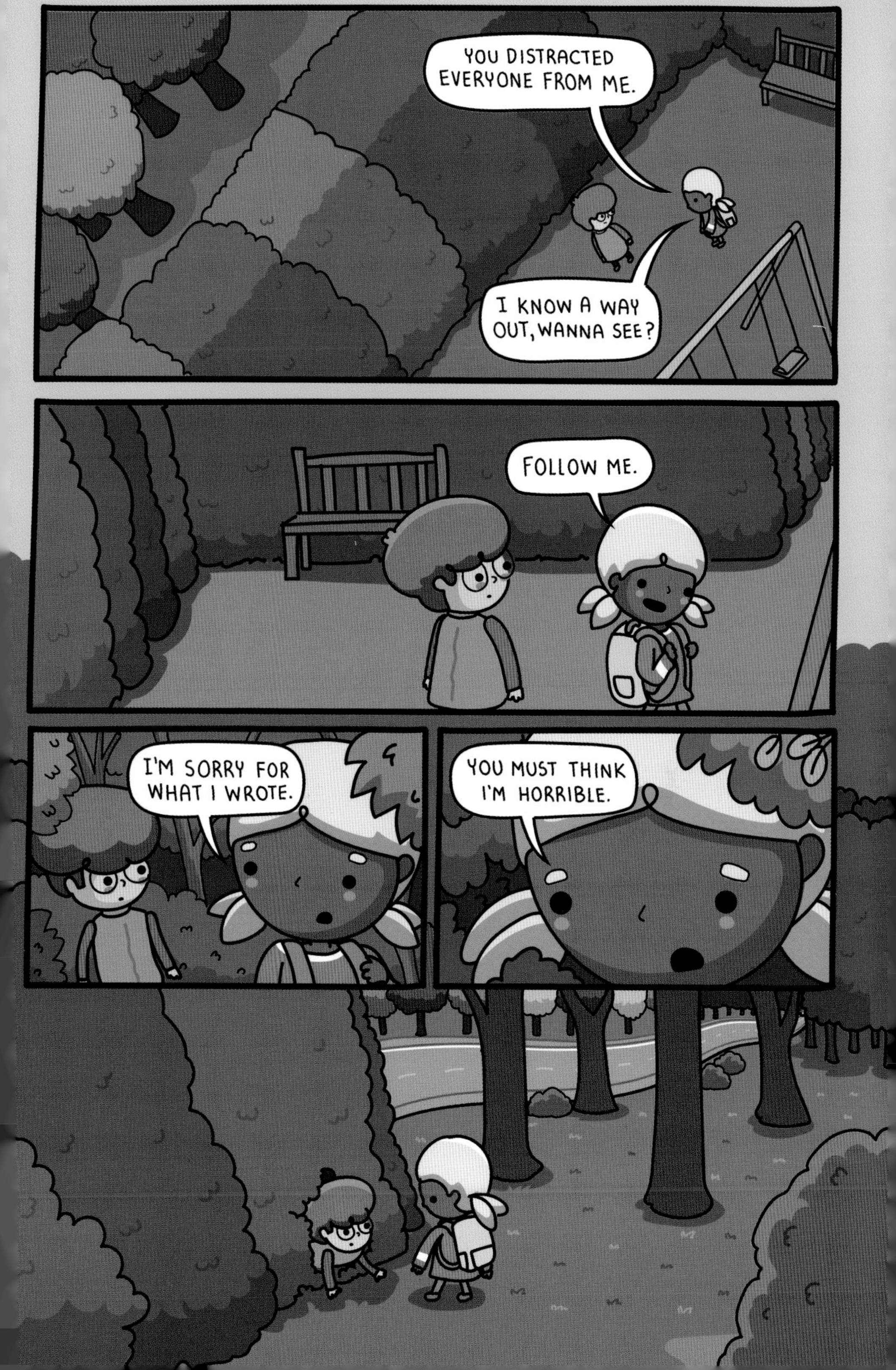
YOU DISTRACTED EVERYONE FROM ME.
I KNOW A WAY OUT, WANNA SEE?
FOLLOW ME.
I'M SORRY FOR WHAT I WROTE.
YOU MUST THINK I'M HORRIBLE.

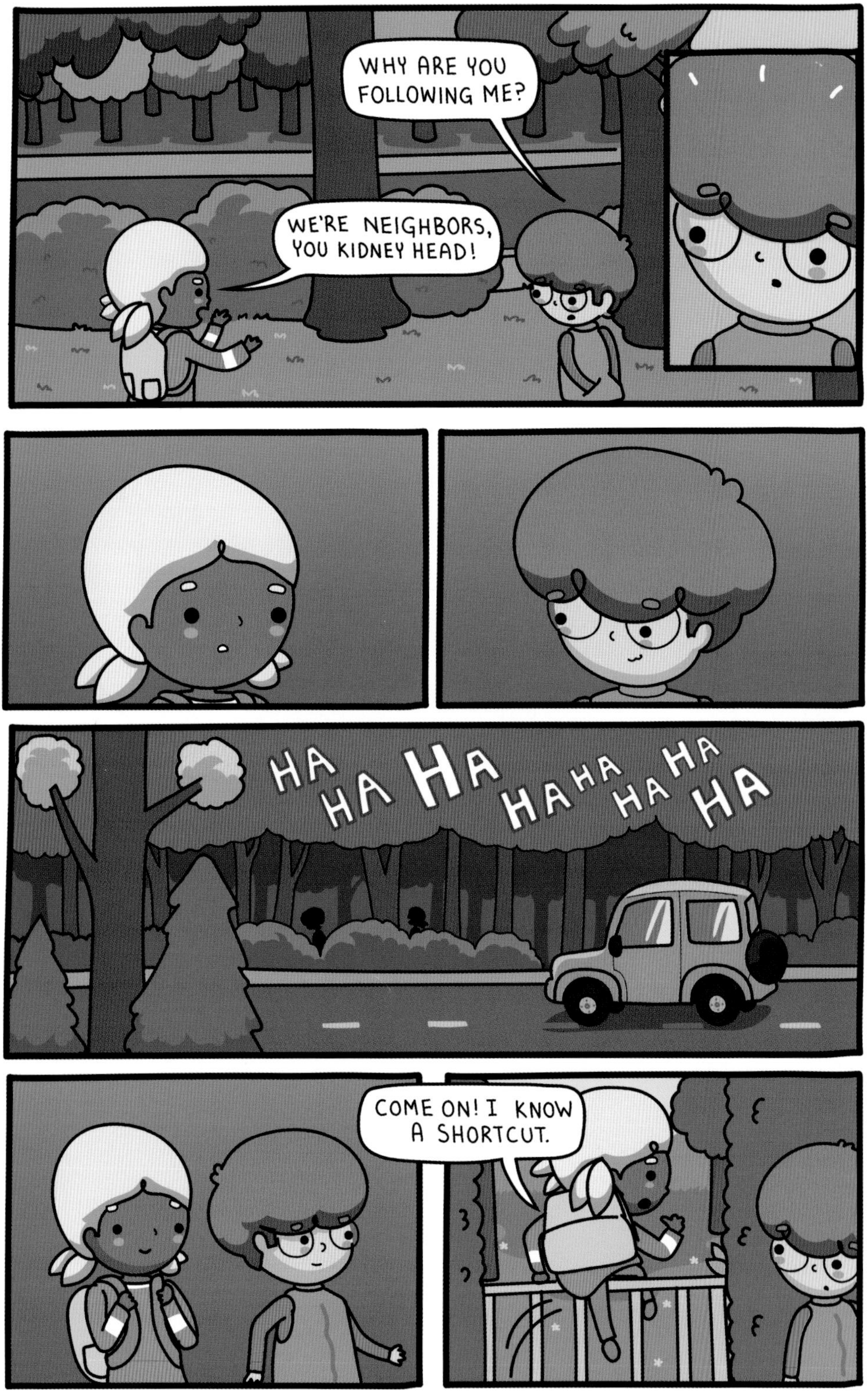
WHY ARE YOU FOLLOWING ME?
WE'RE NEIGHBORS, YOU KIDNEY HEAD!
HA HA HA HA HA HA HA HA HA HA
COME ON! I KNOW A SHORTCUT.

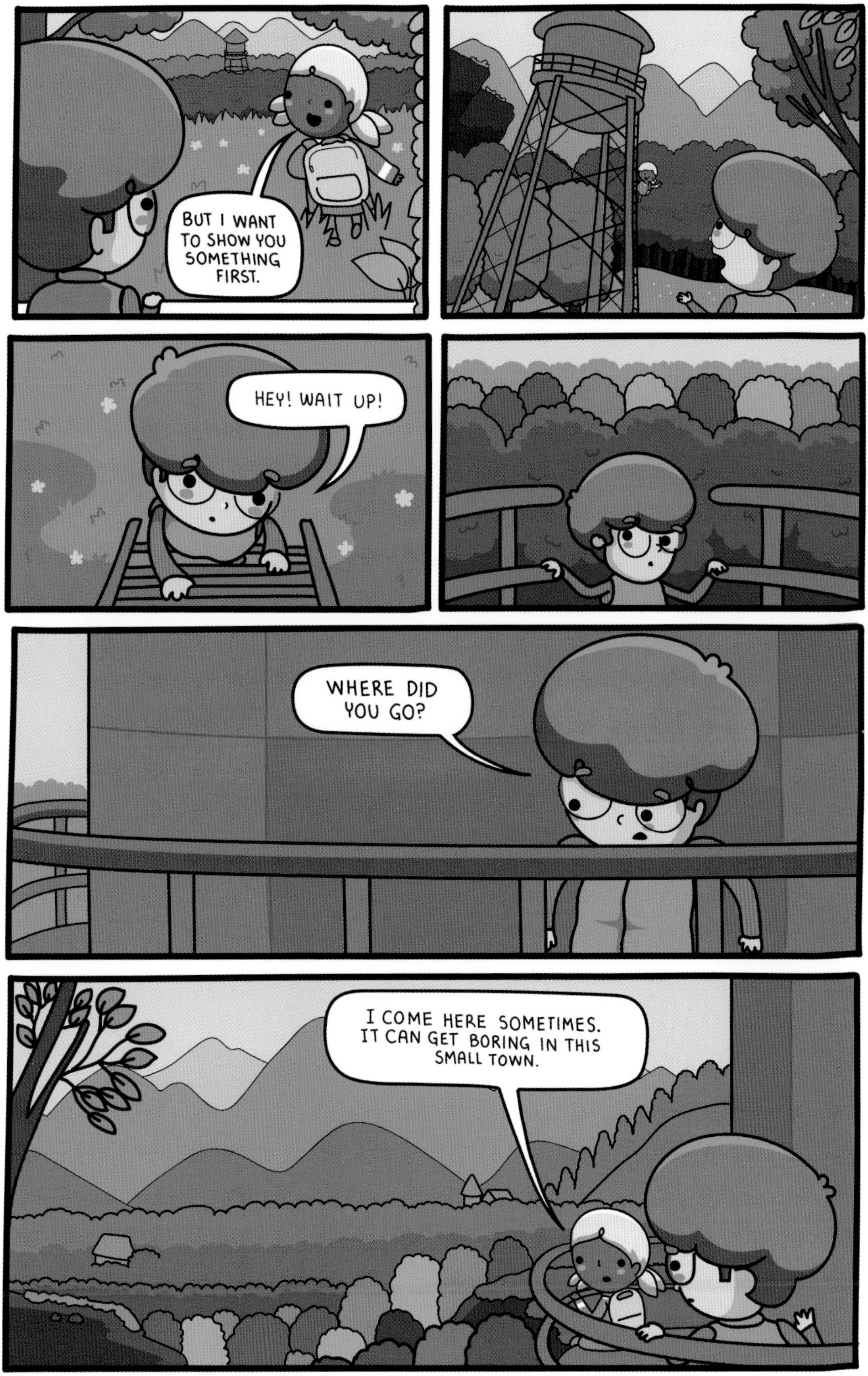
BUT I WANT TO SHOW YOU SOMETHING FIRST.
HEY! WAIT UP!
WHERE DID YOU GO?
I COME HERE SOMETIMES. IT CAN GET BORING IN THIS SMALL TOWN.

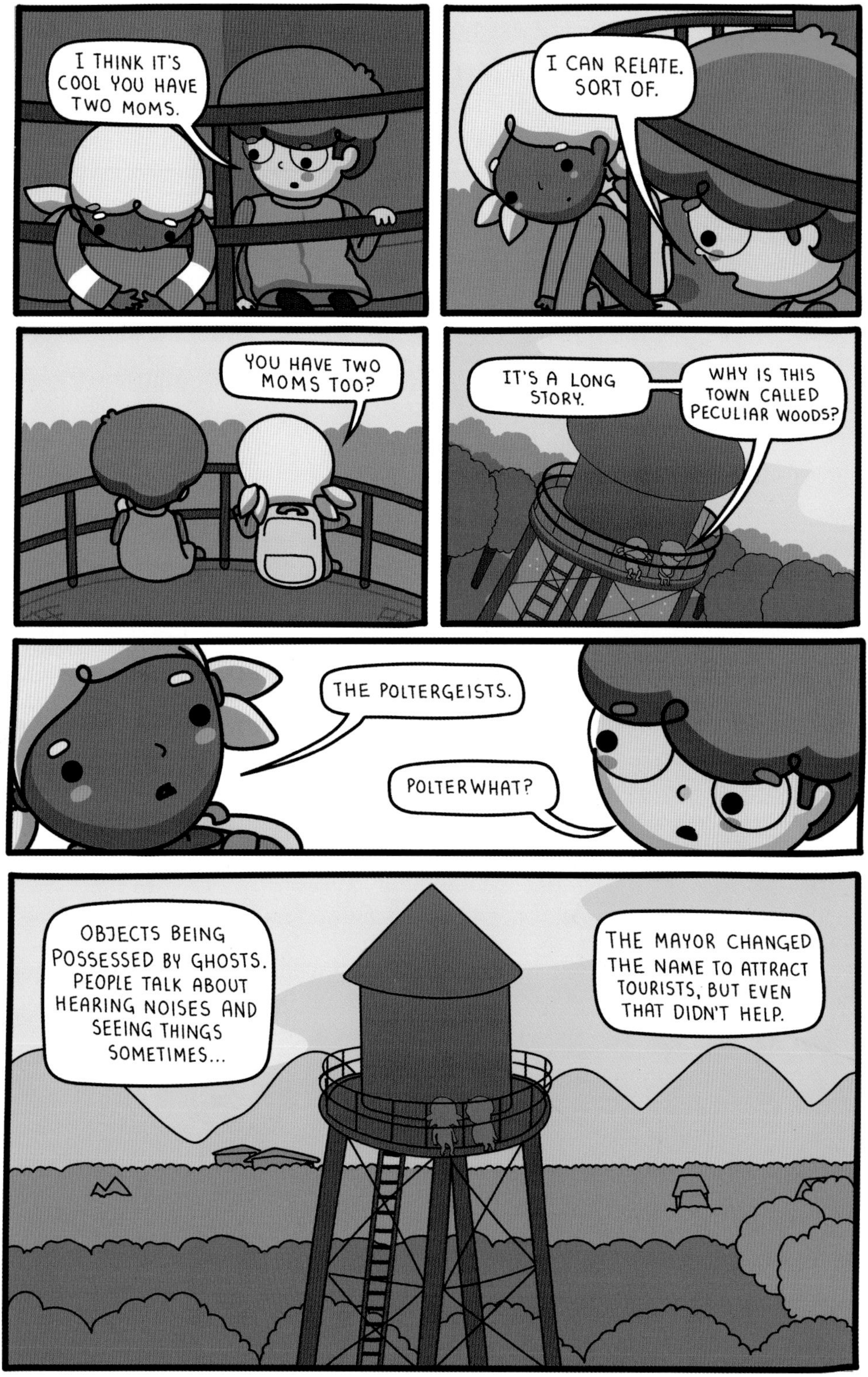
I THINK IT'S COOL YOU HAVE TWO MOMS.
I CAN RELATE. SORT OF.
YOU HAVE TWO MOMS TOO?
IT'S A LONG STORY.
WHY IS THIS TOWN CALLED PECULIAR WOODS?
THE POLTERGEISTS.
POLTERWHAT?
OBJECTS BEING POSSESSED BY GHOSTS. PEOPLE TALK ABOUT HEARING NOISES AND SEEING THINGS SOMETIMES...
THE MAYOR CHANGED THE NAME TO ATTRACT TOURISTS, BUT EVEN THAT DIDN'T HELP.

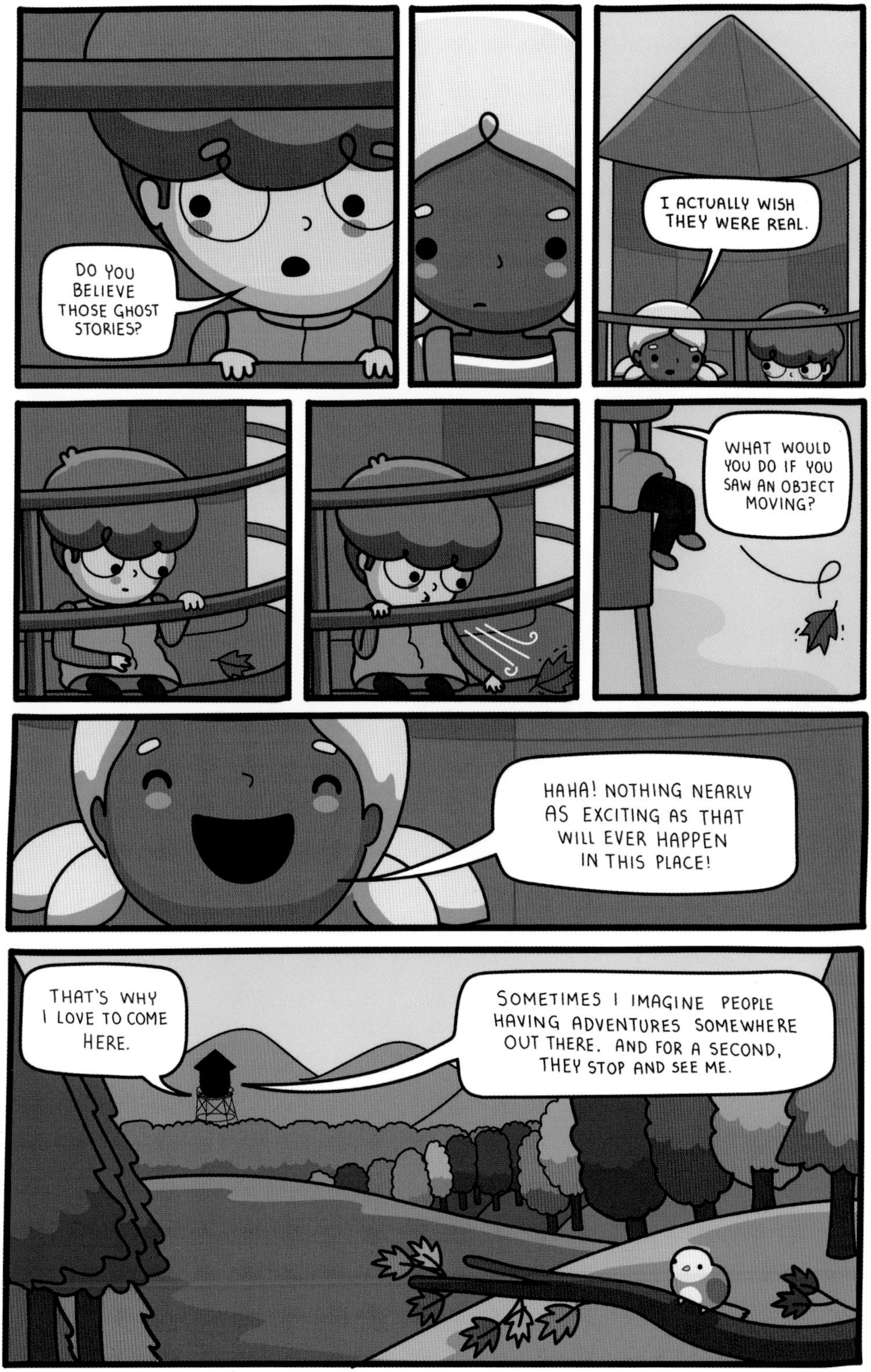
DO YOU BELIEVE THOSE GHOST STORIES?
I ACTUALLY WISH THEY WERE REAL.
WHAT WOULD YOU DO IF YOU SAW AN OBJECT MOVING?
HAHA! NOTHING NEARLY AS EXCITING AS THAT WILL EVER HAPPEN IN THIS PLACE!
THAT'S WHY I LOVE TO COME HERE.
SOMETIMES I IMAGINE PEOPLE HAVING ADVENTURES SOMEWHERE OUT THERE. AND FOR A SECOND, THEY STOP AND SEE ME.

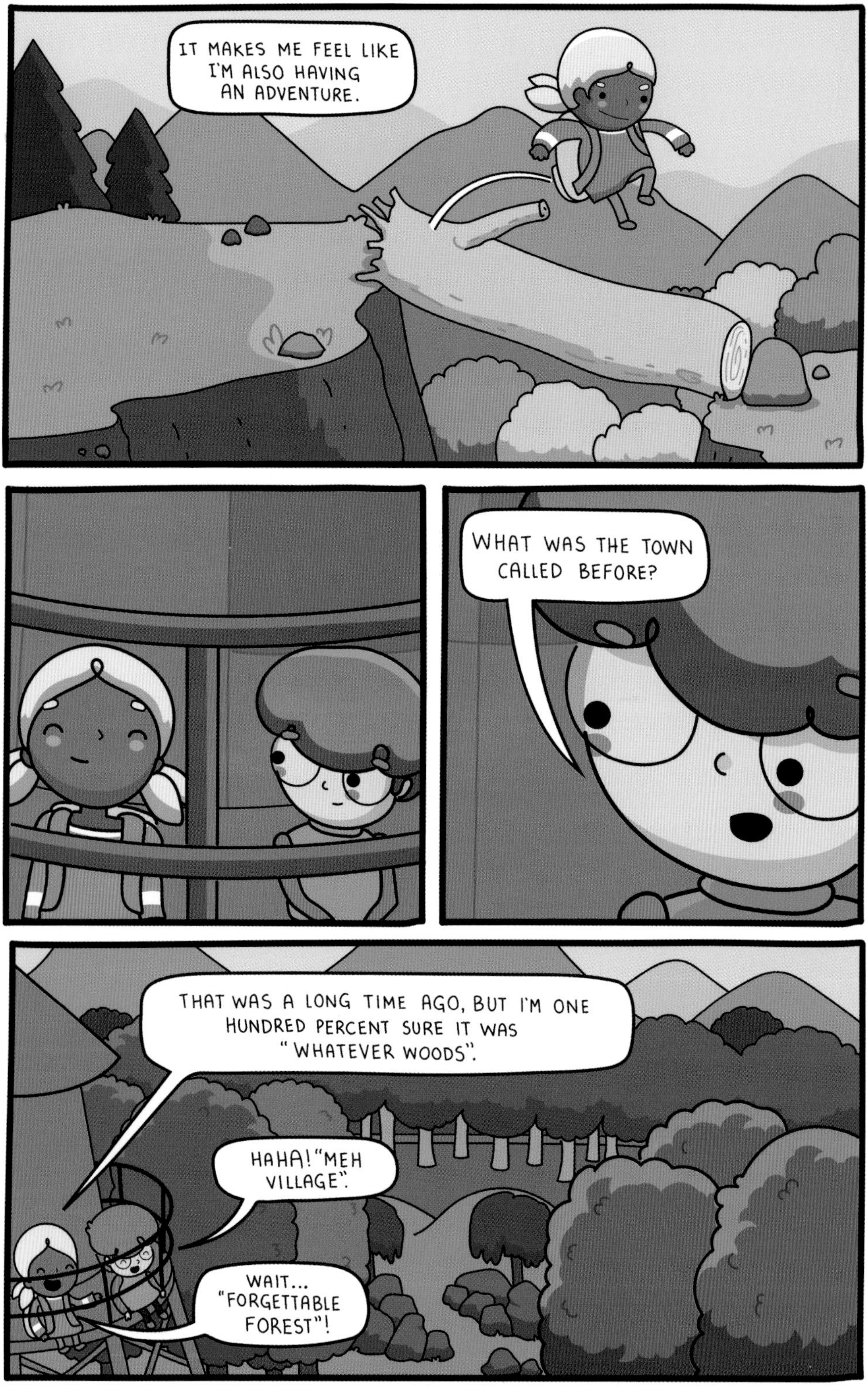
IT MAKES ME FEEL LIKE I'M ALSO HAVING AN ADVENTURE.
WHAT WAS THE TOWN CALLED BEFORE?
THAT WAS A LONG TIME AGO, BUT I'M ONE HUNDRED PERCENT SURE IT WAS "WHATEVER WOODS".
HAHA! "MEH VILLAGE".
WAIT... "FORGETTABLE FOREST"!

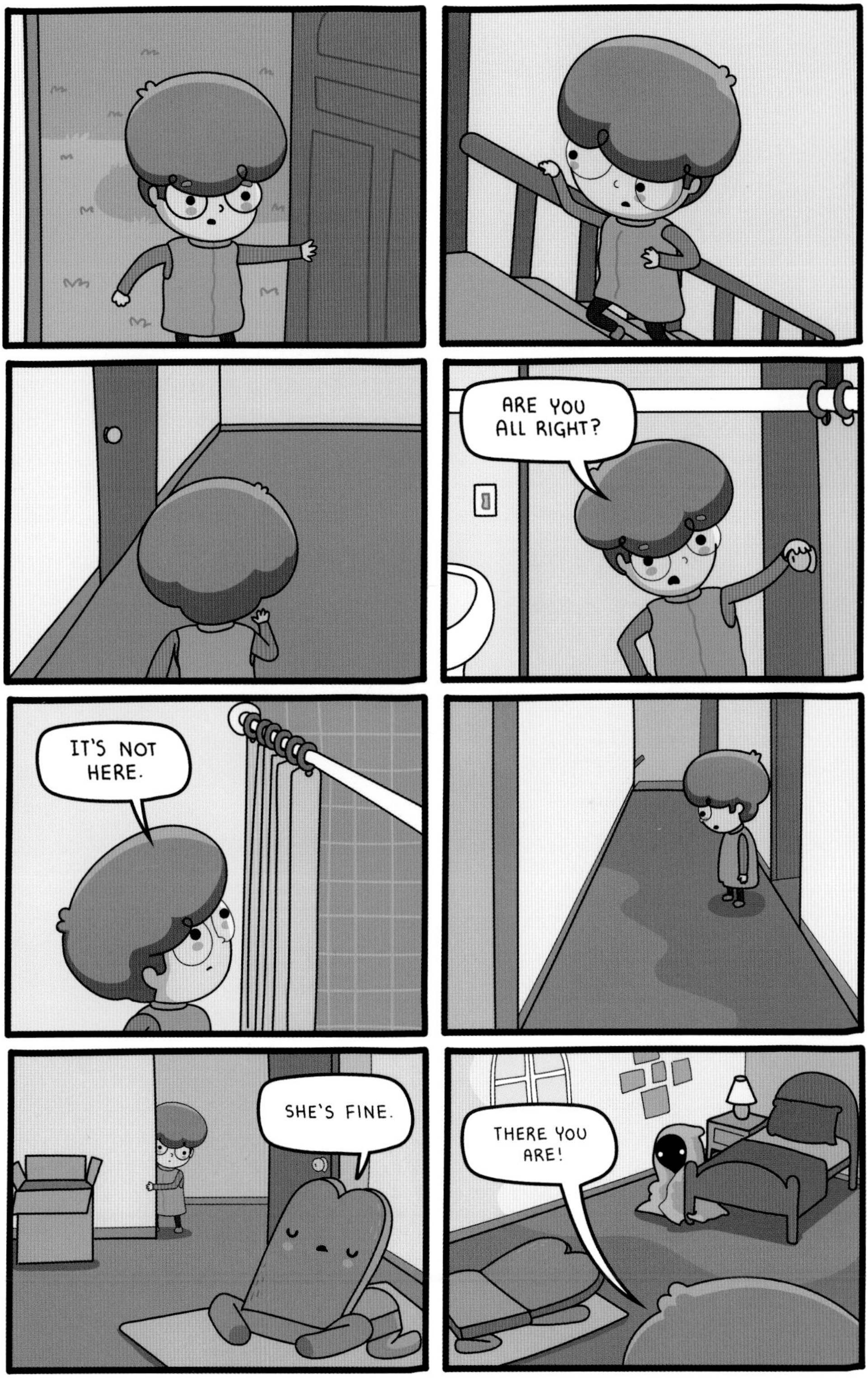
ARE YOU ALL RIGHT?
IT'S NOT HERE.
SHE'S FINE.
THERE YOU ARE!

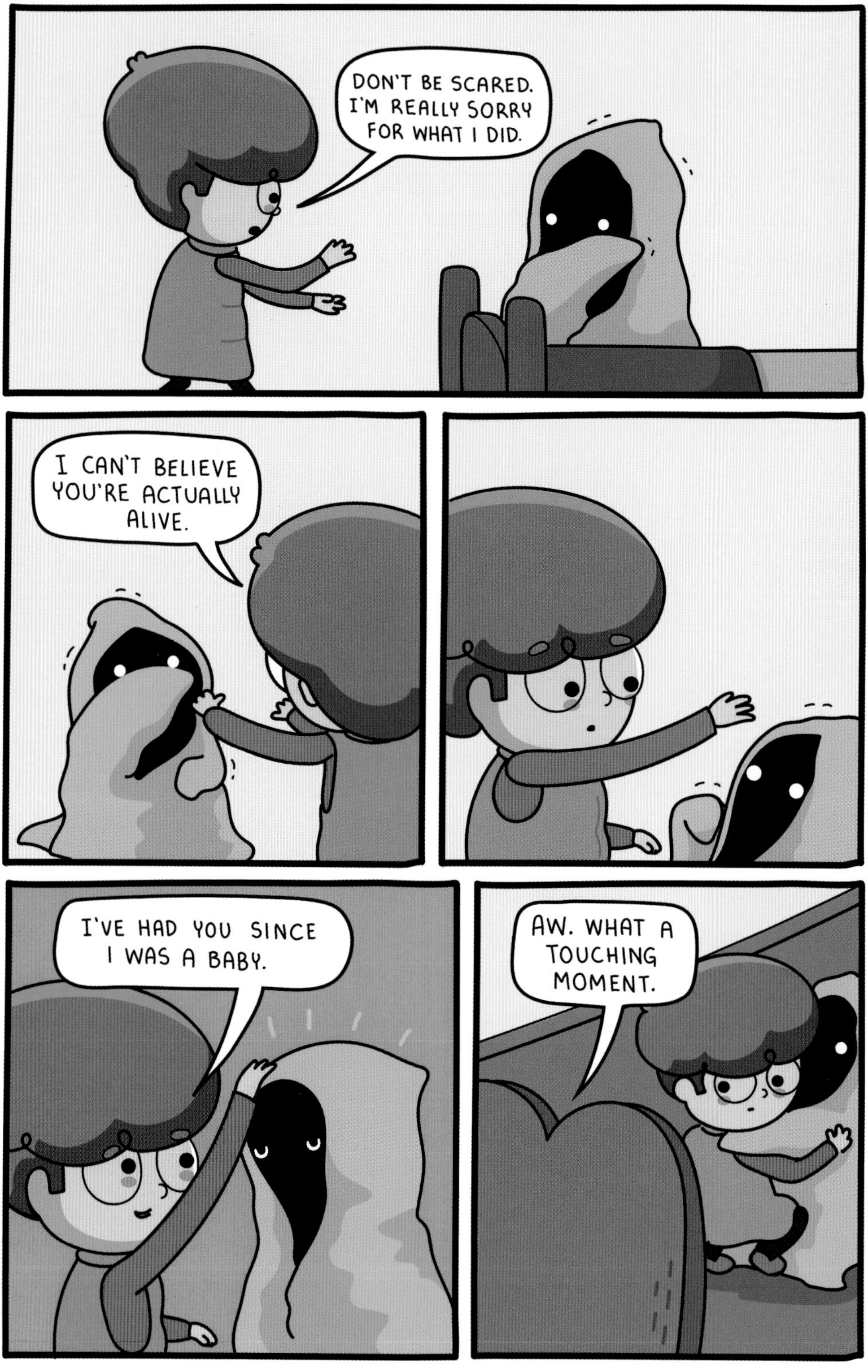
DON'T BE SCARED. I'M REALLY SORRY FOR WHAT I DID.
I CAN'T BELIEVE YOU'RE ACTUALLY ALIVE.
I'VE HAD YOU SINCE I WAS A BABY.
AW. WHAT A TOUCHING MOMENT.

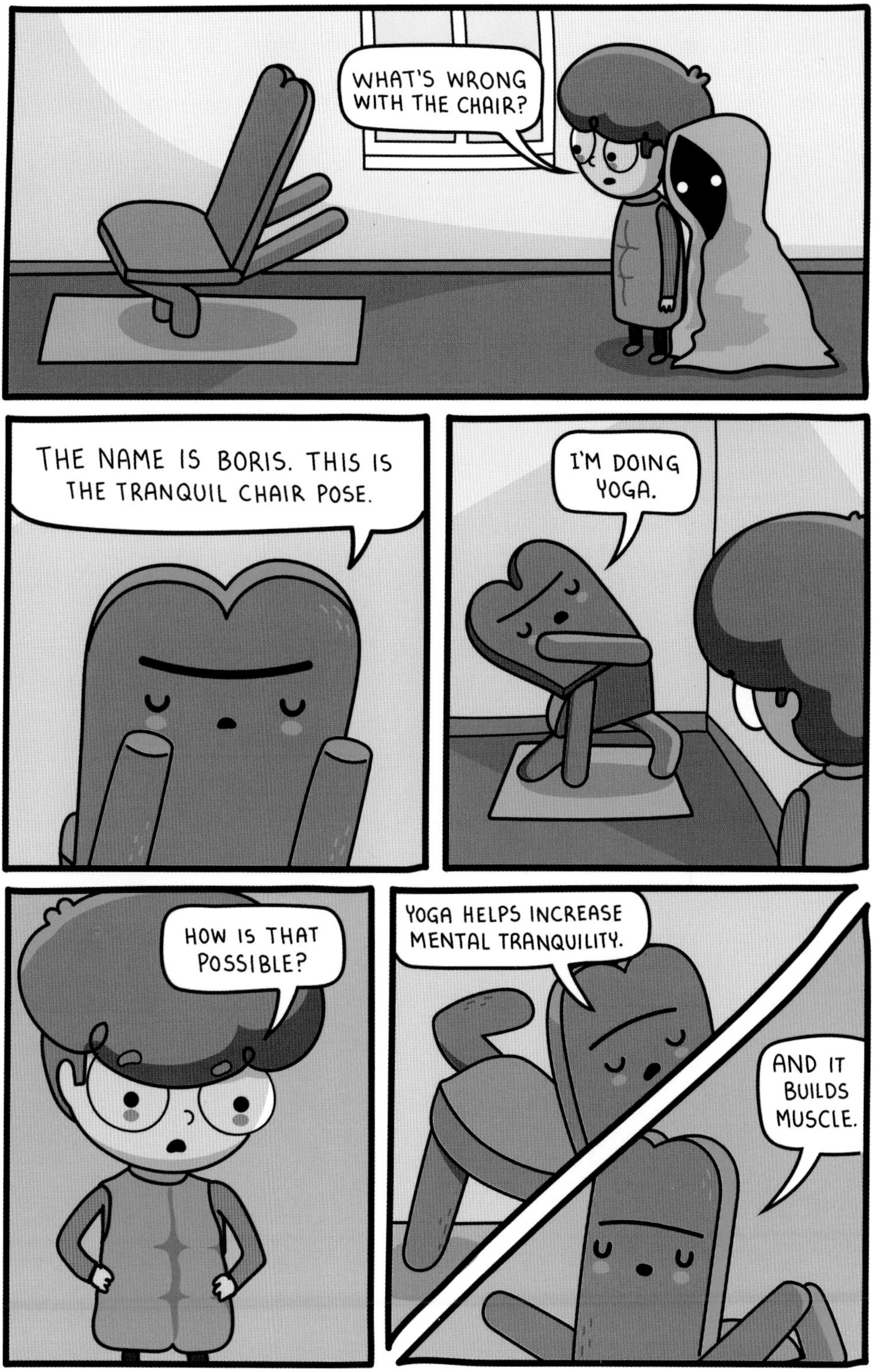
WHAT'S WRONG WITH THE CHAIR?
THE NAME IS BORIS. THIS IS THE TRANQUIL CHAIR POSE.
I'M DOING YOGA.
HOW IS THAT POSSIBLE?
YOGA HELPS INCREASE MENTAL TRANQUILITY.
AND IT BUILDS MUSCLE.

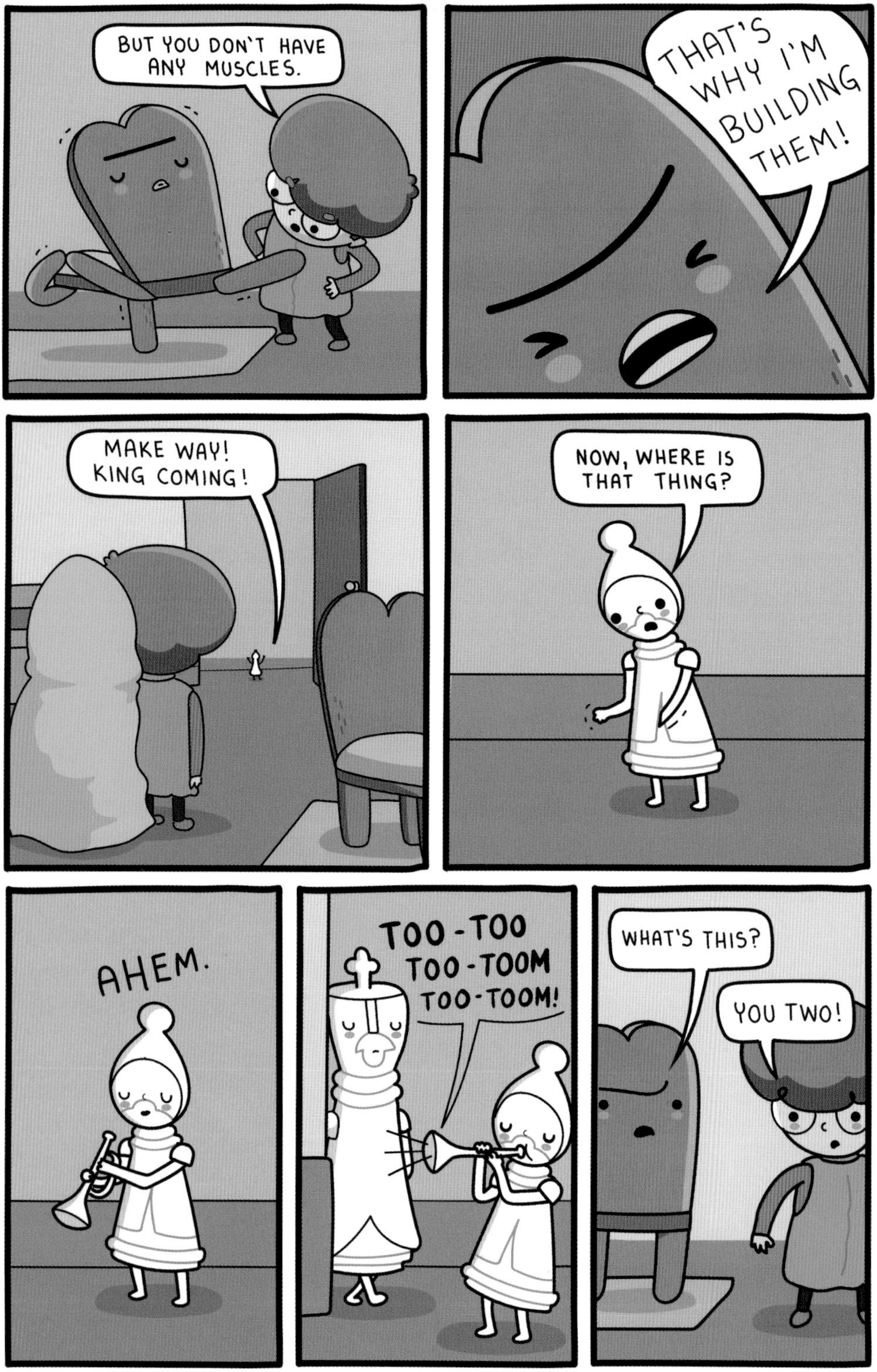
BUT YOU DON'T HAVE ANY MUSCLES.
THAT'S WHY I'M BUILDING THEM!
MAKE WAY! KING COMING!
NOW, WHERE IS THAT THING?
AHEM.
TOO-TOO TOO-TOOM TOO-TOOM!
WHAT'S THIS?
YOU TWO!

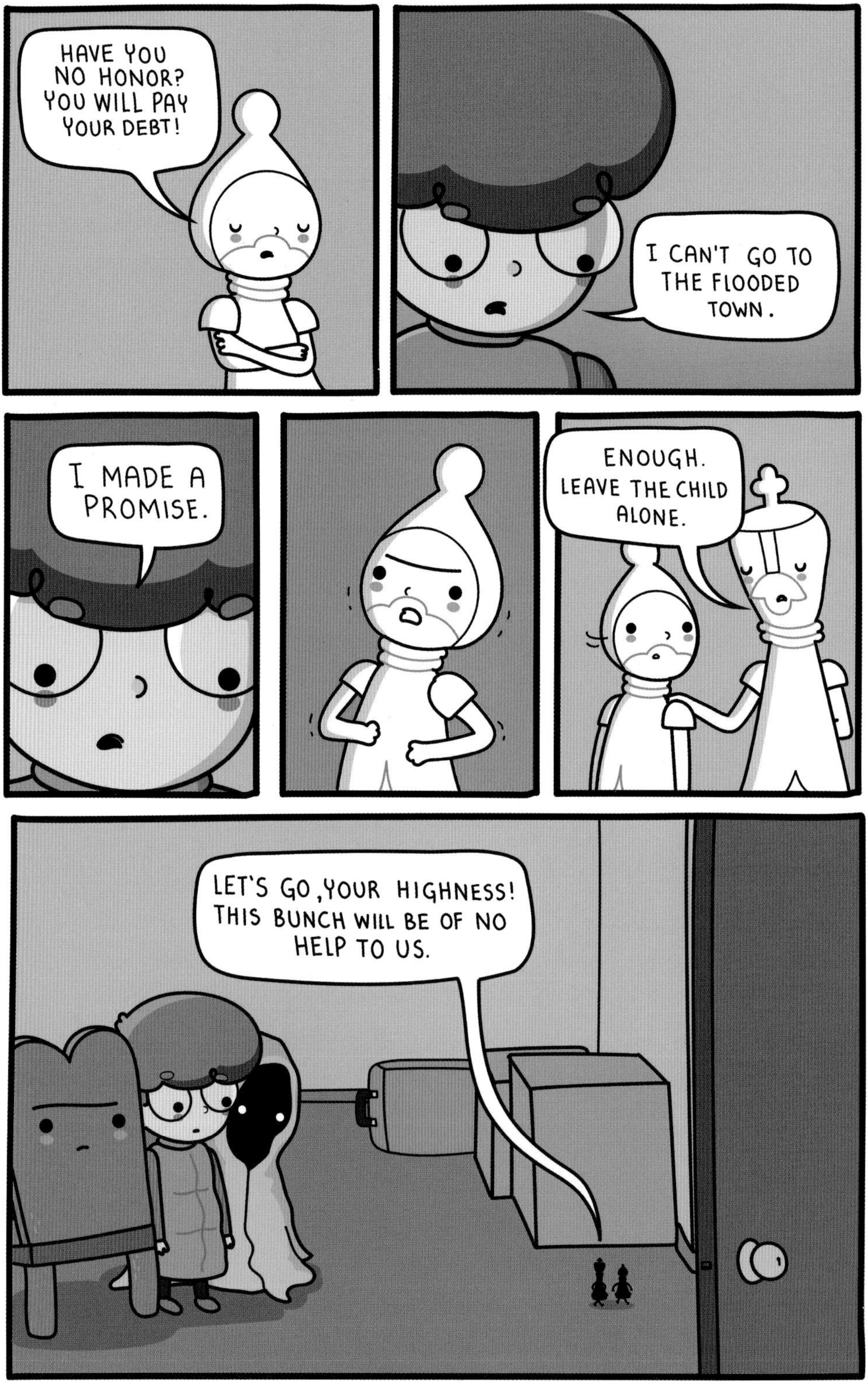
HAVE YOU NO HONOR? YOU WILL PAY YOUR DEBT!
I CAN'T GO TO THE FLOODED TOWN.
I MADE A PROMISE.
ENOUGH. LEAVE THE CHILD ALONE.
LET'S GO, YOUR HIGHNESS! THIS BUNCH WILL BE OF NO HELP TO US.

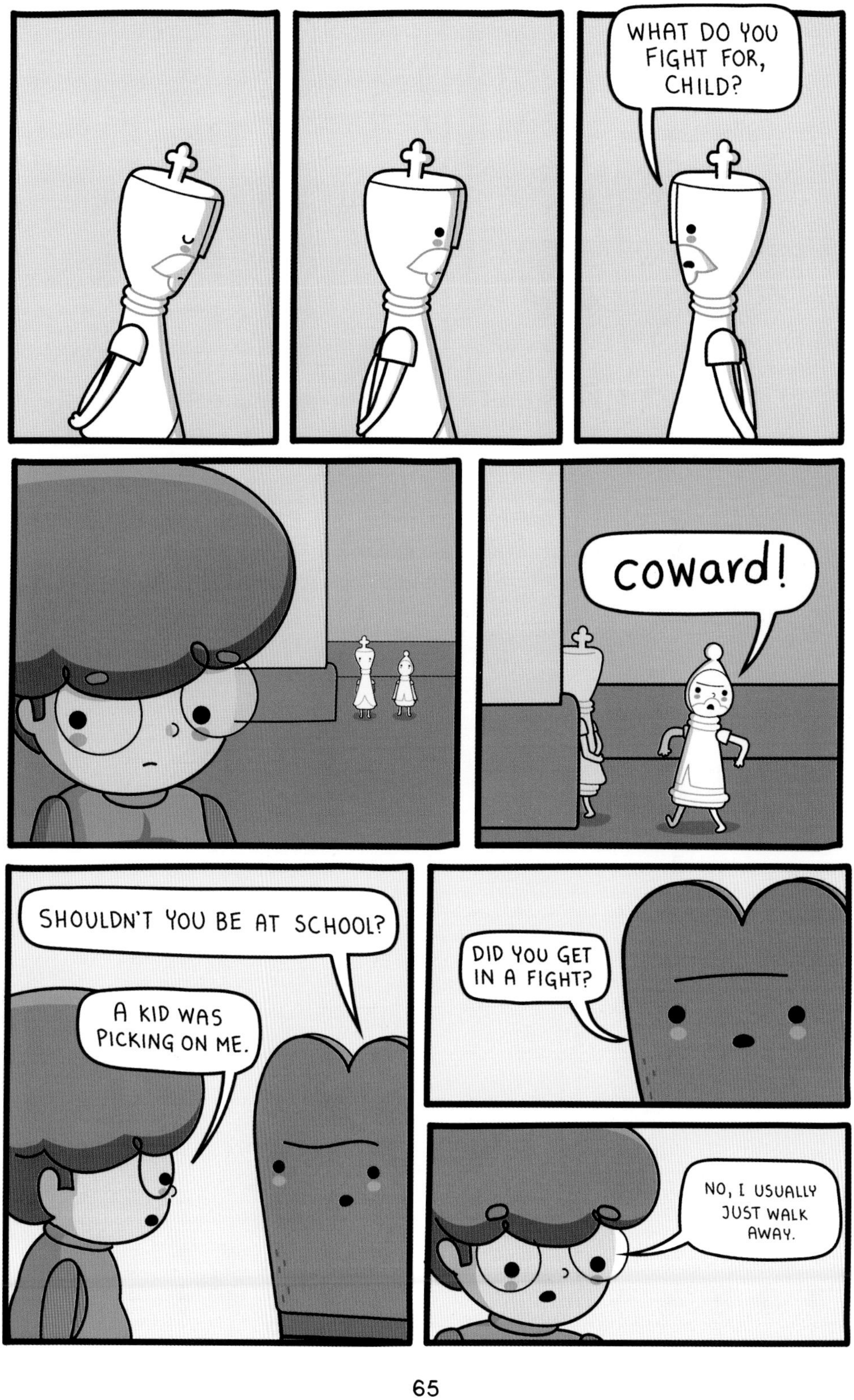
WHAT DO YOU FIGHT FOR, CHILD?
coward!
SHOULDN'T YOU BE AT SCHOOL?
A KID WAS PICKING ON ME.
DID YOU GET IN A FIGHT?
NO, I USUALLY JUST WALK AWAY.

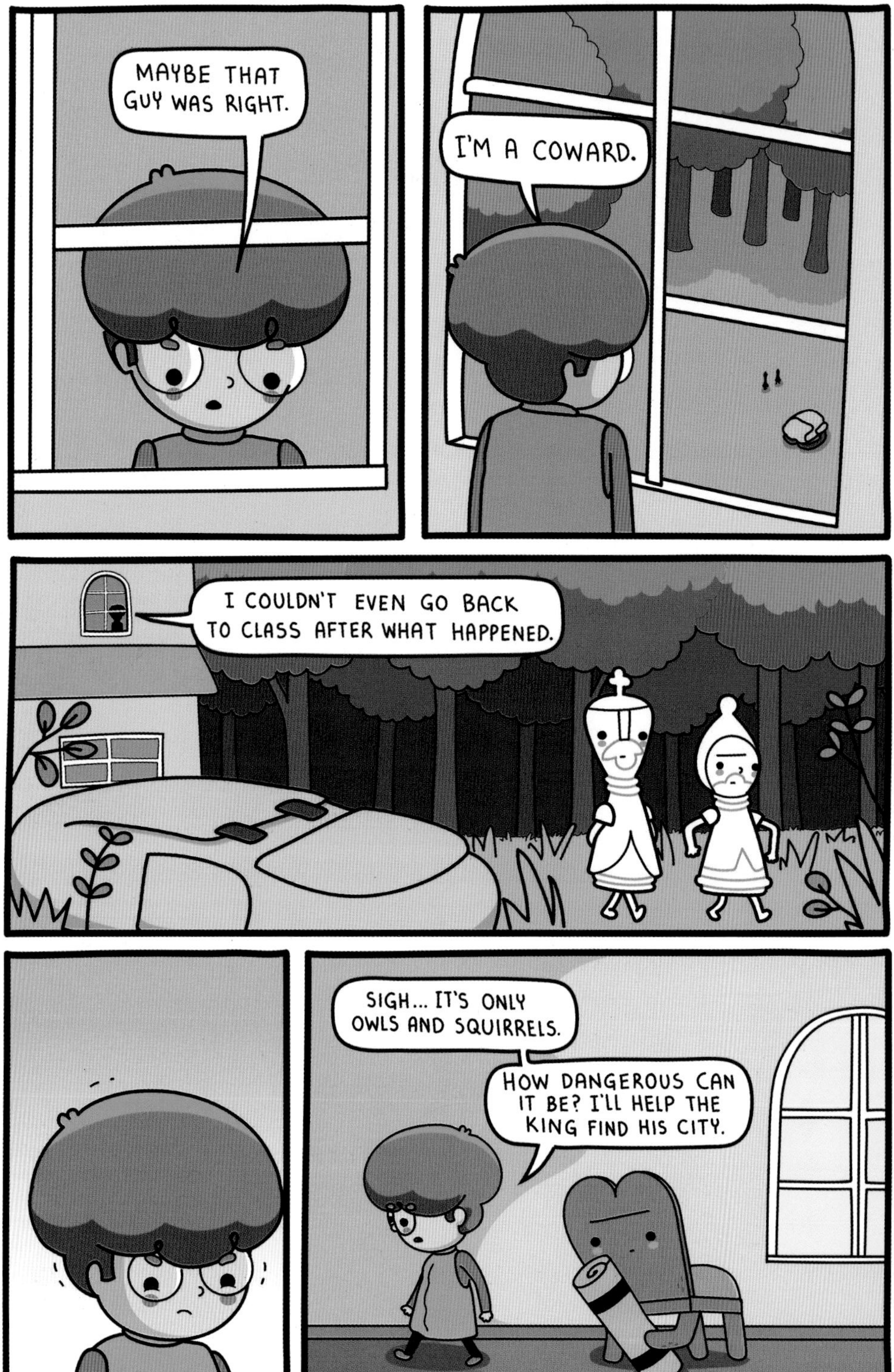
MAYBE THAT GUY WAS RIGHT.
I'M A COWARD.
I COULDN'T EVEN GO BACK TO CLASS AFTER WHAT HAPPENED.
SIGH... IT'S ONLY OWLS AND SQUIRRELS.
HOW DANGEROUS CAN IT BE? I'LL HELP THE KING FIND HIS CITY.

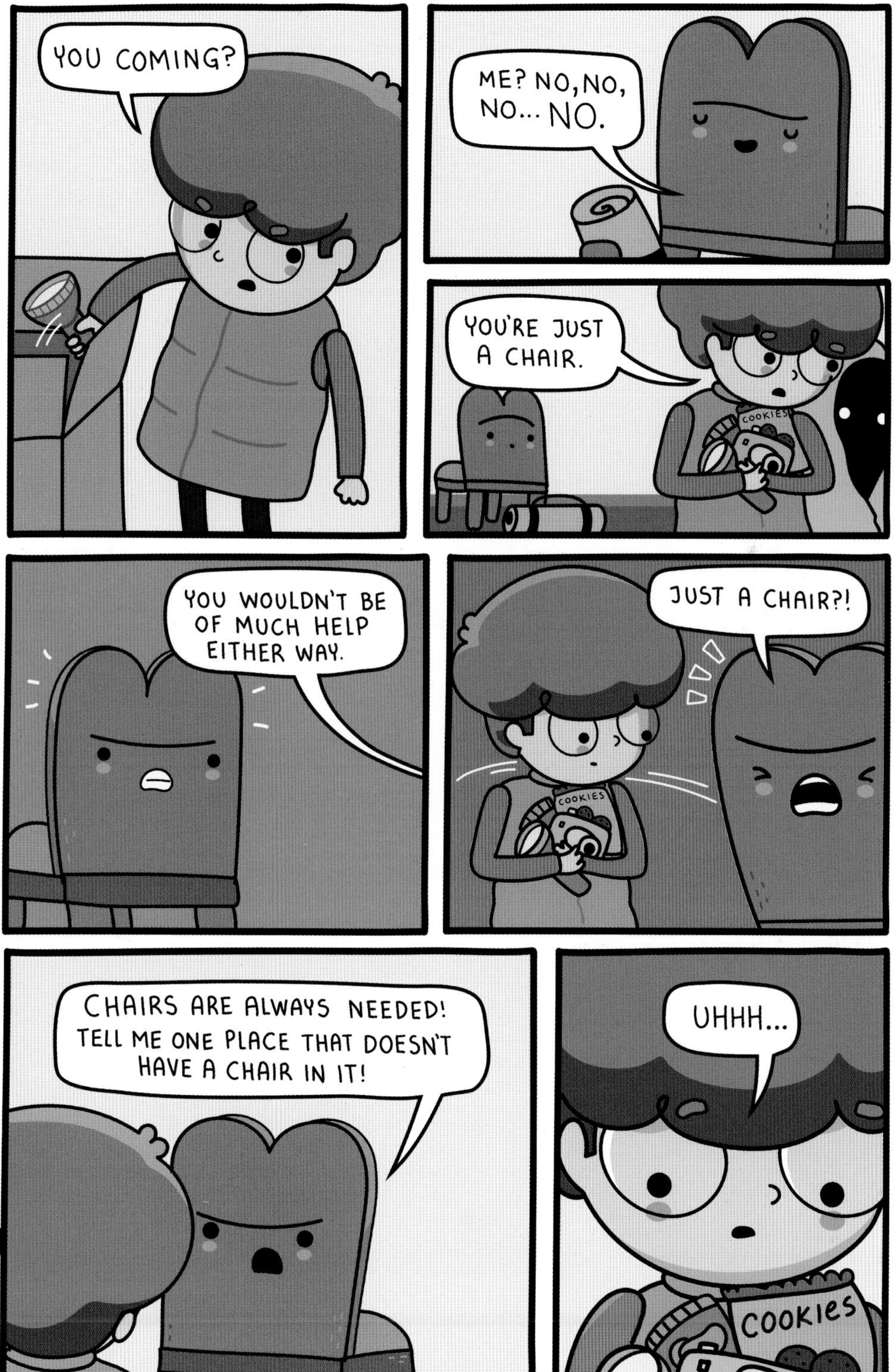
YOU COMING?
ME? NO, NO, NO... NO.
YOU'RE JUST A CHAIR.
COOKIES
YOU WOULDN'T BE OF MUCH HELP EITHER WAY.
JUST A CHAIR?!
COOKIES
CHAIRS ARE ALWAYS NEEDED! TELL ME ONE PLACE THAT DOESN'T HAVE A CHAIR IN IT!
UHHH...
COOKIES

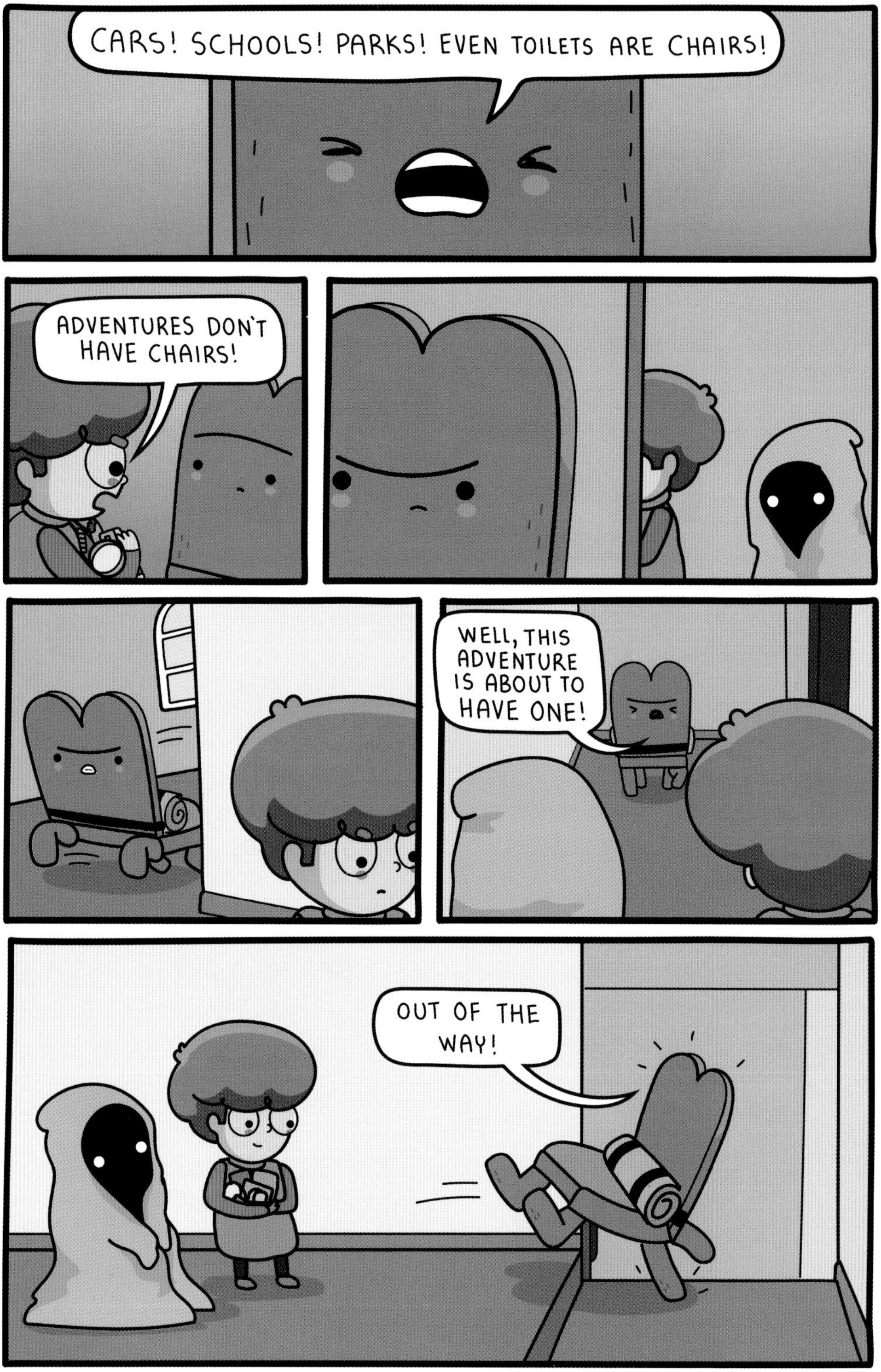
CARS! SCHOOLS! PARKS! EVEN TOILETS ARE CHAIRS!
ADVENTURES DON'T HAVE CHAIRS!
WELL, THIS ADVENTURE IS ABOUT TO HAVE ONE!
OUT OF THE WAY!

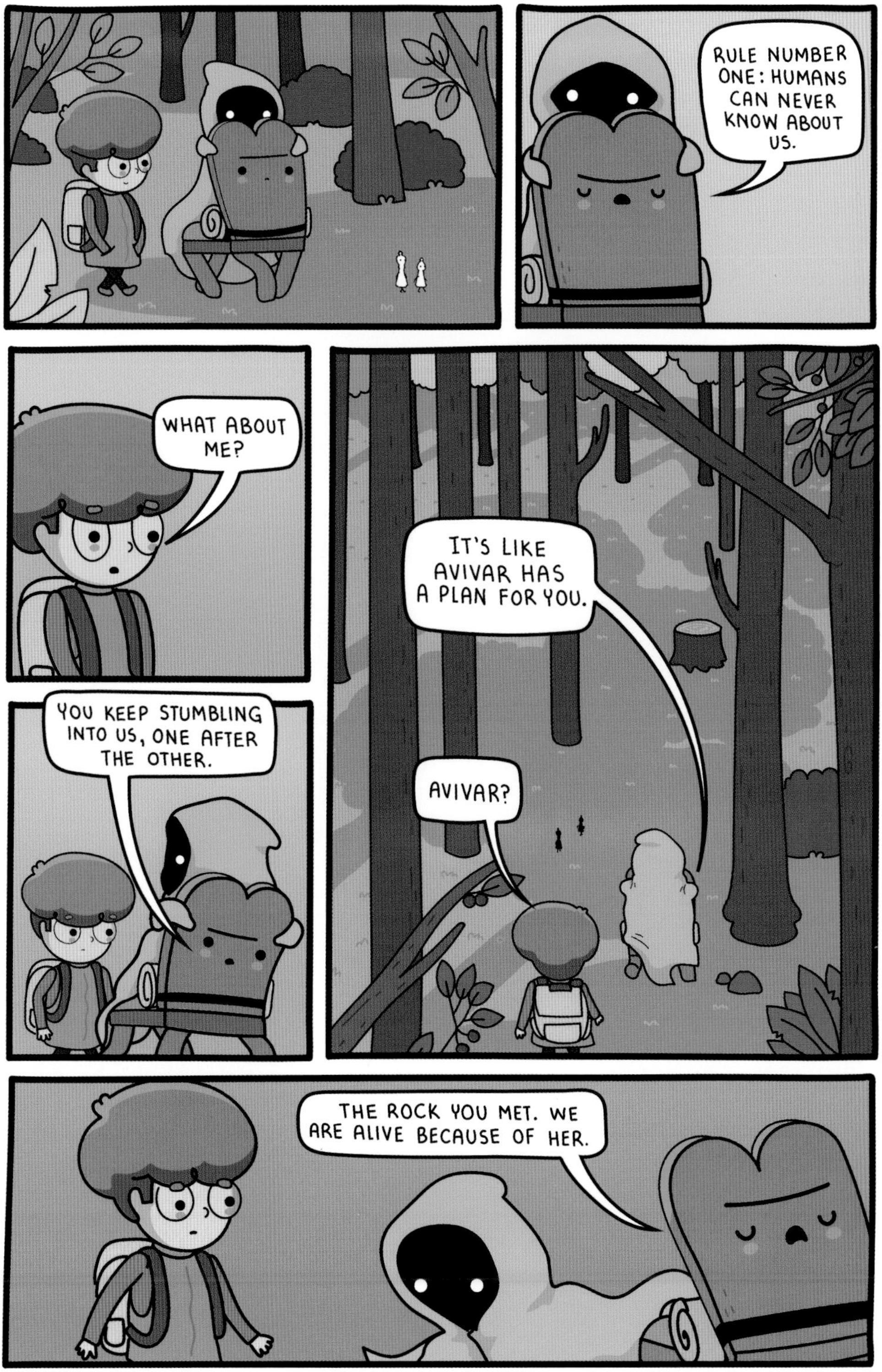
RULE NUMBER ONE: HUMANS CAN NEVER KNOW ABOUT US.
WHAT ABOUT ME?
YOU KEEP STUMBLING INTO US, ONE AFTER THE OTHER.
IT'S LIKE AVIVAR HAS A PLAN FOR YOU.
AVIVAR?
THE ROCK YOU MET. WE ARE ALIVE BECAUSE OF HER.

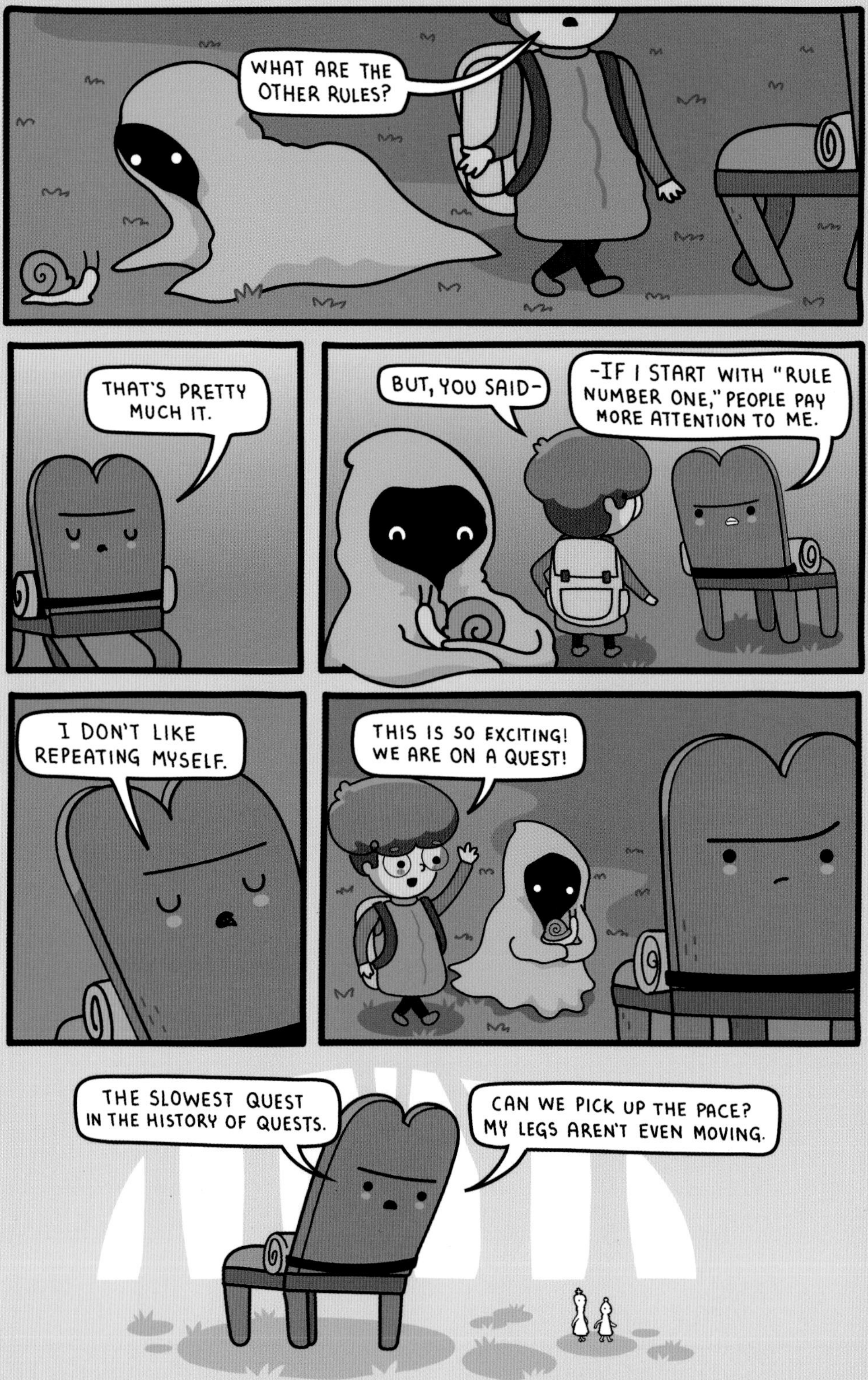
WHAT ARE THE OTHER RULES?
THAT'S PRETTY MUCH IT.
BUT, YOU SAID-
-IF I START WITH "RULE NUMBER ONE," PEOPLE PAY MORE ATTENTION TO ME.
I DON'T LIKE REPEATING MYSELF.
THIS IS SO EXCITING! WE ARE ON A QUEST!
THE SLOWEST QUEST IN THE HISTORY OF QUESTS.
CAN WE PICK UP THE PACE? MY LEGS AREN'T EVEN MOVING.

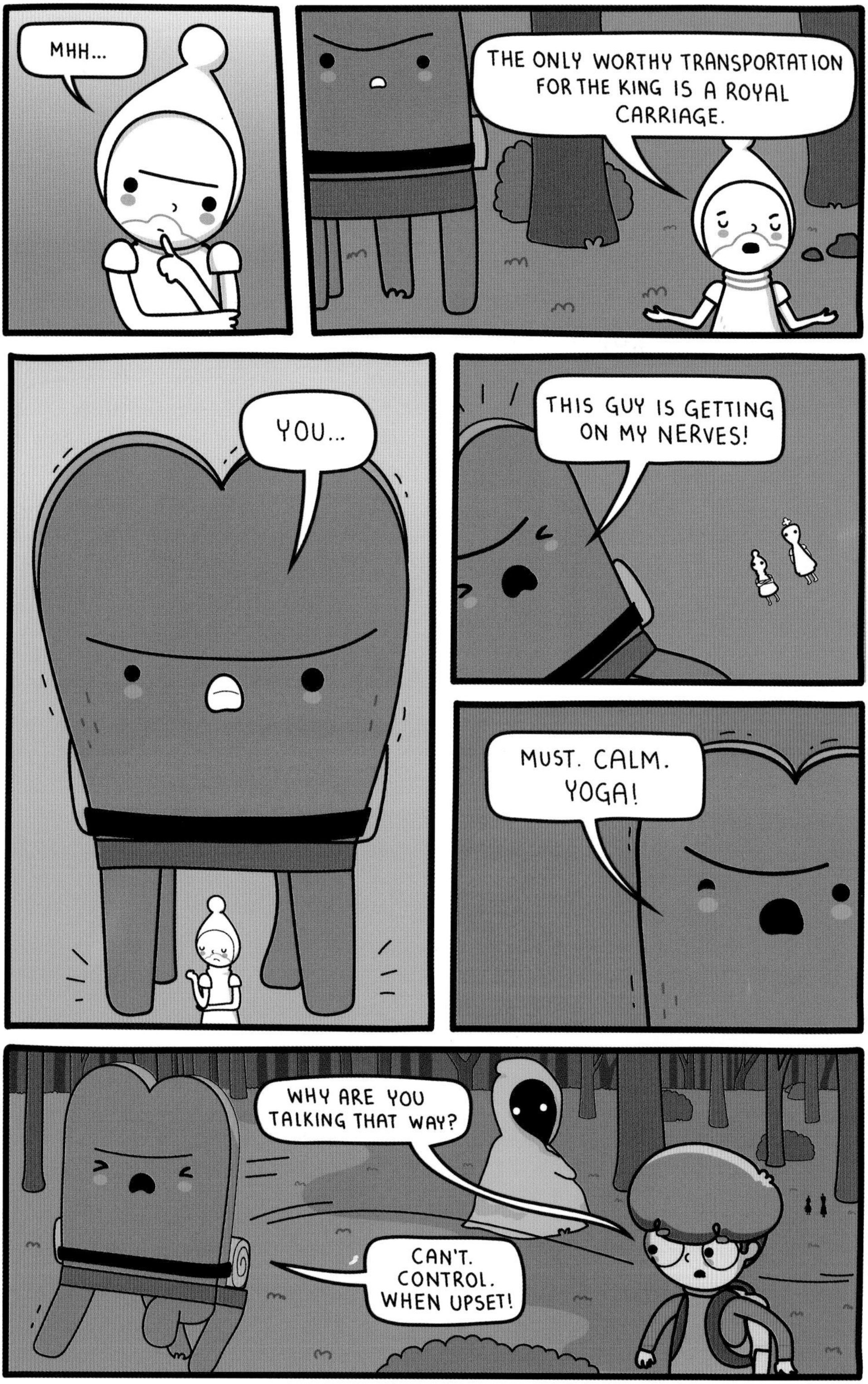
MHH...
THE ONLY WORTHY TRANSPORTATION FOR THE KING IS A ROYAL CARRIAGE.
YOU...
THIS GUY IS GETTING ON MY NERVES!
MUST. CALM. YOGA!
WHY ARE YOU TALKING THAT WAY?
CAN'T. CONTROL. WHEN UPSET!

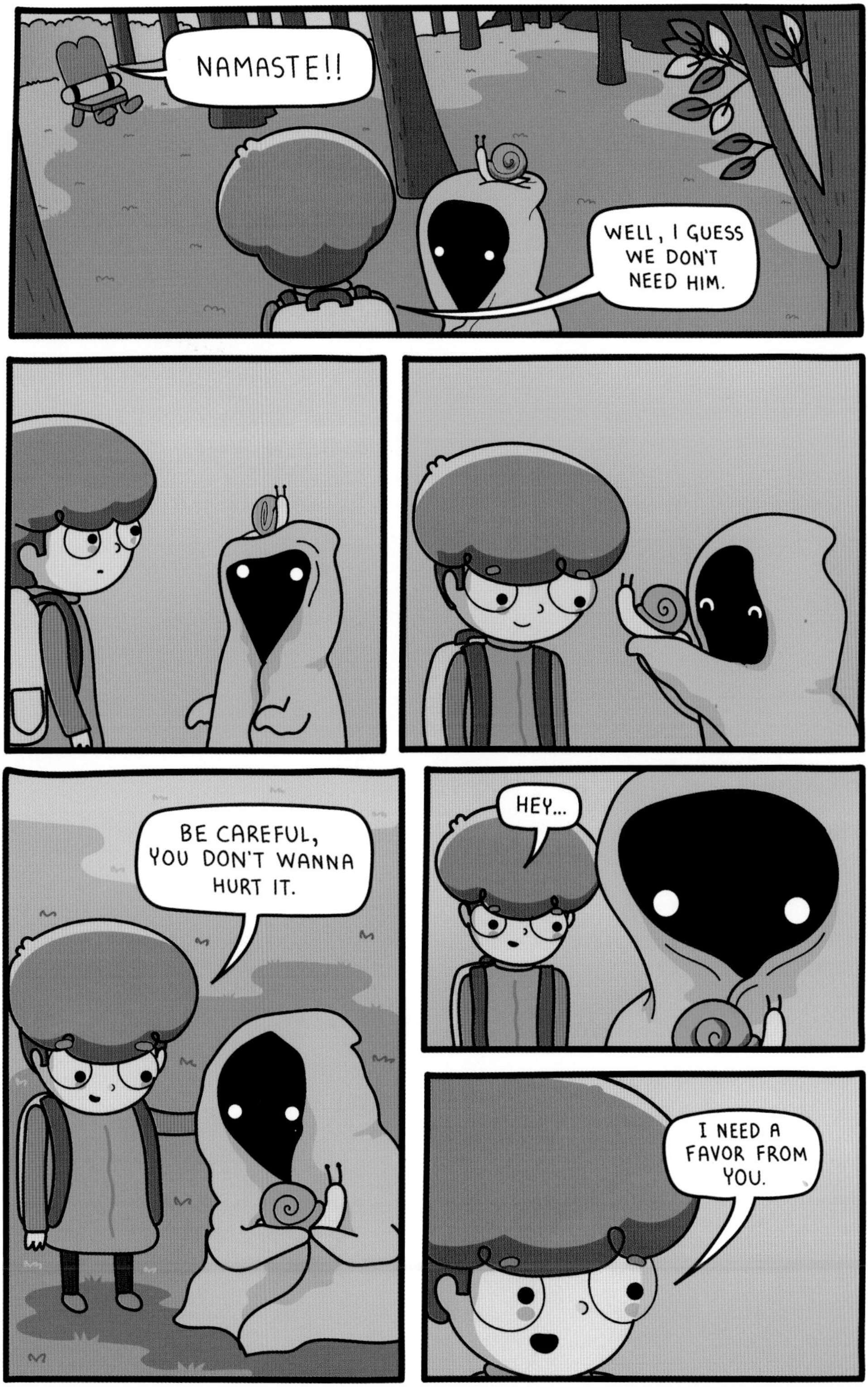
NAMASTE!!
WELL, I GUESS WE DON'T NEED HIM.
BE CAREFUL, YOU DON'T WANNA HURT IT.
HEY...
I NEED A FAVOR FROM YOU.

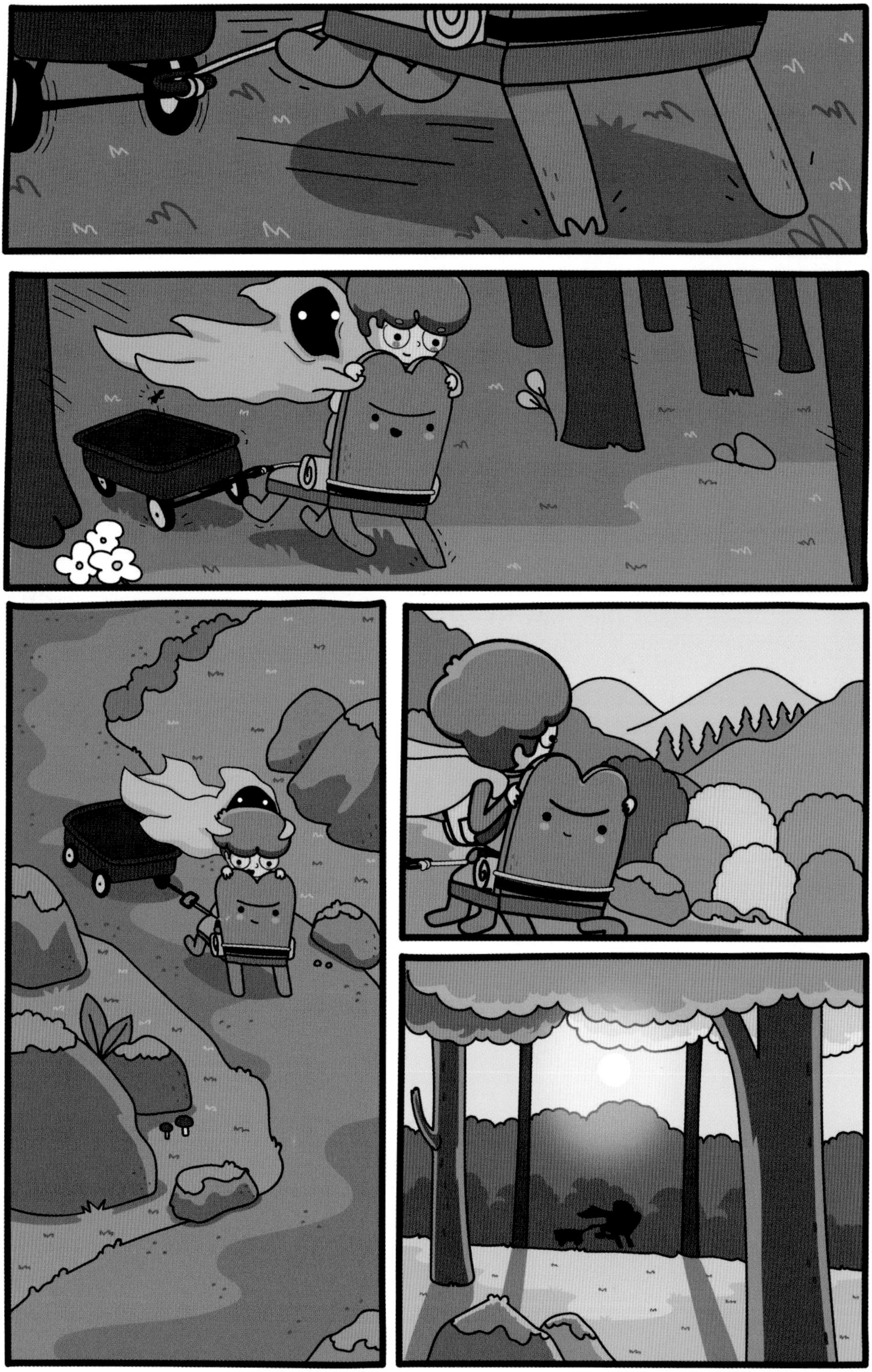

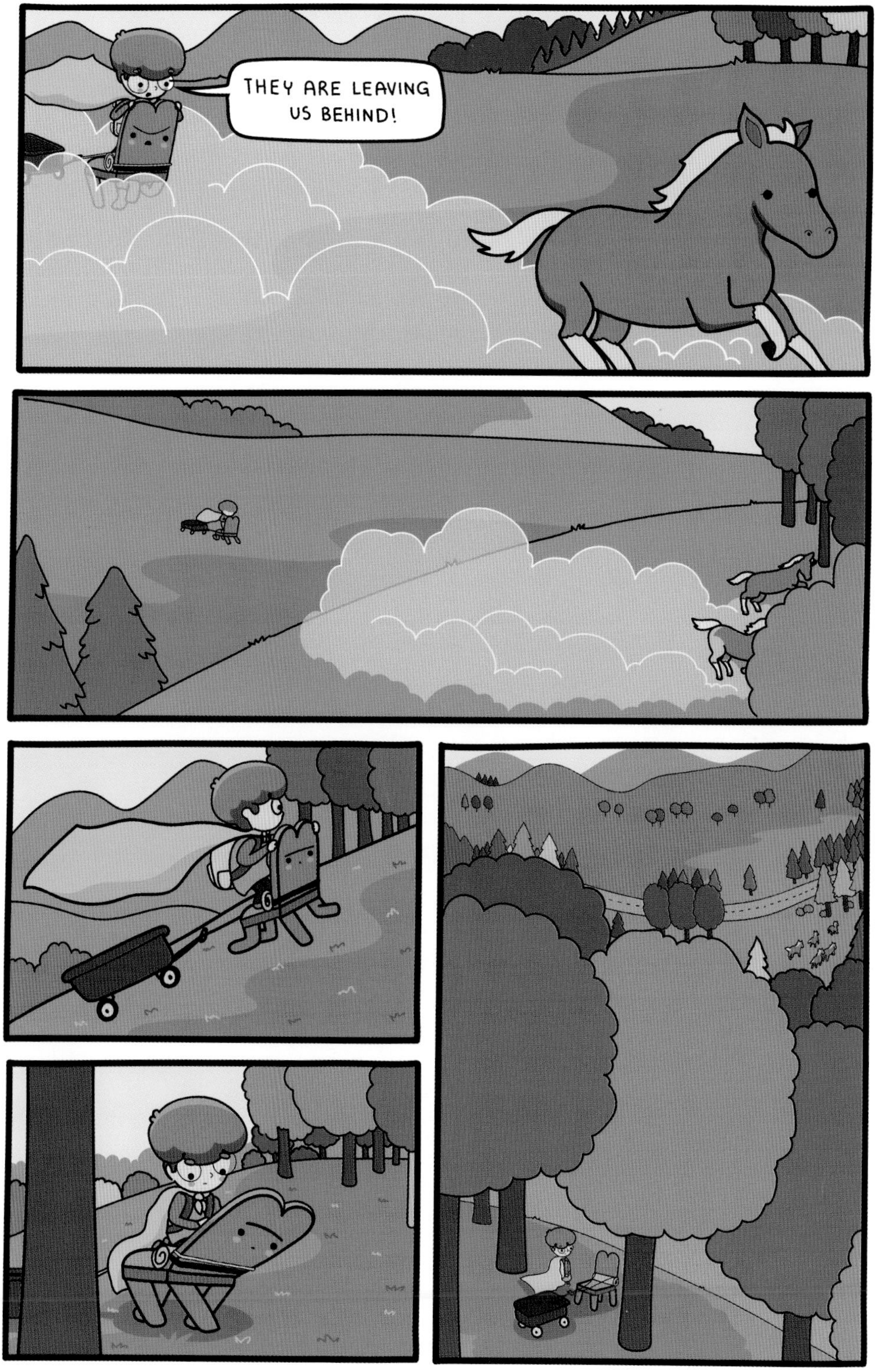
THEY ARE LEAVING US BEHIND!

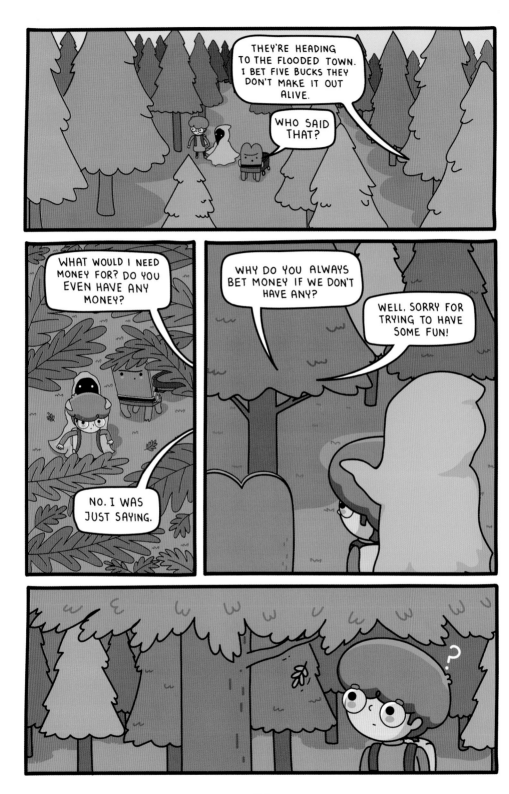

84

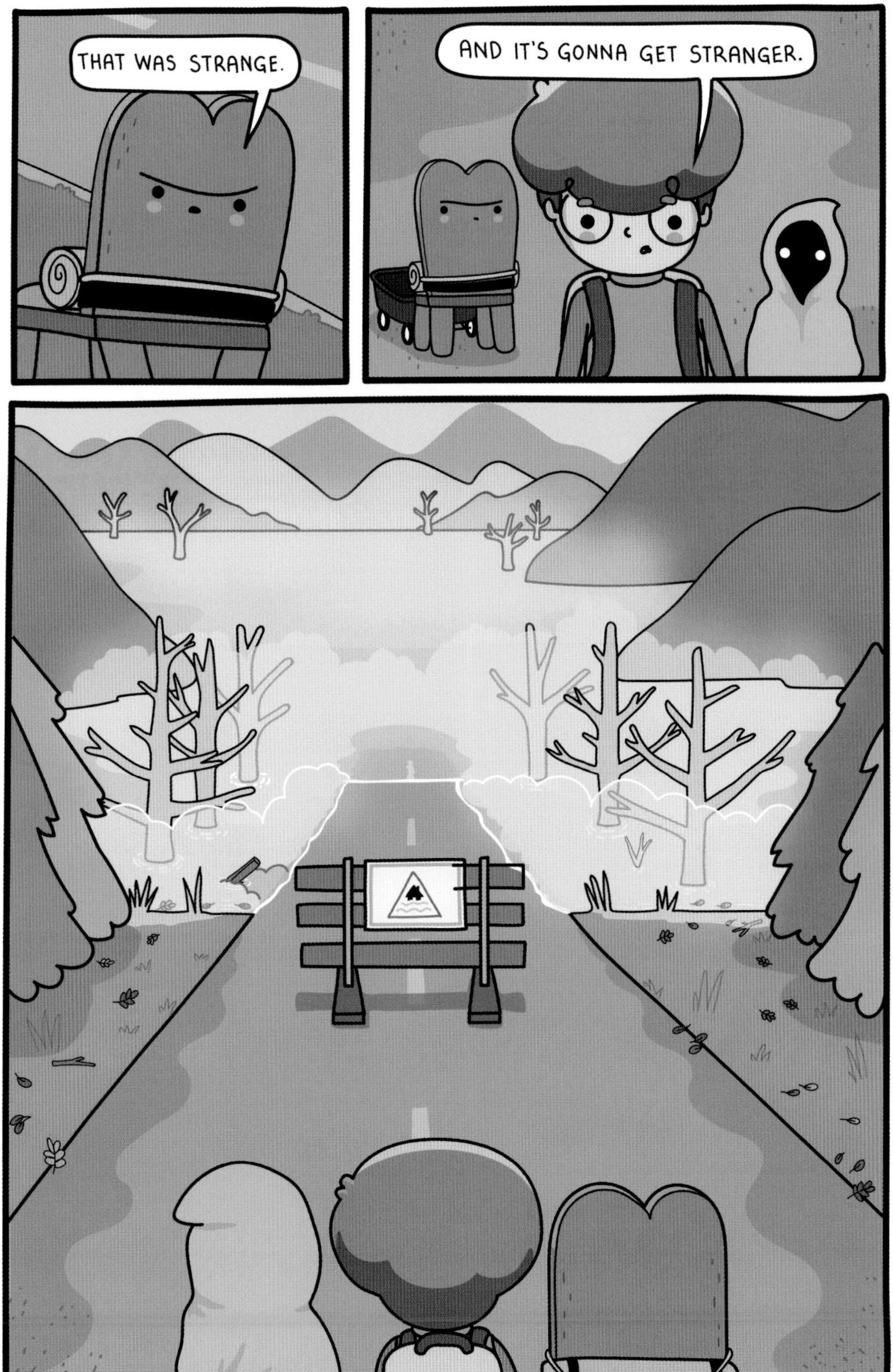
THAT WAS STRANGE.
AND IT'S GONNA GET STRANGER.

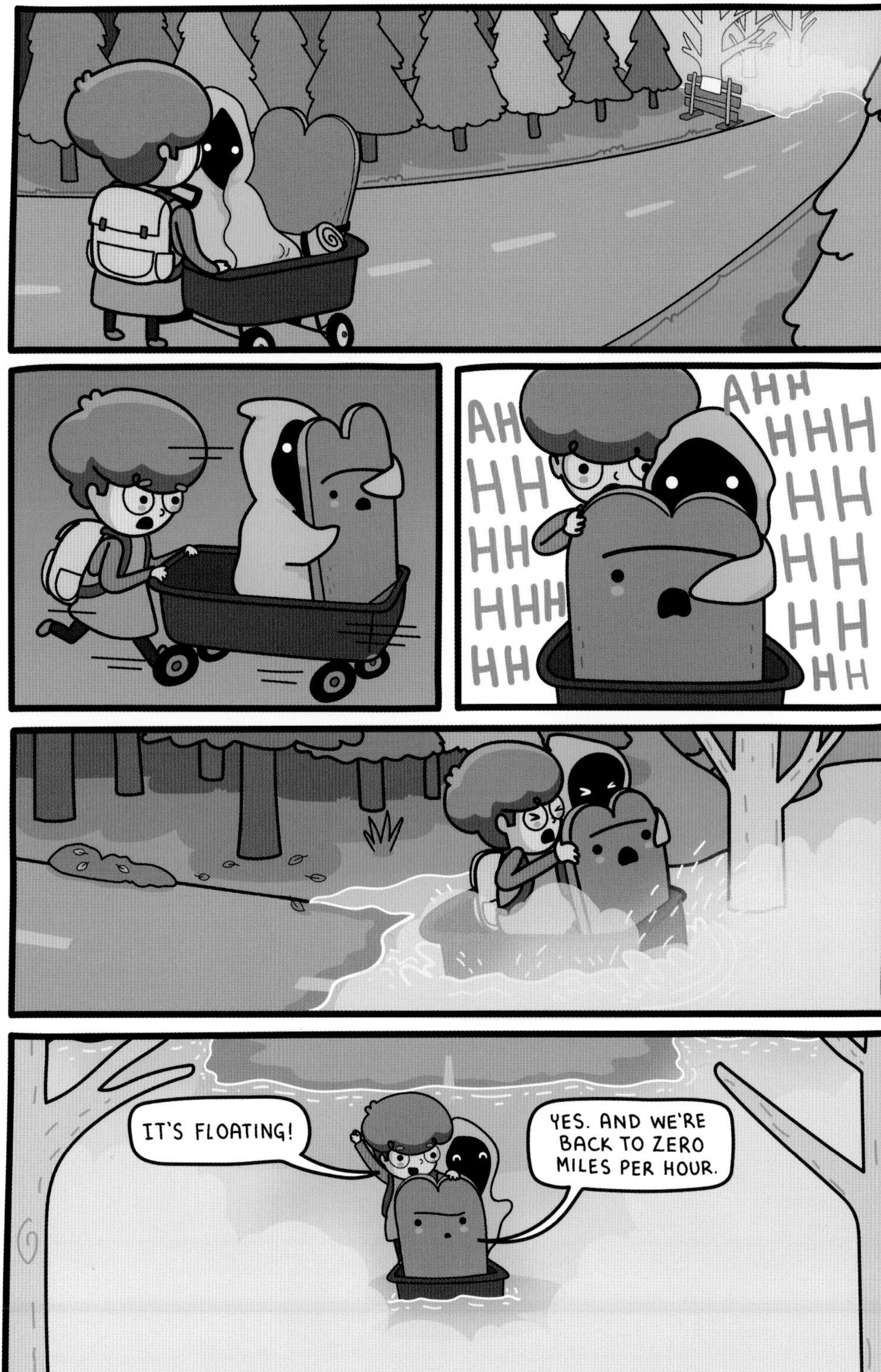
AHHHHHHHHHHHH
AHHHHHHHHHHHHHHH
IT'S FLOATING!
YES. AND WE'RE BACK TO ZERO MILES PER HOUR.

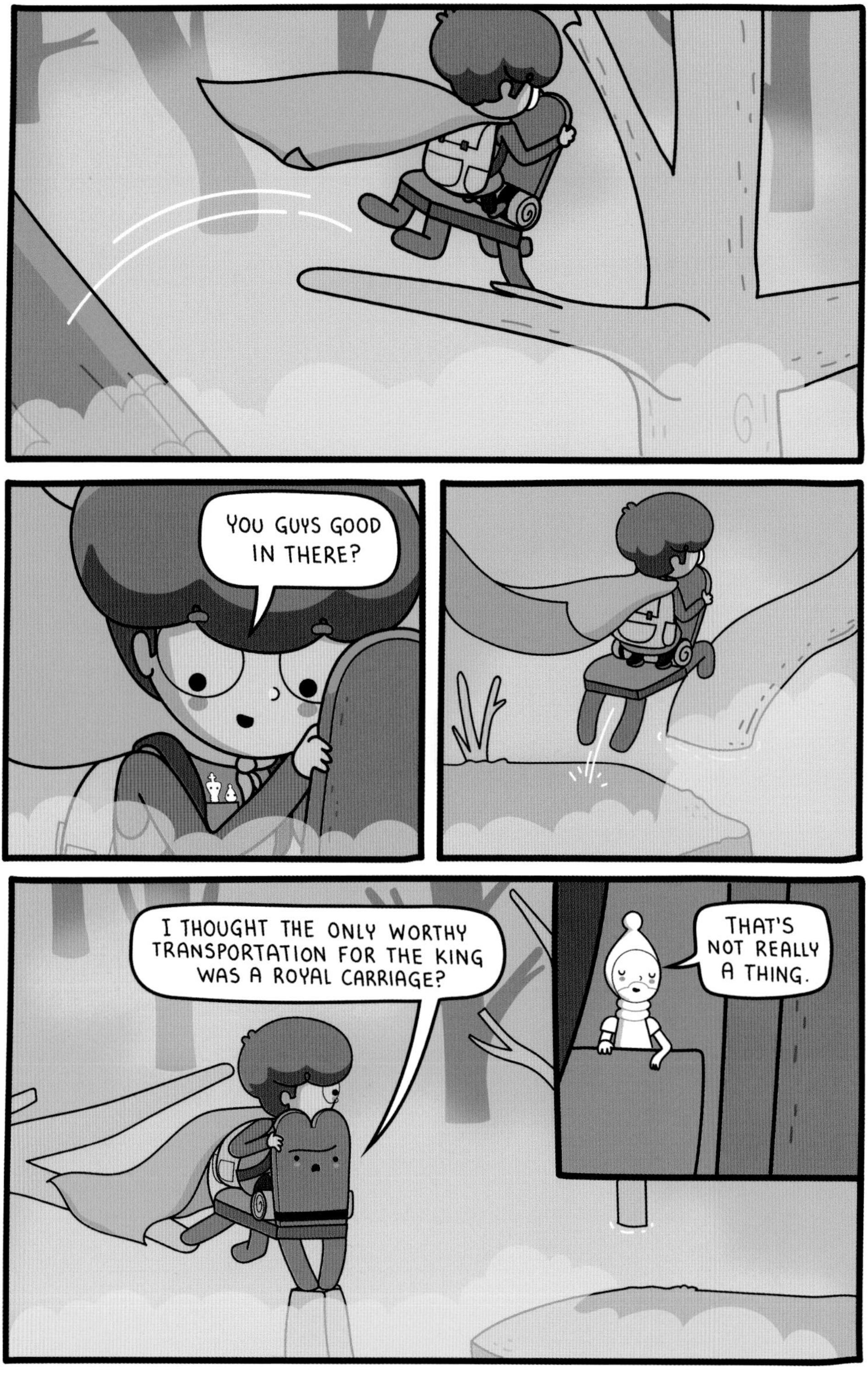
YOU GUYS GOOD IN THERE?
I THOUGHT THE ONLY WORTHY TRANSPORTATION FOR THE KING WAS A ROYAL CARRIAGE?
THAT'S NOT REALLY A THING.

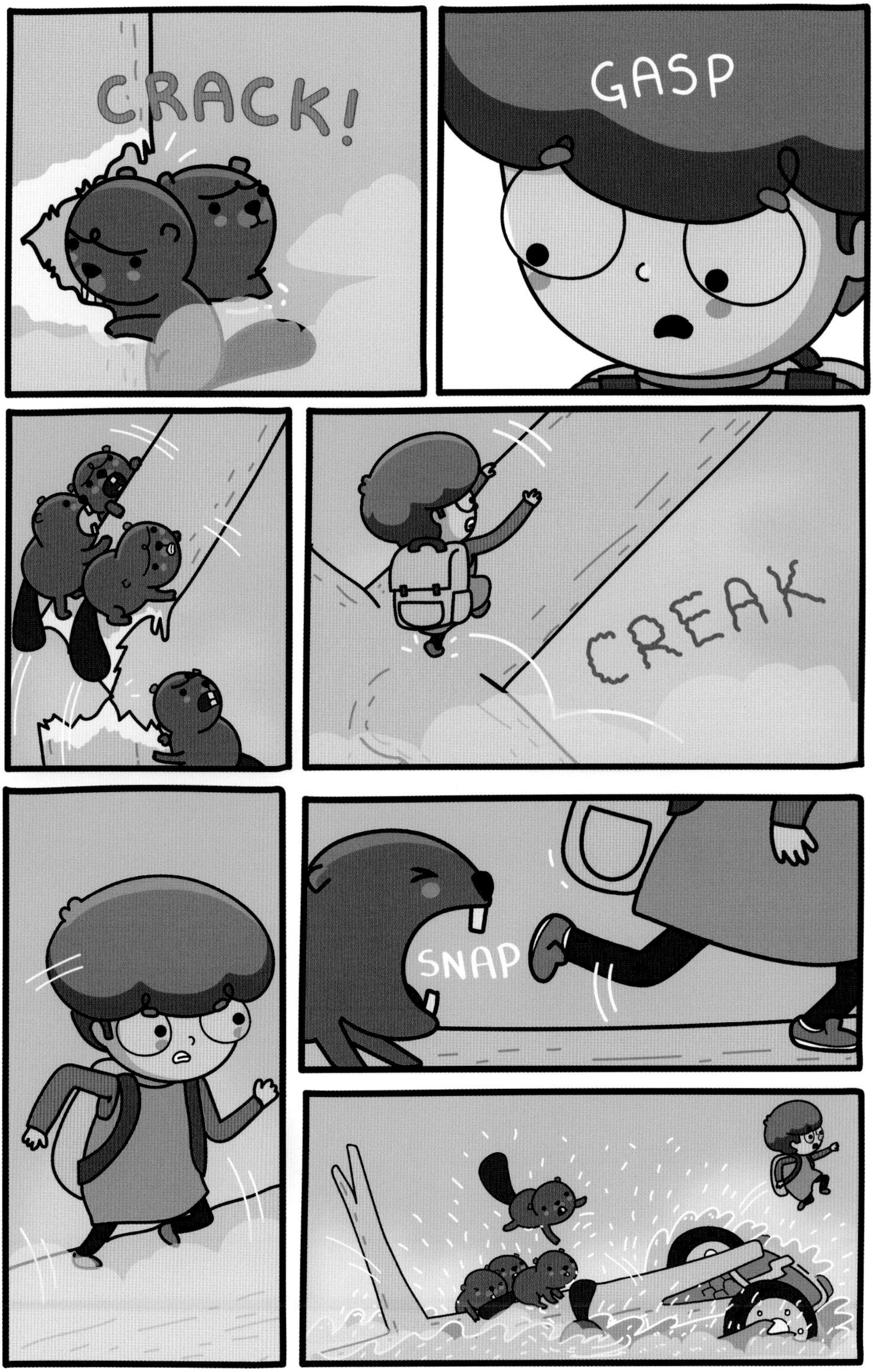
CRACK!
GASP
CREAK
SNAP

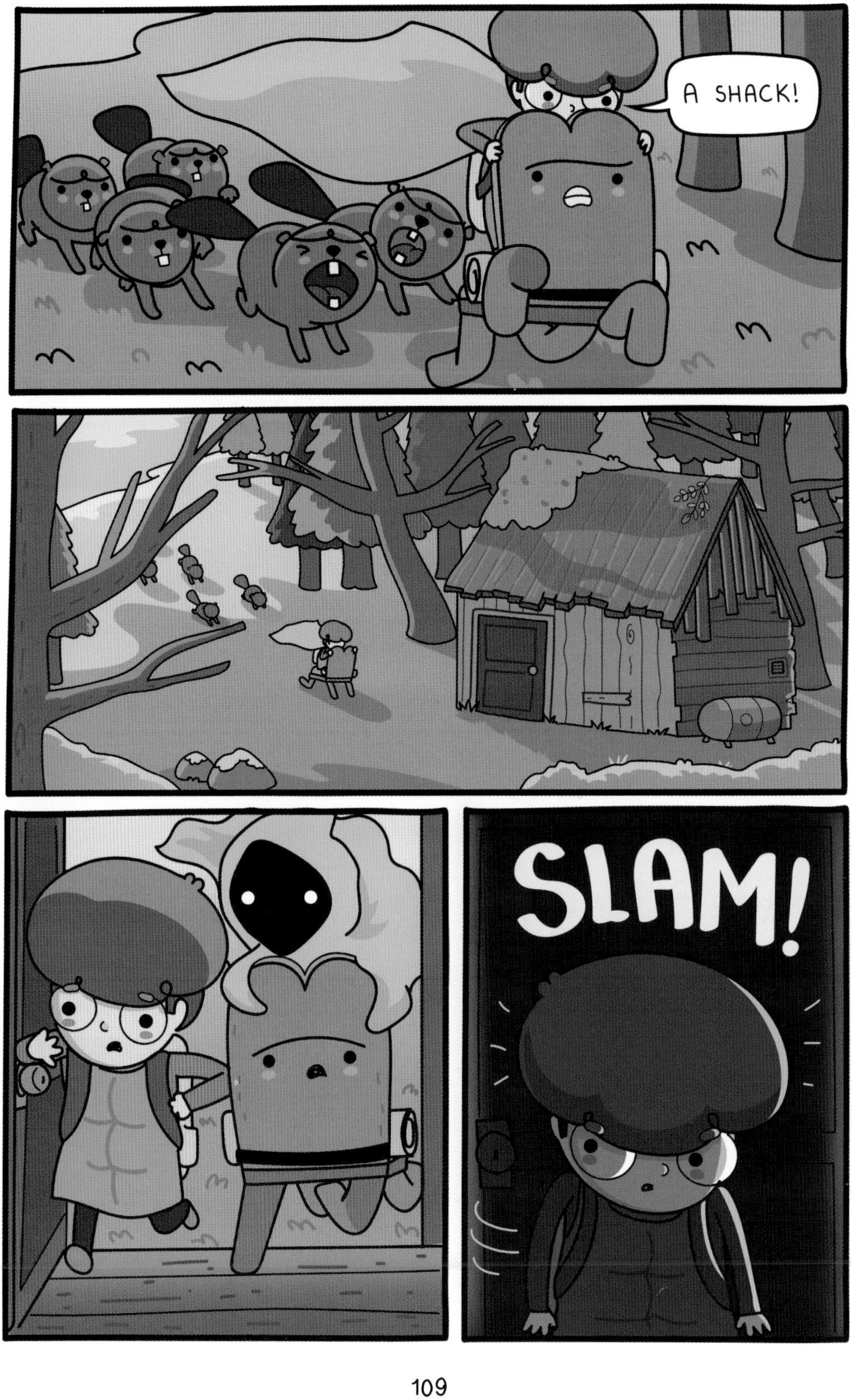
A SHACK!
SLAM!

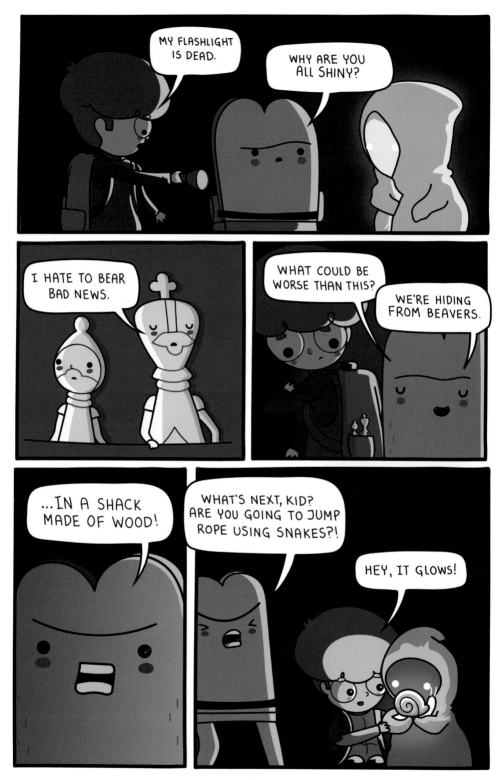

110

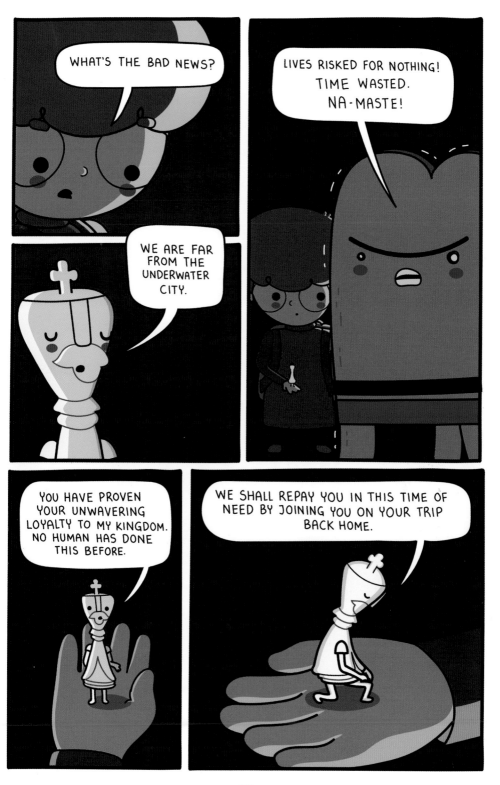

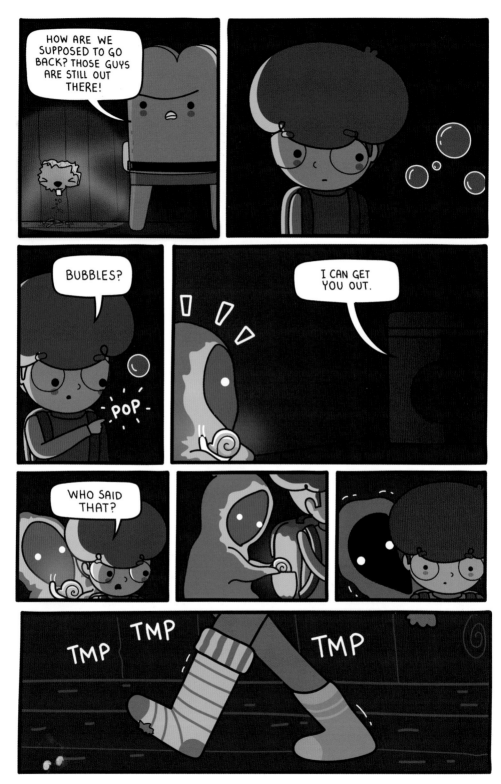

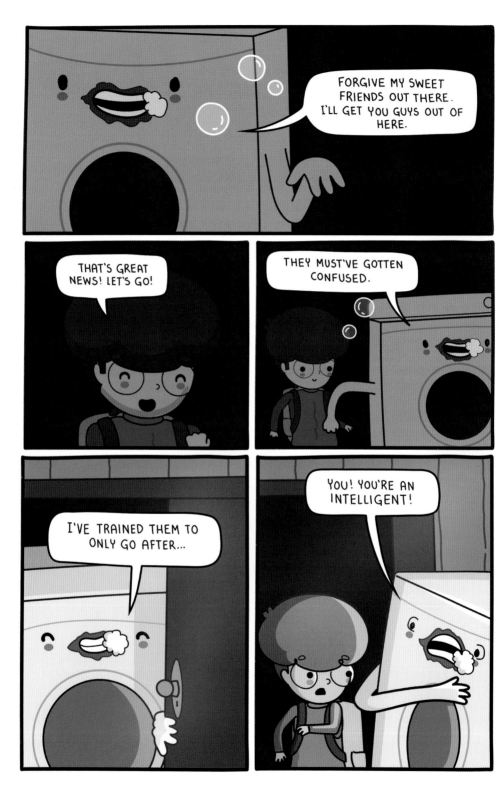

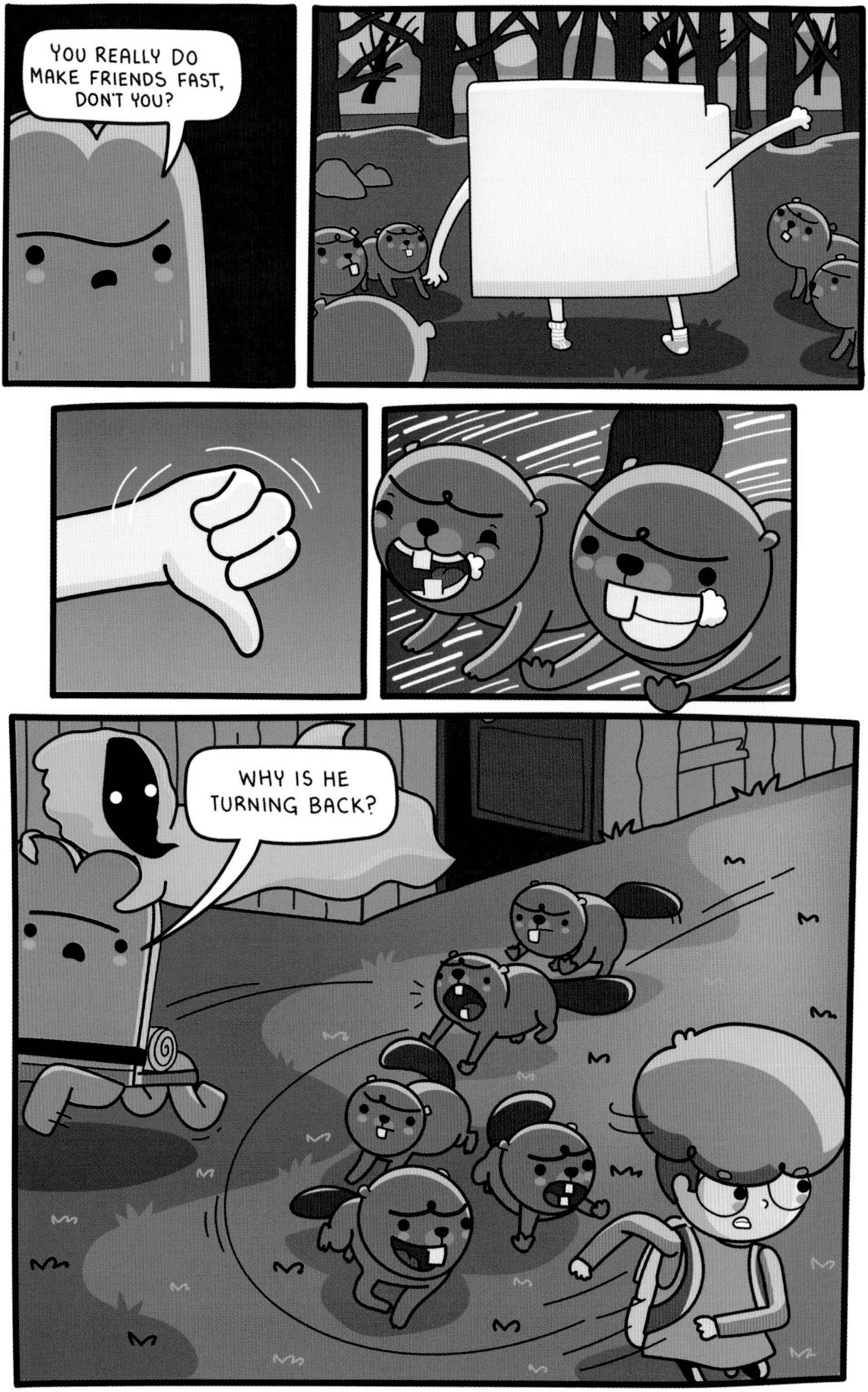
YOU REALLY DO MAKE FRIENDS FAST, DON'T YOU?
WHY IS HE TURNING BACK?

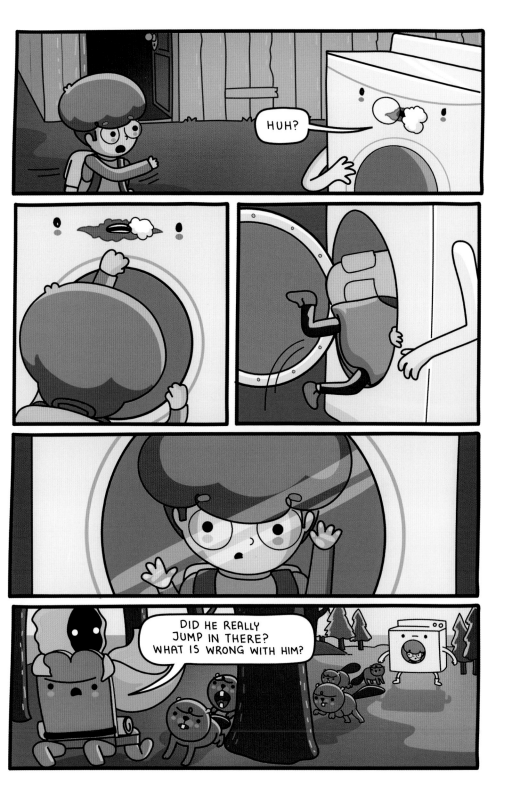

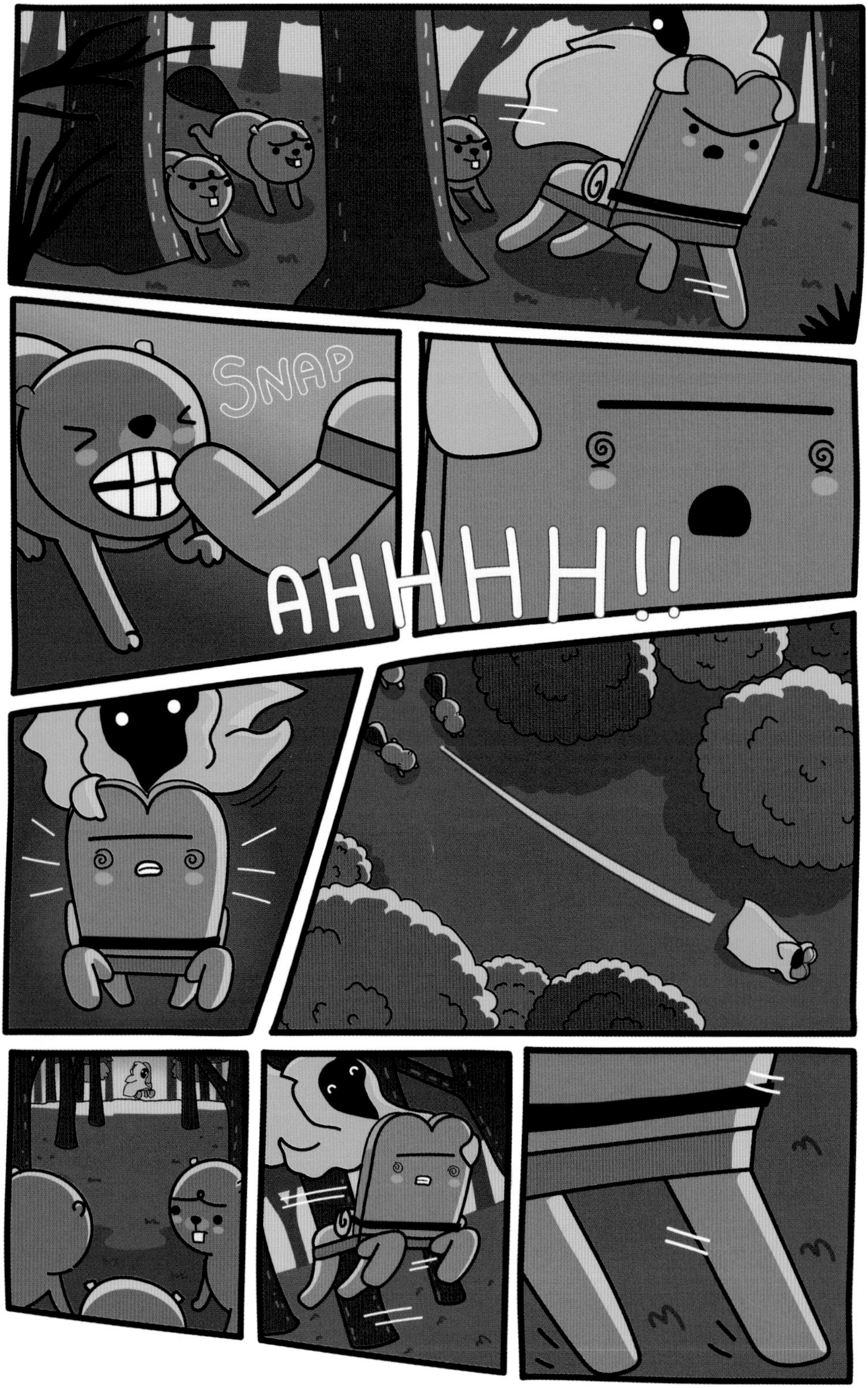
SNAP
AHHHH!!

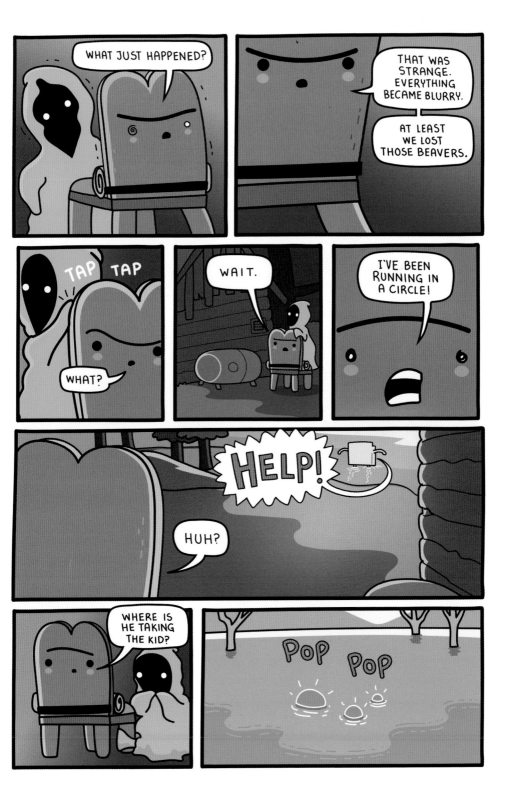

119

122

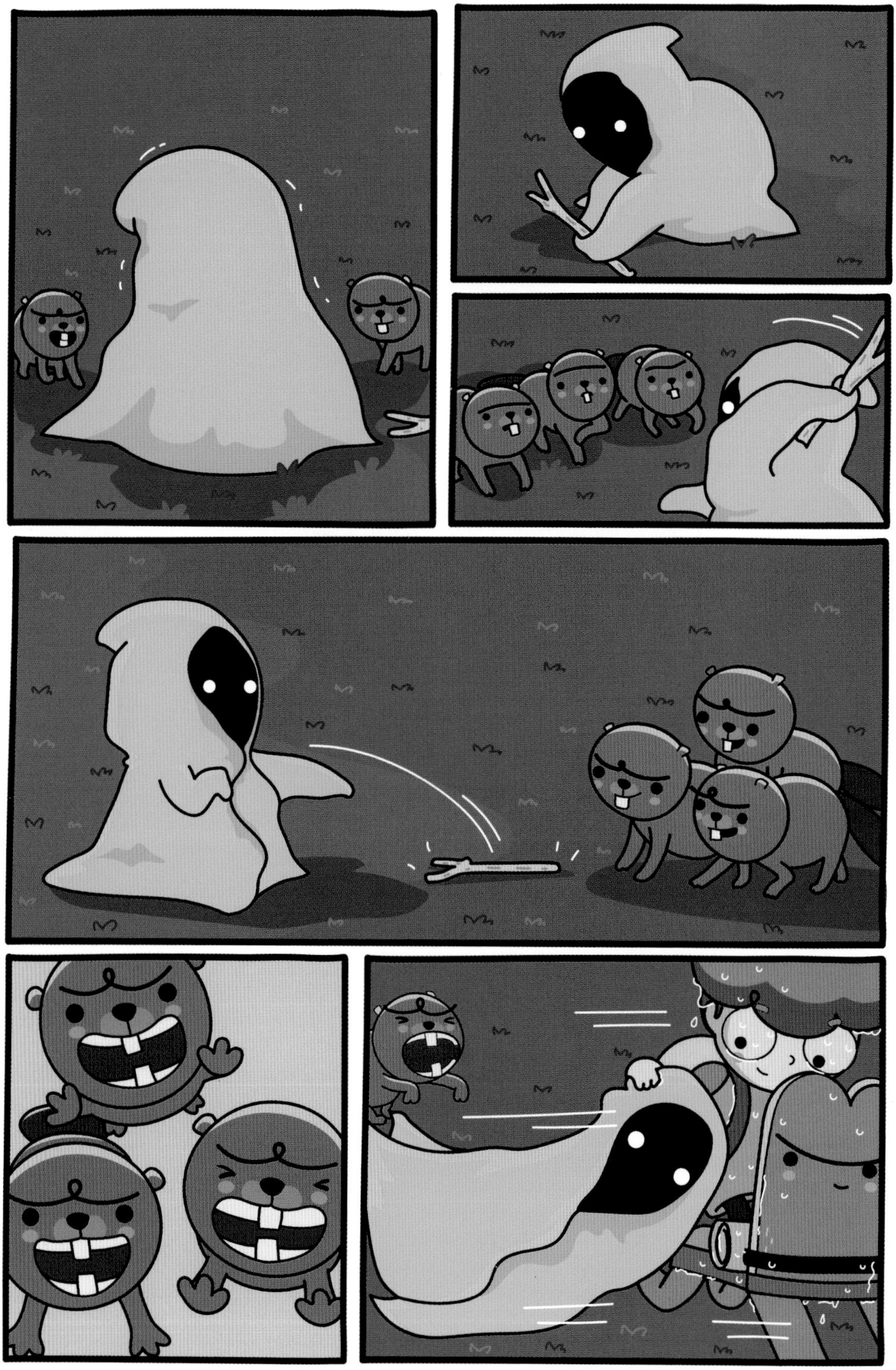

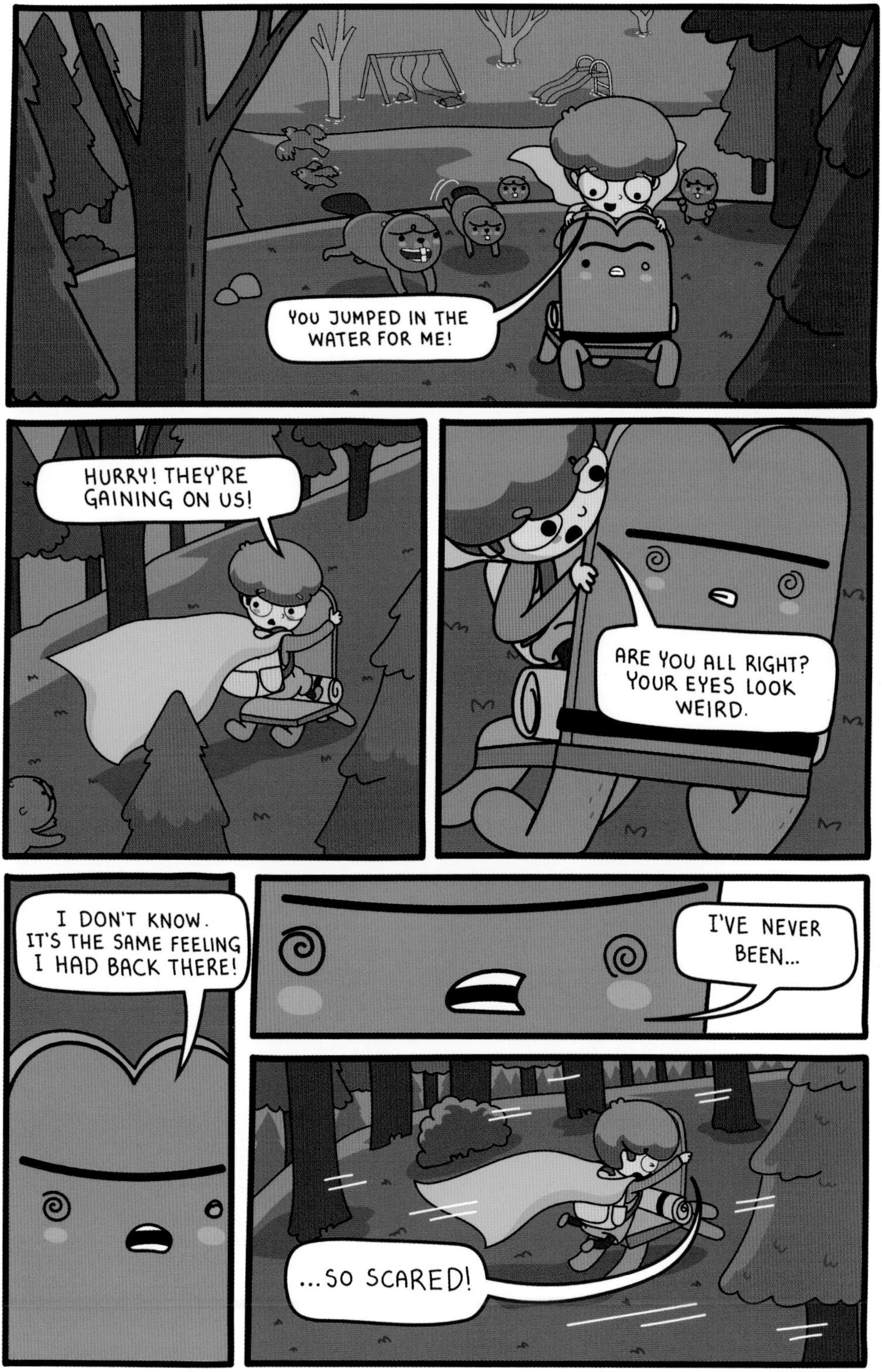
YOU JUMPED IN THE WATER FOR ME!
HURRY! THEY'RE GAINING ON US!
ARE YOU ALL RIGHT? YOUR EYES LOOK WEIRD.
I DON'T KNOW. IT'S THE SAME FEELING I HAD BACK THERE!
I'VE NEVER BEEN...
...SO SCARED!

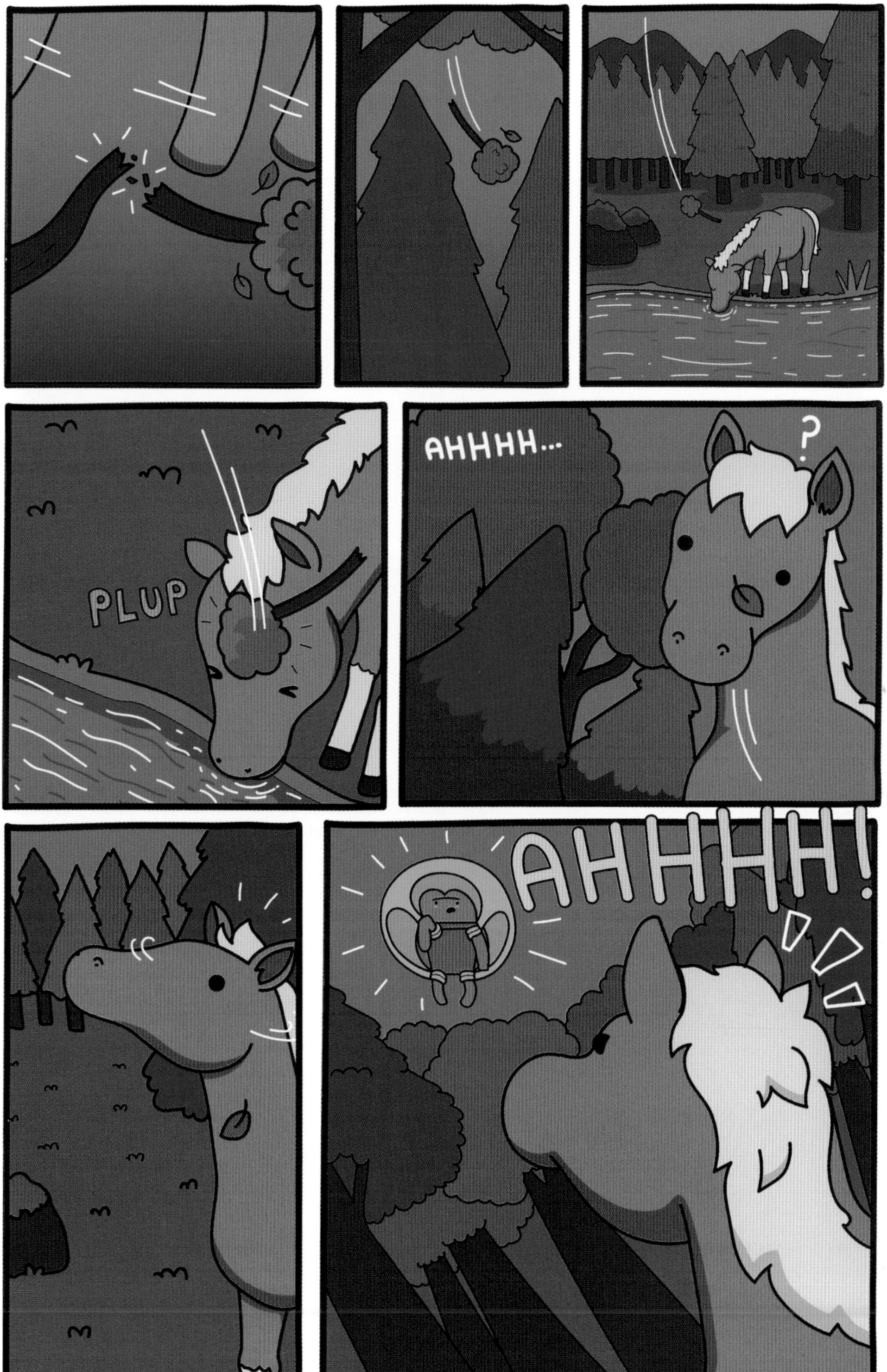
PLUP
AHHHH...
?
AHHHH!

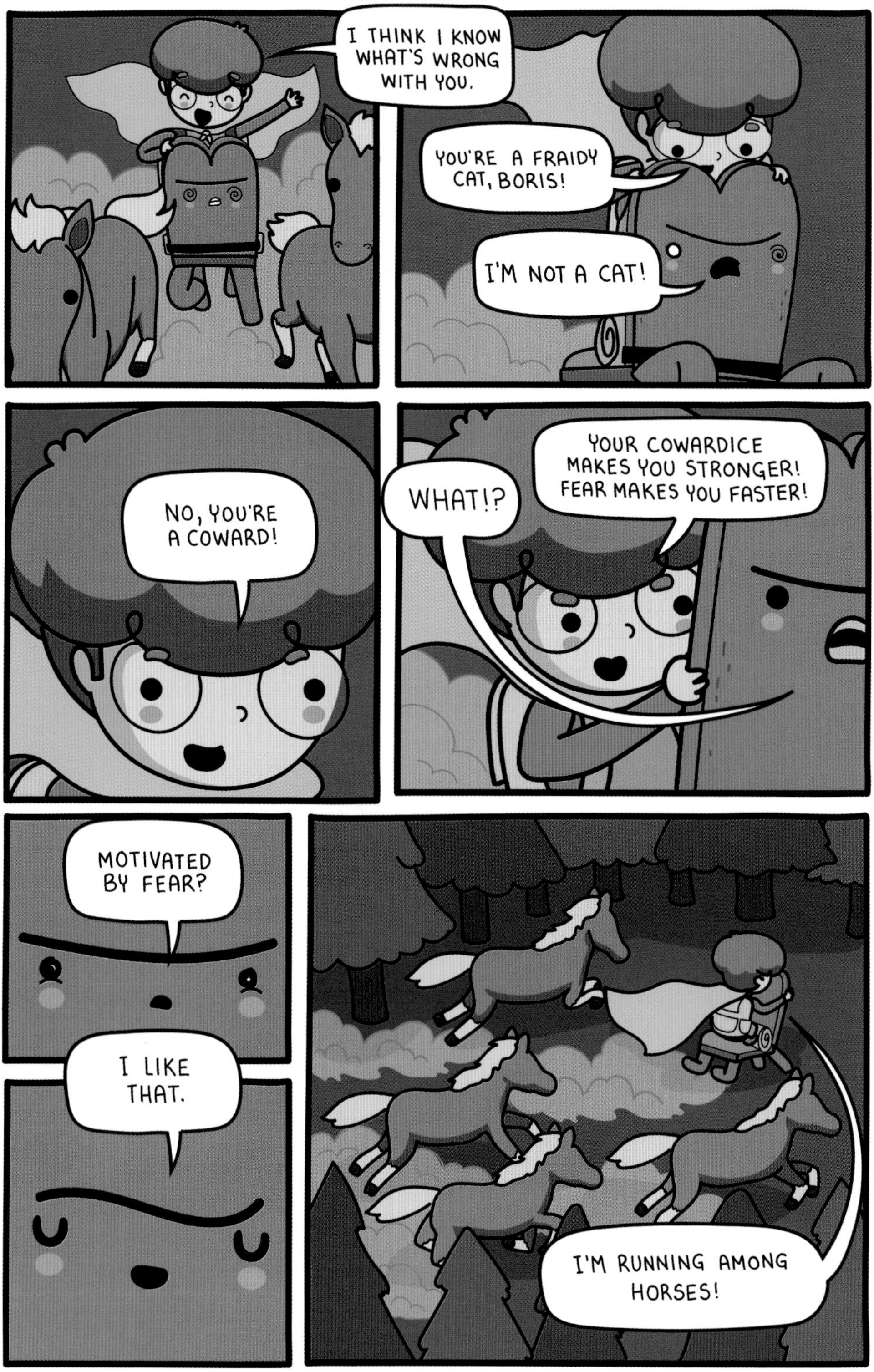
I THINK I KNOW WHAT'S WRONG WITH YOU.
YOU'RE A FRAIDY CAT, BORIS!
I'M NOT A CAT!
NO, YOU'RE A COWARD!
WHAT!?
YOUR COWARDICE MAKES YOU STRONGER! FEAR MAKES YOU FASTER!
MOTIVATED BY FEAR?
I LIKE THAT.
I'M RUNNING AMONG HORSES!

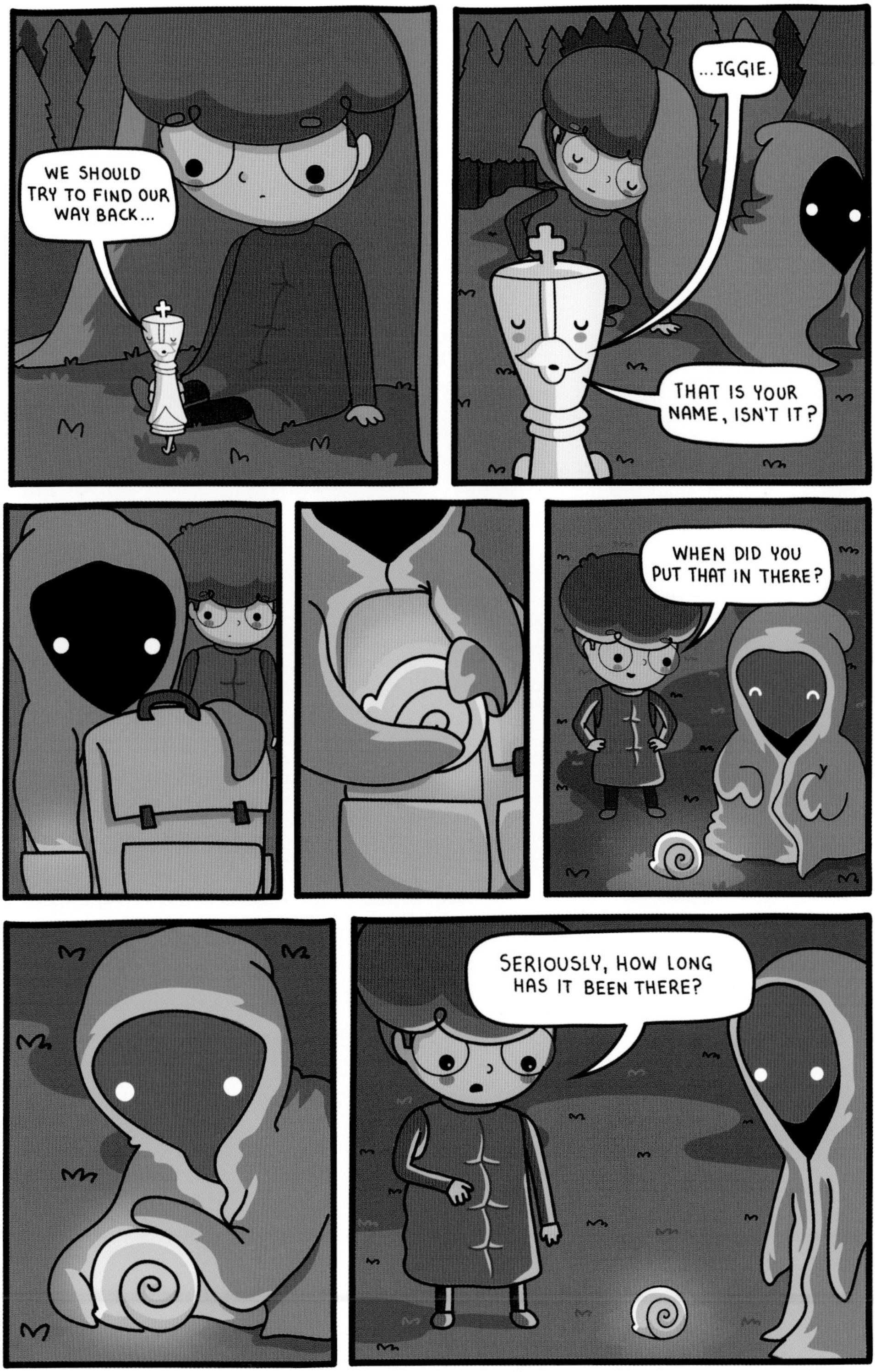
WE SHOULD TRY TO FIND OUR WAY BACK...
...IGGIE.
THAT IS YOUR NAME, ISN'T IT?
WHEN DID YOU PUT THAT IN THERE?
SERIOUSLY, HOW LONG HAS IT BEEN THERE?

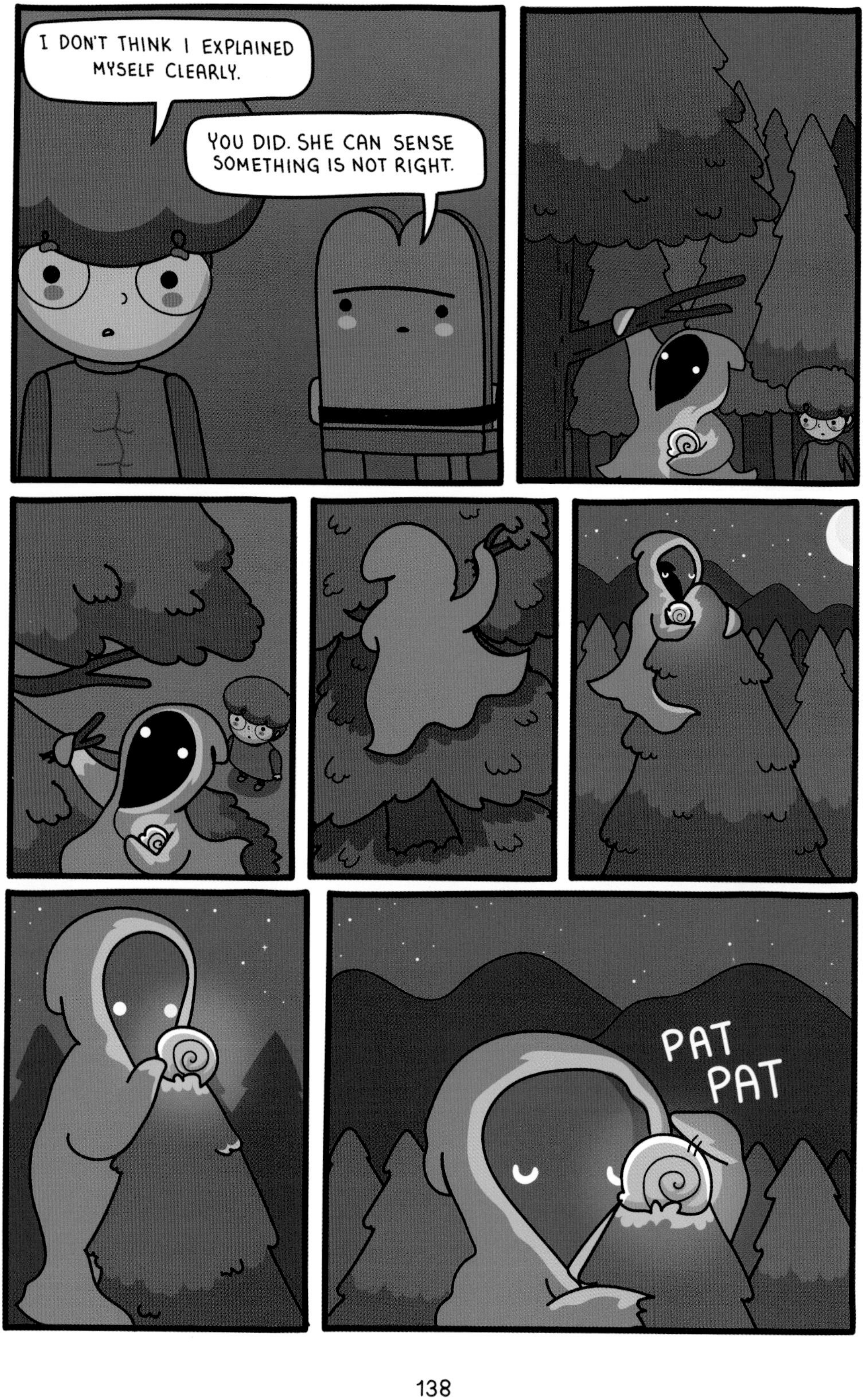
I DON'T THINK I EXPLAINED MYSELF CLEARLY.
YOU DID. SHE CAN SENSE SOMETHING IS NOT RIGHT.
PAT PAT

139

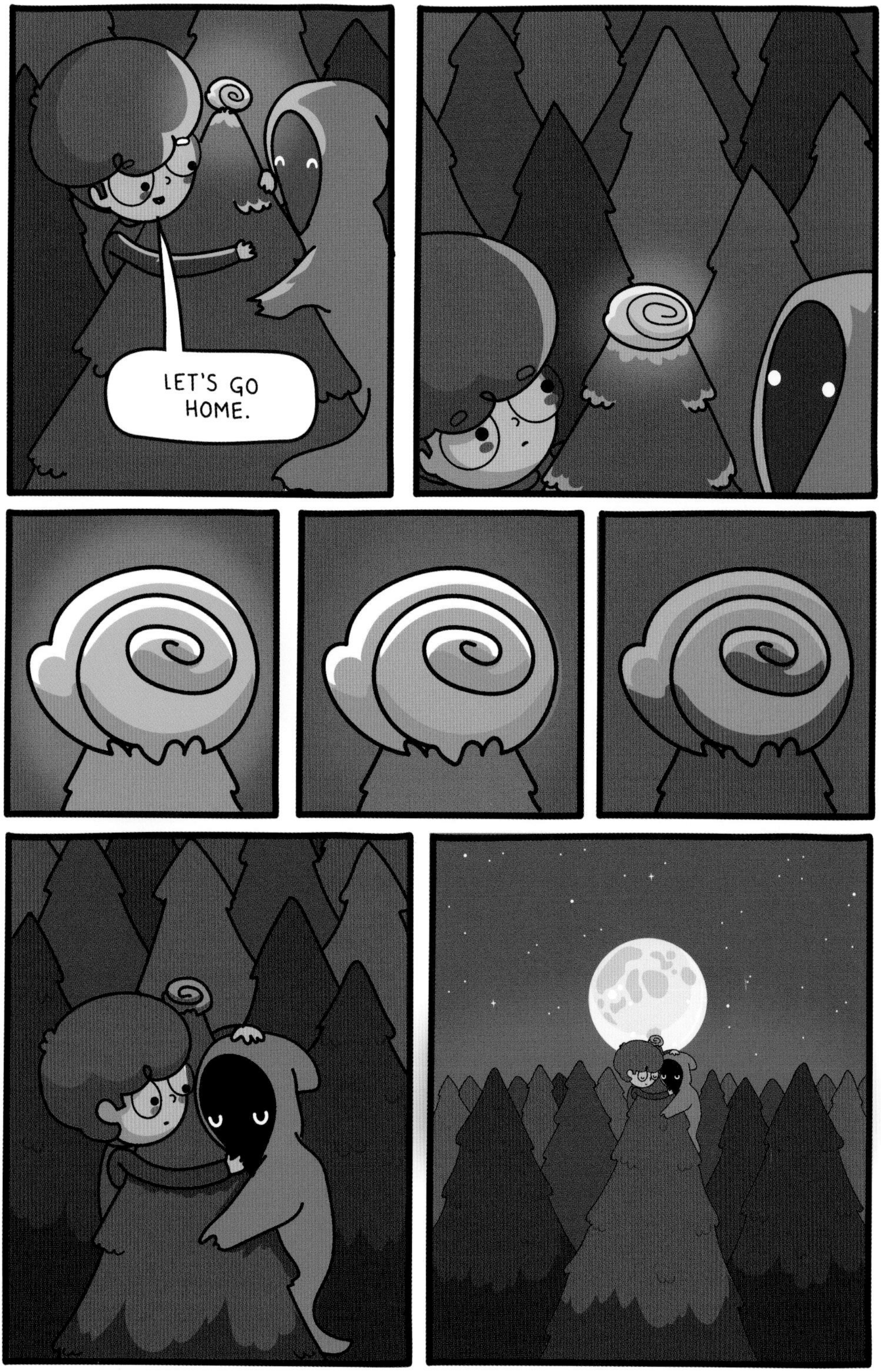
LET'S GO HOME.

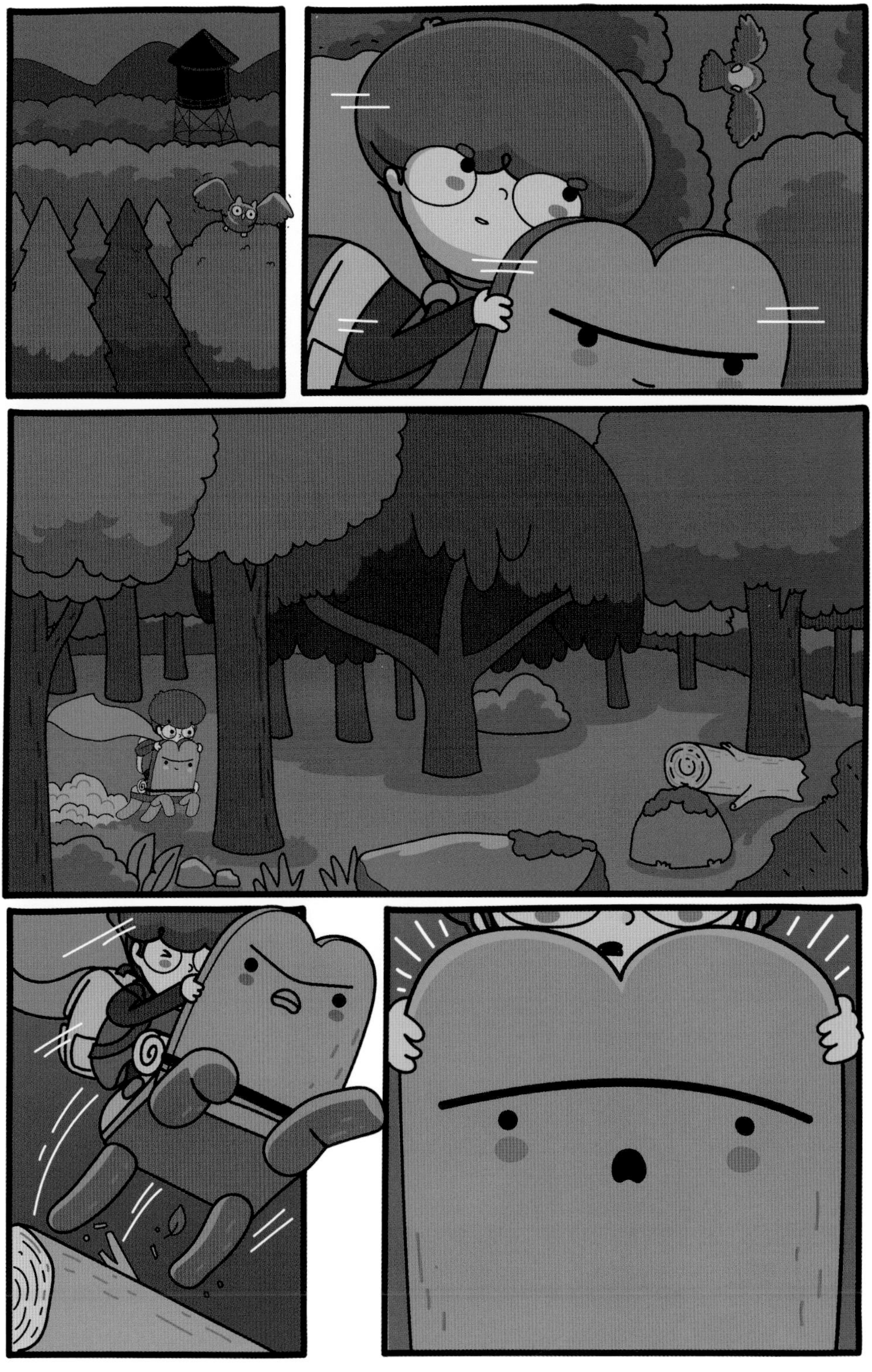

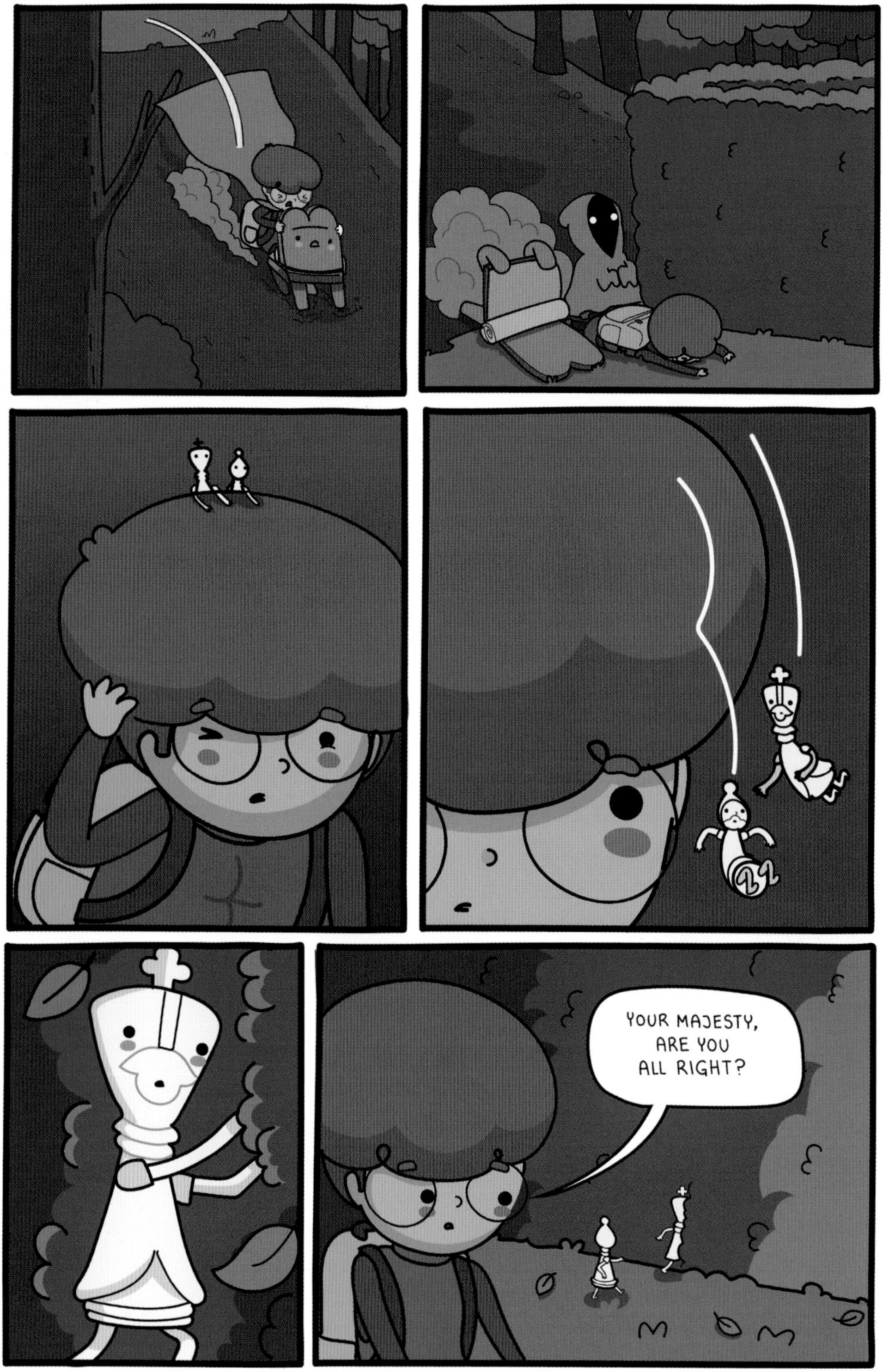
YOUR MAJESTY, ARE YOU ALL RIGHT?

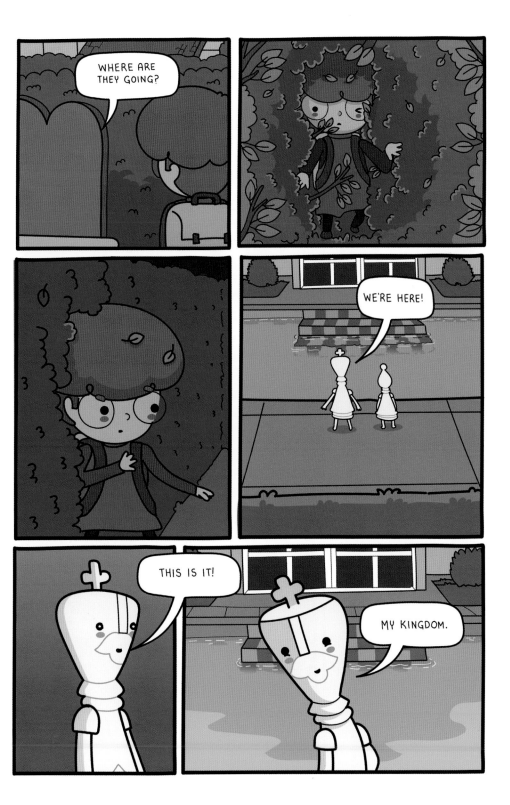

145

149

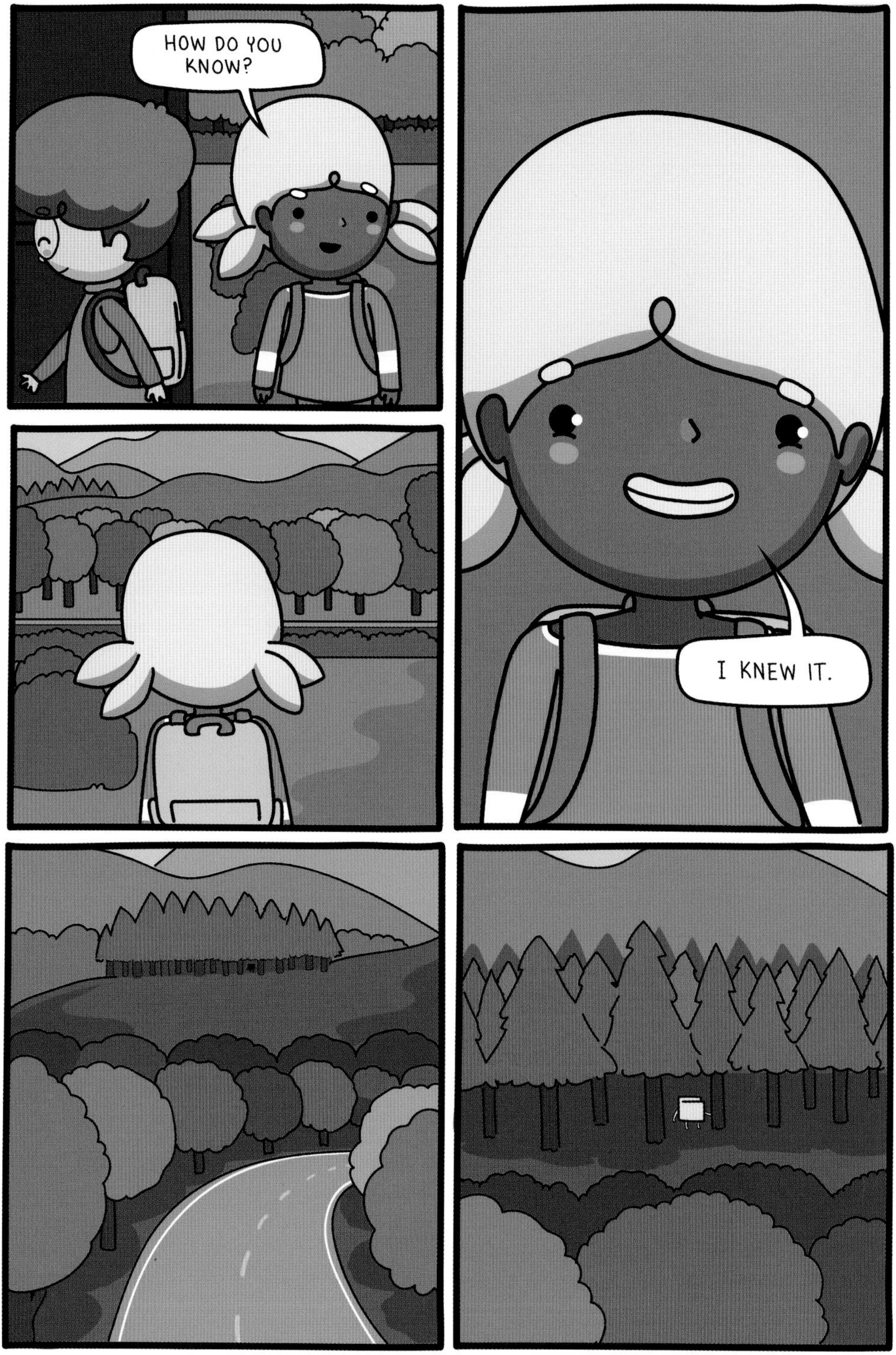
HOW DO YOU KNOW?
I KNEW IT.

TO BE CONTINUED...

⌁ ACKNOWLEDGMENTS ⌁

To my wife, Viviana, who is still by my side even after my nonstop talking about this project for months. Your unconditional love and advice have helped me through this process more than anyone can imagine.

To my two kids, who constantly inspire me and my characters.

To my editor, Lucas Wetzel, whose hundreds of razor-sharp notes were exactly what I needed to organize my thoughts. And all the people at Andrews McMeel Pulishing who were involved in *Peculiar Woods*, making this book possible and giving me their valuable feedback.

To Oscar Colmenares, his assistance coloring pages and the insightful suggestions made it possible to finish the book on schedule.

To Kathleen Ortiz, for being the amazing agent who never doubts my work and always fuels my crazy ideas.

To my readers: This book exists because of you. Please never stop sharing, caring, and showing love.

And last but not least, I would like to express great thanks for the support and warmth over the years to my chair and blanket.

About the Author

Andrés J. Colmenares is a Colombian
self-taught illustrator and the creator of
Wawawiwa Comics, which he describes as
being like a "visual hug" for his millions of
readers around the world. He lives in Bogota,
Colombia, with his wife, Viviana Navas,
and their two children.

Andrews McMeel Publishing
a division of Andrews McMeel Universal
1130 Walnut Street, Kansas City, Missouri 64106

23 24 25 26 27 TEN 10 9 8 7 6 5 4 3 2 1

Paperback ISBN: 978-1-5248-7929-7
Hardback ISBN: 978-1-5248-8491-8

Library of Congress Control Number: 2022947525

Editor: Lucas Wetzel
Art Directors: Tiffany Meairs and Lynn Stoecklein
Production Editor: Julie Railsback
Production Manager: Tamara Haus

www.andrewsmcmeel.com

Made by:
1010 Printing International, Ltd.
Address and place of production:
1010 Avenue, Xia Nan Industrial District,
Yuan Zhou Town, Bo Luo County, Hui Zhou City,
Guang Dong Province 516123, China
1st Printing—12/26/2022

Look for these books!